There's a Murder Afoot

There's a Murder Afoot

A SHERLOCK HOLMES BOOKSHOP MYSTERY

Vicki Delany

CROOKED LANE

NEW YORK

Copyright © 2019 by Vicki Delany

All rights reserved.

Published in the United States by Crooked Lane Books, an imprint of The Quick Brown Fox & Company LLC.

Crooked Lane Books and its logo are trademarks of The Quick Brown Fox & Company LLC.

Library of Congress Catalog-in-Publication data available upon request.

ISBN (mass market): 978-1-64385-573-8
ISBN (hardcover): 978-1-64385-034-4
ISBN (ePub): 978-1-64385-035-1
ISBN (ePDF): 978-1-64385-036-8

Cover illustration by Joe Burleson
Book design by Jennifer Canzone

Printed in the United States.

www.crookedlanebooks.com

Crooked Lane Books
34 West 27th St., 10th Floor
New York, NY 10001

Mass market Edition: November 2020
Hardcover Edition: August 2019

10 9 8 7 6 5 4 3 2 1

To Nolan Arthur Hartley Webb, who has many years of reading ahead of him.

Chapter One

My sister Phillipa Doyle is a minor functionary in the British government. What that means I'm not entirely sure, and she has never bothered to enlighten me.

Pippa is seven years older than I am, and we have never been close. People tell me I'm smart, but I am—although I'd never admit it—the slow one in my family.

I'd hoped Ryan and Pippa wouldn't meet on this trip, but such was not to be.

She extended her long thin fingers toward him, and for a moment he looked as though he scarcely knew what do to with them. Then he recovered his wits, took her hand in his, and pumped it enthusiastically. "Pleased to meet you," he said.

"Charmed," she drawled.

She wasn't going to make this easy.

When Pippa had come into the hotel bar, where we were gathering for predinner drinks, we'd exchanged air kisses and muttered insincerities. I hadn't seen my sister for five years, not since I'd moved to West London, Massachusetts. She never visited me there, and when I'd come to London to visit my parents, Pippa had been out of town. Or so she'd said.

As a child she'd been overweight and, tired of the snickering of her peers, had set out to change that with the single-minded determination characteristic of the way she does everything. By the time she'd gone to Cambridge, she'd been thin to the point of emaciated. Now, I thought, she'd lost weight since I'd last seen her. She'd probably come straight from her office, dressed in a gray skirt suit that cost in the hundreds, if not thousands, of pounds, a pink silk blouse with a bow at the neck, gray pumps—Manolo Blahnik, possibly—with four-inch heels, and small, but perfect, pearl earrings. Her brown hair, highlighted with streaks of caramel, was perfectly arranged to come to a sleek bob at her chin, and her manicure was fresh.

In contrast, I'd been on a plane all night, and although my friends and I arrived at Heathrow on time, my suitcase had not. I'd had to run out to the shops to buy what I could so I didn't have to go to dinner with my family wearing my traveling jeans, comfortable cardigan, and well-worn trainers. Greeting Pippa, I felt like a country bumpkin in my new black-and-white dress under a black shrug, black leggings, and practical shoes.

My friends had all stood when I had, and I made the introductions. As well as Ryan Ashburton, I'd come with Jayne Wilson, baker and business partner; Grant Thompson, rare-book dealer; and Donald Morris, retired lawyer and active Sherlockian.

Pippa told everyone how *absolutely* delighted she was to meet them and took the chair Grant offered her with a warm smile.

Ryan found my hand under the table and gave it a squeeze. I gave him a grateful smile in return. Our on-again, off-again, on-again romantic relationship was at the moment on again, and I was determined to keep it that way.

I hadn't told him I was nervous about seeing my sister, but I never could fool Ryan. Which was a good part of the reason our relationship was sometimes in the off phase.

"Are you a Sherlock aficionado, Ms. Doyle?" Donald Morris asked Pippa.

She turned to him with a smile. "I greatly enjoyed the Jeremy Brett TV program and some of the modern interpretations, although I wouldn't say I'm an aficionado. It is a passion of my great-uncle Arthur, whom I believe you know."

"Fabulous man, Arthur," Donald said. "His knowledge of the Canon is unparalleled."

"Has Gemma told you about our most famous relative?" she said.

I let out a breath, squeezed Ryan's hand, and then released it. So Pippa had decided to play nicely tonight. That came as an enormous relief.

Donald's eyes grew wide beneath his thick spectacles. "You mean Sir Arthur?" He turned to me. "Gemma, you always said that wasn't true. That you aren't related to the great man himself. The creator of Sherlock Holmes."

"Opinions on that differ," I said.

Pippa had instantly taken Donald's measure and decided to play along. Great-Uncle Arthur insisted that Sir Arthur Conan Doyle was a distant relative of ours. My father maintained there wasn't the slightest bit of evidence to support that.

Although, I suppose if you go back far enough, most everyone is related in some way or another, particularly those who share a name.

Pippa had never shown any interest at all in the tales of Sherlock Holmes, and I assumed she was pretending to in order to be polite to Donald. That Donald was a devotee of the Great Detective was obvious.

Not only was he here in London the night before a Holmes conference, but he wore a pin attached to his jacket indicating he was a member of a Sherlockian society. His ulster was tossed over the back of his chair. That type of garment—a calf-length coat with a small cape—had last been fashionable around the time Holmes and Watson were dashing through the fog-shrouded streets of London hunting for the origins of the goose that swallowed a priceless jewel.

The waiter placed another small bowl of nuts and wasabi peas onto the table. "Can I get you something from the bar, madam?"

"A soda water, please," Pippa said. "With a slice of lemon."

"Good beer, this," Grant Thompson said. "I've missed a good English beer."

Pippa turned her smile on him, and this time genuine interest flashed in her eyes. "You're obviously an American, but you've spent time in England. How marvelous. Oxford would be my guess."

"I did my PhD in English lit there, yes," Grant said.

A middle-aged couple came into the bar, and I leapt to my feet. "Here they are now." I ran across the room and gathered the newcomers into a deep hug.

My mother hugged me in return and then stepped away so my dad could shake me with enough enthusiasm to make my teeth rattle. "Gemma," he said when we finally separated. "Here you are. Gosh, but I've missed you."

"I missed you too, Dad. Come and meet my friends." I led my parents to our table. "Everyone, this is Mum and Dad. Anne and Henry Doyle."

We were having drinks in the downstairs bar of the Bentley Hotel in Kensington. My American friends and I were in London for the weekend-long

Sherlock Holmes in the Modern World conference being held at a big convention hotel a few doors down the street.

I'd come because I was giving a talk on Holmes's influence on popular culture, Grant because he was on the lookout for rare books at a good price, and Donald because Sherlock Holmes was his life. Jayne was here for the vacation, and Ryan had come because he was Ryan.

I noticed my mother glancing between Ryan and Grant, sizing them both up, wondering which one was with me. They were similar in age, and both extremely handsome. Ryan, all six foot three of him, had the look of his Black Irish ancestors, with warm blue eyes and thick dark hair cut very short. Grant was slightly shorter but also fit and lean, with brown hair curling around his collar and hazel eyes containing flakes of green that danced when he smiled.

Greetings over and introductions made, my parents took their seats. We occupied a large round table in a corner with enough space for us all. A plush banquette, covered in red silk with a pattern of tigers and cheetahs etched in gold thread, was tucked into an alcove, and the chairs around the table were upholstered in green and gold velvet. Paintings of big cats hung on the walls, and the doorways and alcoves were trimmed in gilt. Being in the basement, the room had no windows; a soft golden light, the type that makes everyone look good, came from lamps and the candles on each table.

This time, it was my turn to give Ryan's hand a squeeze. He was anything but the nervous sort, but he'd been nervous at meeting my parents for the first time. Earlier, he'd called me down to his room to help him choose what to wear. He didn't want to look too formal, as though he were trying to impress anyone, or too casual, as though he couldn't be bothered to make the effort. I'd told him to take off the suit and tie and wear jeans and a leather jacket and just be himself. He looked so good tonight.

Of course, he looked good all the time.

I gave him a smile and his blue eyes twinkled in response. My mother noticed and she nodded in approval.

The waiter brought Pippa's drink and asked what the newcomers would have. Mum ordered a Kir Royale and Dad a single-malt scotch. My mother had come straight from court and was dressed in her regular uniform of black suit with white blouse and black shoes with low heels. Dad, recently retired, wore neatly pressed beige trousers and an oatmeal sweater. In contrast, Donald looked like an unmade bed—which he was, as he still wore the clothes he'd slept in on the plane—in many-times-washed jeans and a rumpled T-shirt under his equally rumpled sports jacket. Jayne looked lovely, as she always did no matter how jet-lagged she might be, in a navy-blue dress with a thin white belt. Grant, like Ryan, had dressed suitably for a casual dinner.

When the waiter left to fetch the drinks, Dad asked Donald if this was his first time in London, and Donald erupted with enthusiasm. "I can't believe I've never been to England before. Imagine, I'm treading the very streets frequented by Sherlock Holmes and Dr. John Watson."

"You do know they weren't real people, don't you, Donald?" I teased. Donald knew, but his enthusiasm got the better of him sometimes.

"Imaginatively speaking, of course," he said. "But Sir Arthur himself trod these ancient cobblestones." Donald's eyes shone, and I thought of the construction work we'd had to detour around on the approach to the hotel. Not many ancient cobblestones left in Kensington.

"On the cab ride here," he continued, "we drove right past Gloucester Road station. I couldn't believe it! The very place where, in *The Bruce-Partington Plans*, Holmes himself walked along the rails, intent on a mission of the utmost national importance, to ascertain if the houses backing onto the rail track had windows looking over it. I was so excited to see more, I didn't take the time to unpack but rushed off to have a closer look." He leaned over and pulled a leather briefcase off the floor. "Would you like to see my pictures?"

"Of Gloucester Road station?" Mum said. "Perhaps not right now."

Undeterred, Donald pulled a small compact camera out of his case and switched it on. He leaned closer to Jayne and held the camera in front of her face. He flicked happily through it. "I particularly loved the flower seller. QUEEN OF GLOUCESTER ROAD spelled out in flowers. Isn't that clever?"

"Very clever," Jayne agreed, suppressing a yawn. London time is five hours ahead of Massachusetts, and we'd been on a late flight last night. I should probably have put dinner with the family off for another day, but the conference began tomorrow and we'd be busy over the weekend.

"What time's your talk, Gemma?" Dad asked.

"Two thirty tomorrow."

"We'll be there," he said.

"You don't have to come if you don't want to," I replied. "It's not going to be very exciting."

"A lecture on Sherlock Holmes pastiche," Pippa said. "What could possibly be more thrilling?"

Donald didn't catch my sister's sarcasm. "I totally agree! Gemma is going to be fascinating, and her talk will be about far more than just books. I printed out the schedule for the weekend, and I've marked off the lectures and panels I'm planning to attend." He rummaged around inside his bag. "Would you like to see?"

"No, thank you," she said.

He pulled the sheets of paper out anyway. "The weekend will be all about the conference, but on Monday I'll be free to visit Baker Street and the Sherlock Holmes Museum. I'm scheduled for a walking tour of Holmes's London on Monday afternoon."

I sipped my glass of prosecco. "I assume you're too busy to come and hear me speak, Pippa."

"I wouldn't miss it," she replied.

Jayne glanced between us.

"And you, Grant," Pippa said. "Will you be speaking also?"

"Not me," he said. "I'm here to check out the books for sale. I'm a rare-book dealer, and I specialize in Victorian and Edwardian crime fiction. I have several clients at home who might be interested in some of the items on offer this weekend."

"Book collecting must be *so* interesting," she said.

He straightened in his chair and adjusted his shoulders. "I find it so."

Pippa was seated on the other side of the table from me. Too far away for me to give her a solid kick in the shins. Instead I gave her a warning look. She smiled in return before turning back to Grant. "Do tell me about your time at Oxford. I myself went to Cambridge."

"We're rivals, then," he said.

"So we are."

"Did you remember to get us banquet tickets, dear?" my mother asked.

"I did, and it's a good thing, because they told me they're almost sold out. Are you sure you want to come? I can probably sell the tickets back to the organizers."

"Of course we want to come," Dad said. "Arthur is being honored."

My great-uncle Arthur Doyle had opened the Sherlock Holmes Bookshop and Emporium at 222 Baker Street, West London, Massachusetts. A few years later, I'd joined him in the business, and I was now the manager and co-owner. He was being given an award at the conference's Saturday night banquet for helping to spread the love of Sherlock Holmes beyond Britain's shores. Actually, I was being given the award and would be saying a few words of thanks in his place. Arthur had considered attending the conference until he heard he'd be expected to give a speech, so he'd suggested I (more like forced me to) come instead.

"I reserved us a table at a place not far from here." My father scooped up a handful of nuts and popped them into his mouth.

"Thanks," I said. "Jayne had a nap when we checked in, but we'll all want an early night."

Jayne attempted, and failed, to smother another yawn.

Pippa flirted with Grant, and Grant flirted back. Mum asked Jayne if she had plans for the visit apart from the conference. Dad asked Ryan what he did for a living, and my father, a retired officer in the Metropolitan Police, was absolutely delighted to hear that Ryan was a West London police detective.

It was early, just after five, but the bar was filling up. I caught quite a few American accents and wondered if those people were here for the conference.

A burst of loud laugher came from the stairwell and a group of men came in. They were a mixture of nationalities—American, English, French, a Scotsman—but they had one thing in common: they weren't here for their first drink of the day.

They grabbed a table in the center of the room and, with much shouting and laughing, pulled up chairs.

"Do you live nearby, Mrs. Doyle?" Jayne asked.

"Call me Anne, please. We're not far at all. The location of this conference of yours turned out to be very convenient for us."

"Things have changed a lot on the force since my day," Dad said to Ryan. "Even though that wasn't long ago."

"What do you do, Pippa?" Grant asked.

"A minor clerical position with the Department for Transport," Pippa said with a light laugh. "I'm basically just a pencil pusher." She ran her hands across her glass as she talked. She was, I knew, keeping them busy and out of the nut dish.

I sipped my prosecco and glanced around the room. The waiter had brought tall glasses of beer and bowls of nuts for the newcomers at the center table. The men lifted their glasses, clinked, and said, "Cheers," before taking a hearty swig. One of them did not join the others in the toast. Instead, he stared intently at our table. He caught me watching but did not turn away.

I leaned across Ryan and spoke to my dad in a low voice. "Center table. Big guy in a blue shirt. He seems to be watching you."

Beside me, I felt Ryan stiffen. Dad stretched his shoulders with a groan. He leaned over to speak to Jayne, which, not at all incidentally, gave him a view of the room behind him.

Shock, followed by anger, crossed his face.

The big man in the blue shirt grinned.

My dad turned back to our table. He picked up his glass and finished his drink. "Time to be off. The restaurant won't hold our place much longer."

"Excellent," Donald said. "I'm starving. Perhaps we could go to a genuine English pub one night?"

"I know the perfect place," I said.

"Is something the matter?" my mother said to my father.

"No." He got to his feet, his face set in tight, angry lines.

Ryan jumped up, ready to follow him.

"The walking tour should be fascinating," Donald said to Jayne. "I hope it doesn't rain."

The man at the center table watched us gather our coats and bags. The waiter hurried over with our bill. I grabbed it. "I'll sign for it." If Donald had to calculate his share of the bill, determine the exchange rate, work out a suitable tip, and then examine every pound note and coin in his wallet, we'd never get out of here.

Dad stepped back and allowed Mum and Jayne to precede him. Mum was telling Jayne she must visit the food hall at Harrods, which was within easy walking distance of our hotel.

"What's wrong?" Pippa asked in a low voice. "Why the sudden rush?"

"Nothing's wrong," Dad said. "I'm hungry. Let's go."

I gestured to Grant and Ryan to go with Pippa, Jayne, Mum, and Donald. Dad and I followed. As we passed the big table in the center of the room, the man in the blue shirt stood up. "Henry Doyle."

"Randolph." Dad's voice contained not a touch of warmth. "What brings you to this part of town?"

"Business, what else?" Randolph studied me, his hand resting on his chin, his head cocked slightly to one side. "It's been a while, Henry. Don't tell me this is sweet little Phillipa, all grown up."

"I'm not Phillipa." I took my cues from Dad. He was not at all friendly with this man, so I wouldn't be either.

"You must be her sister, then. You look very much like your mother when she was your age. Anne's as beautiful as I remember, although *you've* aged a lot, Henry. Nice to see you two are still together. And they said it wouldn't last." A small smile touched the edges of Randolph's mouth. He was about the same age as my parents, late fifties, well groomed and casually yet expensively dressed. His companions' conversation died as they looked between us and their friend in confusion. One of the men wore a Baker Street Irregulars lapel pin. So he, at least, was here for the conference. Which might mean this Randolph, whoever he might be, was as well.

Ryan and Pippa hadn't left the room with the others. They stood in the doorway, watching.

"Anne didn't recognize me," Randolph said. "I guess I've changed a lot over the years. But you knew me right off, Henry."

"I've seen your mug shots," Dad said.

Randolph laughed heartily. "I bet you made a point of searching for them. Oh, yes, I've followed your career too. Now that we've run into each other, let's keep in touch." He opened his wallet and took out a business card. He held it out, but my father didn't accept it.

"If you'll excuse us," Dad said. "I'm going to dinner with my family." He walked away. I followed. I couldn't resist glancing over my shoulder as I passed through the doorway.

Randolph had picked up his beer, but he hadn't taken his seat. He lifted his glass in a toast and gave me a broad wink.

I grabbed Dad's arm at the bottom of the stairs and spoke in a low voice. "What was that about?"

"Best not mention this to your mother," he said.

"Why not? Who was that?"

"An old case," he said.

"No it wasn't. He knew Mum and he knew your children's names, Pippa anyway. He said I look like Mum, but he looks more like her than I do. The same accent, the same eyes and chin. They even have the same mannerisms, that way of cocking the head to one side when studying something."

Dad grinned at me. "I see living in America hasn't dulled your wits any. Which one of those young men is your boyfriend? The police officer, I suspect. A good choice. The other was clearly smitten by your sister, yet you didn't seem to mind overly much."

"Dad. Tell me what's going on. Those men Randolph is with are here for the conference, so I suspect he is too."

My father hesitated for a moment before he said, "That, my dear, is your uncle Randolph. The family called him Randy."

"I have an uncle named Randolph? Why have I never heard of him before?"

"He's your mother's younger brother. The black sheep of the Denhaugh family. He and I never did like each other much. I haven't seen Randy since the night he stole the Constable your grandfather had put away to provide him and your grandmother with some much-needed income for their old age. Shall we join the others?"

Chapter Two

The Sherlock Holmes in the Modern World conference was a big affair. Sherlockians had come from all over the world to attend a weekend of all-Holmes, all-the-time.

I'm not an excessively enthusiastic Sherlockian myself. I enjoy the original Conan Doyle stories and many of the offshoots, and confess to having a small weakness for Benedict Cumberbatch's portrayal of the Great Detective. But I can't discuss the minutiae of the Canon in great detail, argue over the finer points, or identify which obscure quote comes from which obscure story.

I leave that to my father's uncle Arthur, founder and co-owner of the Sherlock Holmes Bookshop and Emporium. Retired after a long and successful career in the Royal Navy, acting totally on impulse, Great-Uncle Arthur bought the building at 222 Baker Street in West London, Massachusetts, for its address, whereupon he turned it into a shop dedicated to all things Sherlock Holmes. He loved setting up the store, searching for and purchasing stock, and chatting with potential customers, but he soon tired of the actual running of the business and tried to sell it. He couldn't find a buyer for such a specialized bookstore.

Whereupon I arrived on the scene, fresh from getting rid of my partnership in a mystery bookshop near Trafalgar Square and looking for a fresh start. Now I own half the business and run it. Uncle Arthur is a silent partner, in the bookstore as well as in the bakery next door, which we call Mrs. Hudson's Tea Room and own along with Jayne Wilson, who also serves as head baker and restaurant manager.

At this moment, Great-Uncle Arthur was at the shop, keeping an eye on things with the help of my assistant, Ashleigh, and caring for our cocker spaniel, Violet. Our shop cat, Moriarty, pretty much looks after himself. It was mid-January and business was slow, so I hoped they'd be able to manage without me. Jayne had reluctantly left the tearoom in the hands of Fiona and Jocelyn, her helpers. It hadn't been easy, but I'd managed to convince her to come. She's been working nonstop since opening the bakery a year and a half ago; she needed the break.

Donald had heard of the conference some time ago and made plans to attend. Without asking my permission, which I would not have given, he'd proposed my name as a speaker. When I received the invitation, I'd been about to refuse, but Uncle Arthur suggested I accept the award in his place. The timing was perfect: January, when business in the shop is at its slowest. Donald told Grant about the event, and Grant decided to come along. Ryan then decided to come too, saying he had vacation time to use up. (I hoped he wasn't with us because he wanted to keep an eye on Grant, who had once had feelings for me.) As our group got larger and larger, I managed to convince Jayne to join us as a delayed birthday treat. Jayne's birthday is January 6, which I remember only because it's the same date as

Sherlock Holmes's. Not that the Sherlock of Sir Arthur Conan Doyle's imagination has a birthday, but for some reason fans have settled upon that day.

When I discovered that Donald had done nothing at all about planning how to get to the conference, never mind where to stay once he arrived, I took over managing the details of the trip. By the time I made up my mind to come, the conference hotel was fully booked, so I put us all in the Bentley, also located on the street named Harrington Gardens, wanting to be as near the action as possible. Jayne had balked at the expense and wanted to back out of the plan, so I'd had to talk her into sharing a room with me by telling her it was my birthday gift to her.

That left Ryan in a room one floor below us, bunking in with Donald.

He hadn't complained about that *too* much.

As well as delivering my talk on Sherlock Holmes and popular culture on Friday afternoon and accepting Uncle Arthur's award at the Saturday evening dinner, I planned to check out things I might want to stock in the shop. We're primarily a bookstore, but over the years we've gradually accumulated all the paraphernalia that goes with the name of the Great Detective these days: coloring books, socks, teacups, coffee mugs, puzzles, dolls, calendars, life-sized cardboard cutouts; the list is practically endless.

My lecture was scheduled for two thirty on Friday, the first day of the conference. I planned to relax in the morning and tour the exhibit hall before giving my talk.

*   *   *

The restaurant prices at our hotel were well out of my comfort zone, so first thing Friday morning Jayne and

I went in search of breakfast. We ended up at Garfunkel's, located in a small arcade off Gloucester Road, where I enjoyed a proper English breakfast with an excellent cup of tea before heading to the conference.

"Let's check out the exhibit floor," I said. "I'm looking for items we can stock in the Emporium. Nothing our regular customers would find too expensive and nothing we'll have trouble importing into America."

We walked into the exhibit space. The room was large and well lit, with a high ceiling, ornate ballroom chandeliers, and a practical multicolored carpet. Tables and booths had been laid out in rows, every one of them covered in some variation of Holmes-related merchandise, ranging from costumes to art to books to scale replicas of the sitting room at 221B or Baskerville Hall. Quite a few people, vendors as well as those browsing, wore some variation of Victorian attire. I saw one person dressed as Data role-playing Sherlock from the old TV show *Star Trek: The Next Generation*.

"Donald's going to be in heaven," Jayne said.

"Speaking of heaven, always nice to see you two in a morning." Grant Thompson popped between us.

"Good morning. How are you today?" I asked.

"Just great." He was almost sparkling. The green flakes in his hazel eyes shone in the light from the chandeliers. He was freshly shaven and smelled of good soap. I recognized the scent; before turning in last night, Jayne had switched on the jets in the deep tub in our room and poured in the entire bottle of hotel-provided bath salts.

"I hope you didn't get back to the hotel too late," Jayne said. After dinner, my parents had bid us good night and headed home. Grant and Pippa had gone for another drink, while the rest of us staggered our weary way back to the hotel and collapsed into our baths or beds.

"Not too late," Grant said with a grin. I swallowed a sigh. Pippa was, sometimes, not a nice person. I don't mean she intended to be cruel, but she didn't always (like ever) pick up on other people's unspoken signals, and the only thing in her life that mattered to Pippa was Pippa, followed by her job and our parents. I reminded myself that Grant would be on the flight home with the rest of us on Tuesday, so she couldn't do too much damage to his heart. Besides, he was a big boy. He didn't need my well-meaning advice.

"Have you seen Ryan and Donald this morning?" I asked.

"They were having coffee in the hotel restaurant when I came down. Donald couldn't stop complaining about the price of the breakfast."

"Welcome to London," I said.

"Ryan wants to see the Parliament buildings," Grant said. Ryan had not the slightest interest in Sherlock Holmes. "So he set off by himself as soon as he finished one cup of coffee. He asked me to tell you he'll try to get back in time for your talk. Did you hear your dad say he's going to see if he can arrange a visit to Scotland Yard?"

"I did. That'll make Ryan happy."

"Speaking of happy," Jayne said, "here comes Donald."

Our friend had dispensed with the ulster this morning and was dressed in jeans and a T-shirt that proclaimed, You Know My Methods. "I see people are dressing up already," he said with a pout. "I thought they'd only do that for the banquet on Saturday."

"Are we supposed to wear costumes?" Jayne said. "I didn't bring anything."

"Neither did I," I said. "And I have no intention of playing dress-up."

"Catch you later," Grant said, and we went our separate ways. Donald had his face buried so deeply in the program book he bumped into a young woman in full Victorian dress complete with aisle-filling bustle. He almost knocked her into a display of Sherlock-themed teacups. He carried on, not noticing the poisonous glare she threw after him.

Jayne and I walked down the closest row of tables and booths. I wasn't ready to get into buying conversations yet, just having a first look. But one of the largest displays had me stopping dead in my tracks.

The walls of the foldable partitions were covered in pencil and pen-and-ink sketches illustrating scenes from the Canon. Holmes leaping nimbly across the moors. Holmes and Watson having tea in 221B or relaxing with their newspapers and pipes on a train. Holmes's walking stick slashing frantically at a bedside bell pull. A visit by the unruly young mob of street urchins he called the Baker Street Irregulars. Mrs. Hudson ushering in a darkly cloaked visitor.

The drawings were exceptionally well done. The representations were faithful to the spirit of the Canon and to its earliest illustrators. Even out of context and out of costume, this Holmes would be instantly recognizable—the lean face, the hook nose, the piercing intelligence in the eyes. Holmes and Watson wore the dress of Victorian gentlemen: hat, cane, cloak. The women, Mrs. Hudson, Irene Adler, and Violet Hunter recognizable among them, were in long dresses with either hats or aprons.

On first look, the pictures were standard Holmes fare, although exceptional in their quality. But look again, and something modern lay beneath the surface. The window out the train carriage showed a glass-and-concrete high-rise in the distance. An iPad was falling off the edge of the breakfast table. Mrs. Hudson had trainers, what Americans call sneakers, peeking out from beneath her dress. Look once more, and the modern became disturbing. The high-rise was all shattered windows and crumbling concrete; the iPad showed an image of an ambulance outside a hospital at night; Mrs. Hudson's laces were undone and her shoes covered in mud.

"Those are good," Jayne said.

"Slightly creepy, though," I replied.

"Then you perceive my intent," said a deep voice. "Many don't on first glance. But then again, I'd expect nothing else from Henry Doyle's daughter."

The man who'd spoken was the one my father had talked to in the bar at the Bentley last night. My uncle Randolph, apparently.

"Are you the artist?" I asked.

He gave me a slight bow. I studied him. The resemblance to my mother was there, but on him, I thought, the familiar features had a touch of meanness about them. Meanness and bitterness.

Then again, maybe I was being influenced by my father's reaction to this man.

He held out his hand. I took it in mine. His grip was strong. I kept mine firm without trying to engage in a battle of wills.

"Randolph Denhaugh, at your service." Denhaugh was my mother's maiden name. "My friends call me Randy."

"I'm Gemma Doyle, and this is my friend Jayne Wilson."

He didn't even glace at Jayne. That was unusual. Men liked to look at Jayne. "Ah, yes. Gemma. I'd heard Anne and Henry had a second daughter some years after Phillipa. My mother's name was Phillipa. Did you know that?"

"I know my maternal grandmother was Phillipa."

"She was a formidable woman. No one ever dared call her Pippa. Or, heaven forbid, Pip."

"Was she still alive when you stole the Constable?"

The edges of his mouth turned up. "So you've heard of me, then. I'm glad to hear it."

"I heard of you last night for the first time."

"I didn't steal the Constable. I took it as part of my inheritance. Although honesty forces me to admit that my parents hadn't died yet."

"A constable's a police rank," Jayne said. "How can you steal one?"

"You brought an American friend. Isn't that nice." Randy held out his hand, and Jayne took it. Her face was a picture of confusion, not only at misunderstanding Constable but at my attitude toward this apparent stranger.

"John Constable is one of England's greatest landscape painters," I said. "If you go to the National Gallery or the Tate Britain, you'll see many of his works."

"He's never been to my taste," Randy said. "I find his paintings too stodgy, too provincial."

"Stodgy," I said, gesturing to the display, "is not a word I'd use for your art."

He grinned. "Sherlock in the modern world. Isn't that what this little gathering is here to celebrate?"

"You don't seem to be celebrating it."

"What I'm attempting to say here, in my own small way, is that Holmes would take one look at our world and flee back to his own. Wouldn't you agree, Gemma?"

"As I know Holmes isn't a real person, I have no opinion on what he might or might not do in any circumstances."

"Fair enough," he said, "but a man has to earn a living. And this is how I am attempting to earn mine these days." He gestured to the metal cashbox, pile of business cards, and receipt pad on the table. "I'm surprised to see you here, at this thing." He dipped his chin to indicate the conference badge on the lanyard around my neck. "Wouldn't have taken a daughter of Anne for a Sherlock fanatic."

"Gemma owns—"

I cut Jayne off. "I'm interested in a great many things."

"I remember hearing something about Henry's eccentric uncle Arthur being convinced he's a relative of Conan Doyle."

"Arthur isn't—"

I cut Jayne off again. "Your work is impressive. I hope you do well here."

"Thank you. Your parents and I might not be close, to put it mildly, but I hope you and I can be friends. Perhaps we can have lunch one day or a drink later."

"Perhaps." I took Jayne's arm and we walked away. I imagined I could feel my uncle's intense stare boring into my back.

"What on earth was that about?" Jayne asked once we were out of Randy's hearing. "Is that guy a relative of yours? You weren't very friendly."

"He's my mother's brother, and I'd never even heard of him before last night. Dad said he's the black sheep of the family."

"Wow. Sounds interesting," Jayne said.

My father had said nothing further about it, despite my questions as we walked through the darkening streets to dinner.

Jayne and I made a circuit of the hall, and I made a mental note of the vendors I wanted to talk to in more detail later.

Jayne checked her watch. "We'd better go if we want to get a seat. It'll be standing room only for Mark Gatiss." Gatiss, who plays Mycroft Holmes on the *Sherlock* TV show as well as being a writer and coproducer, was scheduled to appear at eleven, and I was looking forward to hearing what he had to say about creating and working on the hugely popular show.

Jayne was right, and I picked up my pace. As we passed the aisle where Randy (Uncle Randolph?) had his goods displayed, I was distracted by the sound of raised voices. Heads turned and people stopped walking.

"You owe me big time, and I want it now!"

I also stopped walking. A small woman stood in Randy's space. She was a good foot shorter than him, but she almost pressed herself up against him, so he had to look down at her. She wore an ankle-length multicolored dress, her hair was tied back in a mass of dreadlocks, a row of piercings ran up both ears, and a thick silver band was wrapped around every finger. At the moment, her index finger was extended, and she jabbed it into Randy's chest.

"No," she said. "I will not stop making a scene. I want to make a scene. I want everyone here to know you stole my idea." She whirled around to face the onlookers, her skirt forming a circle of swirling color. Some people ducked their heads and returned to their own business, not wanting to be caught staring. Many kept staring.

I did.

The woman threw out her ringed hands. "All this, all this, was my idea! I had the concept. I made the original sketches. I thought we were friends. And instead"—she turned again and pointed theatrically at Randy, who shrugged—"he went behind my back and stole them."

Two security guards, a man and a woman, approached at a rapid trot. "Come with us, please, madam," the man said.

The short woman glared at Randy. "You haven't heard the last of this."

"Oh, I'm sure I haven't," he said.

She walked away, head high and steps firm. The security guards scurried after her, relieved the scene had ended so easily. Randy lifted his arm and his sleeve fell back. He spun the index finger of his right hand in the air beside his ear. A few people laughed.

"That was interesting," I said to Jayne. "Second time in two days I've heard my long-lost uncle be accused of theft."

Chapter Three

Jayne and I were lucky enough to snag the last two seats in the packed room for Mark Gatiss, off to one side, near the front. We enjoyed his talk very much. He was funny and charming, and answered audience questions with genuine warmth and interest.

Although I caught the occasional slip of his smile and the half roll of his eyes at one in an endless stream of questions about what Benedict Cumberbatch was *really* like.

We filed out of the room amongst a pack of eagerly chatting fans.

"What's next on the schedule?" I asked Jayne.

"Lunch," she said. "Do we want lunch?"

"Not after that big breakfast."

"Which is why Anna, Duchess of Bedford, invented afternoon tea. One of the things I most want to do in London is have afternoon tea. Where do you think's the best place for the whole experience?"

"They do a marvelous tea at the Orangery at Kensington Palace. You could tell everyone at home you had tea in Kensington Palace without adding that you had to pay an exorbitant amount for it and no one from the royal family joined you."

"That would sound impressive, all right."

"The National Portrait Gallery does a nice tea as well, and you get a great view over the rooftops to

Trafalgar Square and down Whitehall. I used to go there when I had American publishers and publicists visiting the shop and I wanted to treat them. By treat them, I mean let them pay."

Jayne clapped her hands. "There's so much to see and do. I wish we were staying longer. Hey, there's your dad." She waved, and my father broke into a huge smile.

He gave me a light kiss on the cheek and said hello to Jayne. "Nervous?" he asked me.

"About what?" I said.

"About giving your talk?"

"Oh, that. Why would I be nervous?"

"Gemma doesn't do nervous," Jayne said. "Instead, I get nervous for her."

The short woman who'd accosted Randy earlier walked swiftly past us, skirt swinging, dreadlocks bouncing, jewelry clanking, paying no attention to anything going on around her. "Do you know who that is?" I asked my father.

He watched her go and then shook his head. "Should I?"

"She's no friend to Randolph Denhaugh."

"Not many people are. He doesn't keep friends for long. No longer than it takes to fleece them, anyway."

"You going to tell me the story there?"

"Someday, perhaps. Can I take you ladies to lunch?"

"No lunch for us, thanks," I said. "But if you're going someplace, we'll join you and have a cup of tea."

"I'm heading back to the hotel," Jayne said, "to check into the times for some of the things I want to do in the city tomorrow and Sunday. I'll be back in time for your talk, Gemma." She wiggled her fingers at us and slipped into the crowd.

"Your friend's nice," Dad said.

"She is definitely that." Jayne had her phone with her and the hotel provided free Wi-Fi for conference attendees. She didn't need to go to our room. She wanted to let my father and me have some time alone together. I slipped my arm through his and we went to the hotel restaurant.

I ordered tea and Dad asked for steak and kidney pie, his favorite.

"Don't tell your mother," he said after he'd handed the waiter his menu.

"Tell her what?"

"That I'm having a pie and mash. Now I'm retired she thinks I'm a prime candidate for a heart attack, and she's put me on a diet."

This was the first I'd heard of any heart problems. I looked at my father in alarm. His color was good, his eyes clear, and he hadn't put on more than a pound or two since I'd last seen him.

He read my face and gave me a big smile. "Don't worry, Gemma. I'm as healthy as I ever was. One of the solicitors in her chambers dropped dead of a heart attack a week after his retirement party. Your mother's convinced retirement killed him, not the fact that he was a two-pack-a-day smoker and he weighed close to twenty stone."

"That'll do it," I said. Twenty stone was almost three hundred pounds. I leaned back to allow the waiter to put my tea things in front of me. I happily breathed in the scent of a perfectly prepared cup of tea. "Now that you've retired, is Mum thinking about doing the same?"

"She's thinking about it, yes. But thinking and doing are very different things. I'm well aware a lot of old cops can't cope very well with retirement, but I've always had my woodworking to keep me focused. I'm selling some pieces now."

"Glad to hear it," I said. Before I'd been born, Dad had set up a woodworking shed in the back garden. When things on the job were particularly tough, he retreated in there and dealt with all the stress and anger by making beautiful sculptures and playful toys.

My mother was a barrister, a trial lawyer. She and her chambers—her law firm—was one of the most highly regarded in the city. My dad had been a cop. Police officer and defense lawyer didn't make for an easy marriage sometimes. But my parents loved each other deeply and they made it work. They were different in many ways. Dad was from a working-class family. His father had been a construction worker and his mother a store clerk, whereas Mum's family was genuine aristocracy—although her extended family had the title and it was a minor one at that. Her family had been penniless since the late nineteenth century, when a drinking, gambling, dissolute son invested everything in a scheme to find gold in the jungles of Borneo.

Gold had not been found in Borneo, and said son had spent the remainder of his days, and the last of the family money, in a mental asylum.

These days the family seat—meaning the house and the land that couldn't be sold off—was crumbling into ruin, and I hadn't seen the current earl, my third cousin twice removed (or was it second cousin three times removed?) since my christening.

"Speaking of families . . ." I said.

"Were we?" Dad asked.

"We are now. Tell me about Randolph. He's here, at this conference, selling sketches in the exhibit room. They're very good."

The waiter brought Dad's lunch: a large round pie with a glistening golden crust, thick brown gravy, a mountain of mashed potatoes drenched in butter, and a side of mushy peas. Dad picked up his knife and fork and cut into the pie. Steam, fragrant with the smell of beef and onions, rose into the air, and the filling spread through the potatoes.

"Want some?" Dad said.

"Oh, yeah." I pushed my side plate over and he served me a healthy portion.

I savored a few bites and then repeated my question. "Randolph?"

"First, what's your take on him, Gemma?"

I thought. "He's been in prison, but probably not for too long. He has at least one poorly applied tattoo, what the Americans call a prison tat, visible above his right wrist." I'd noticed that when he lifted his hands to joke to the onlookers that the woman who'd confronted him was crazy. "His color is fine, for an Englishman in January anyway, so it's been some time since he was in jail. He has a similar accent as Mum, which you'd expect, but slightly different, which means they were educated apart. Mum's dad went to Eton, so his son likely did also, but Randolph didn't attend Cambridge or Oxford."

Dad nodded. "Close enough. He was kicked out of Cambridge first term."

"If he did the drawings I saw this morning—and judging by his attitude to them, he did—then he's highly talented, but he doesn't take his art seriously. I don't think he takes much seriously."

"Except the pursuit of money," Dad said.

"Considering he's staffing his own booth at a fan conference, his career as an artist isn't proving all that lucrative. Meaning, he has to find money another way."

He'd stolen a valuable painting from my grandparents more than thirty years ago. He'd been in prison at least once. He was, judging by his drawings, a highly skilled and highly detailed artist. That, plus the accusations the dreadlocked woman had thrown at him, led me to the logical conclusion. "His past, and maybe his present, is in art forgery?"

Dad grinned at me. "You got it. I've unofficially followed Randy's career for a long time. After he was expelled from Cambridge for forging a letter of recommendation, he went to Camberwell College of Arts. He didn't last there either. Something about paying another student to write a paper for him. He tried to make it in the London art world, but nothing came of it. He has talent to spare, but not a breath of originality."

"Exactly the skill set required for a forger."

"Now he's on police radar as a forger, he can't get much work. Which is why, I assume, he's trying to get by selling his own art." Dad scraped his plate almost down to the pattern.

I poured myself another cup of tea. "You're right he's short of money, and no doubt not at all happy about it."

"Why do you say that?"

"His clothes, both last night and today, were middling expensive, and reasonably new or at least well maintained, but his shoes showed signs of excessive wear. He's keeping up appearances as best he can, but he has to cut corners where he hopes it won't be noticed. He was wearing the same shoes last night, with black dress trousers, as today with khakis." Dad nodded, telling me to go on. "As people have come for this weekend from all around the world, and some pack lighter than others, on most people at the conference I wouldn't consider the lack of shoes matching clothes to indicate a problem, but Randy lives in London."

"How do you know that?"

"He has an Oyster card, a Tube pass. I saw it last night when he opened his wallet to take out his business card. Although, I will admit, tourists buy Oyster cards for temporary visits."

"Randy might seem like a charming old rogue," Dad said. "But he's nothing of the sort."

"I didn't think so," I said.

"I can't help thinking it's not a coincidence he's here, this weekend. Your name is listed on the conference website as a guest speaker, Gemma. Be warned. He broke your grandparents' hearts when he took the Constable and disappeared. They didn't have much money, but they used what they did have to give your mother and her brother a good education. The Constable was an inheritance, one of the only things saved when the family lost everything, and they needed it to help them in their old age."

"What happened to the painting?"

Dad shook his head. "I've no idea. I've never worked in art fraud, but I made a few inquiries over the years. It seems to have simply disappeared. Probably locked in some Middle Eastern art collector's private vault these days. Everyone knew Randy took it, but your grandparents wouldn't help the police investigate, so he was never charged. They hoped he'd have a change of heart and bring it back. That never happened. Keep away from him, Gemma, that's all I ask."

Dad rubbed his face, and he suddenly looked twenty years older. "I only hope your mother doesn't catch sight of him. She adored her little brother. It was an enormous blow to her when he did what he did, and to this day she hasn't forgiven him. Ready to go?"

"Is Mum coming to hear me speak?"

"She'd like to, if she can get away in time."

Dad paid the bill and we left the restaurant. I wanted to check in with Ashleigh at the Emporium, so Dad and I separated in the lobby and I found a seat in a reasonably quiet corner.

"You're calling all the way from England!" Ashleigh bellowed.

I winced and pulled the phone away from my ear. "I can hear you perfectly well. No need to shout."

"Oh, sorry." Her voice dropped fractionally.

"How's everything there?"

"Good. Busy."

"Really?"

"Yes, really. We've been exceptionally busy. A lot of new customers too, which is surprising as the tourists aren't here. Quite a few elderly ladies have been coming in."

"So Uncle Arthur's been helping out."

"He's such fun, Gemma. I haven't laughed so much in years. Did you know he used to be the captain of a battleship?"

"I did know that, yes. About the store . . ."

"He knows everything there is to know about Sherlock Holmes. I'm learning so much!"

"That's good. Have you heard from—"

"He thinks the franchise idea's a good one."

I didn't. Ashleigh was a good employee. She cared about the business and wanted to see the shop doing well. She had more ambition for it than I did. I was happy with the Emporium the way it was. I didn't want to open more branches or set up franchise agreements, both of which Ashleigh thought would be great ideas.

"You might have a whole market we hadn't thought of," she said. "Some ladies from the retirement home came in yesterday. They want Arthur to speak to them about Sir Arthur Conan Doyle."

I grinned to myself. In the over-eighty set, Great-Uncle Arthur, an unmarried, healthy, and active man, was a valuable commodity.

"You're giving a lecture at that conference you're at," Ashleigh said. "Maybe we can open a speakers' bureau. You can make good money on the lecture circuit. Or so I've been told."

"I don't have time for anything like that."

"Sure you do. Now that I'm running the store on my own . . ."

I briefly considered hurrying back to the Bentley, throwing all my things into my suitcase, hailing a cab for Heathrow, and catching the first flight back to America.

My mother came into the lobby. She hesitated at the doors, looking around. Dad didn't want her to run into her long-lost brother. If she was here for my talk and didn't plan on seeing anything else of the conference, such as the exhibits in the dealers' hall, that might be possible.

I stood up and waved my arms over my head to catch her attention. "Gotta run. I'll call again later. Love to Uncle Arthur."

"Oh, one thing. I'm sorry, but Moriarty got into your office. I'm sure I shut the door after me when I went home last night, but maybe I didn't. Sorry. We're trying to dry out your laptop now. The guy at the computer shop says he thinks he can save the hard drive. Maybe."

My mother caught sight of me and headed my way. I said goodbye to Ashleigh and put my phone away. I'd worry about my shop cat and his act of sabotage later.

Moriarty never had liked me.

Mum and I brushed cheeks, and the familiar scent of Chanel No. 5 took me instantly back to my childhood. "Good news," she said. "I was assisting one of my juniors in court this morning. The Crown's star witness admitted on the stand that he might not have been at the bar at the time in question, but if he wasn't, he wanted to be. The case was dismissed, so I will not have to go over her strategy with her, and thus I have the remainder of the weekend free. How about we have a nice afternoon at Harrods tomorrow with lunch first?"

"I'd like that," I said. Shopping, to me, wasn't a recreational activity, but it was for my mother.

"Bring your friend Jayne—she's so sweet—and I'll check with Pippa."

"Are you coming to hear my talk?"

"Wouldn't miss it," she said.

"I have to go someplace quiet and read over my notes," I said. "I'll see you there. Room one ten. Dad's around somewhere."

I didn't actually have any notes to read over. I hadn't made any. I hadn't even thought about what I was going to say to fill an hour in front of a room full of people who'd come from all parts of the world to hear my insights into marketing the modern phenomenon known as Sherlock Holmes. I had about fifteen minutes to write and memorize a speech.

I needed a few moments of quiet to get my thoughts into some sort of order, but the lobby was busy and I feared random people might want to talk to me.

I glanced around, searching for someplace to escape to for a short while. A discreet darkened hallway led off a far corner of the lobby. It ran alongside the restaurant, so probably went to the kitchens. No guests would go there, so it should suit my purposes perfectly.

A few steps in and the cacophony behind me died away. I faced the wall to try to block out all distractions. I wanted to start my talk with an amusing anecdote about an Englishwoman out of her comfort zone in America. Unfortunately, I could think of no amusing anecdotes on the spur of the moment.

Jayne had asked me on the plane if I wanted her to help me write my speech. I told her I had it all in hand and opened the copy of *From Holmes to Sherlock* by Mattias Boström I'd brought for the flight, looking forward to the hours ahead with nothing to do but read.

In retrospect, that might have been a mistake.

Jayne knew plenty of stories about me living in America. Many of them I didn't find at all amusing, but other people seemed to.

Footsteps sounded on the floor behind me. I turned my head slightly, expecting to see a cook's helper or a waiter. Instead it was a large man in jeans and a denim jacket. He had not a strand of hair on his head and his face was clean-shaven. A tattoo of the outstretched talons of an eagle reached up out of his shirt collar on the left side of his thick neck. He studied me through narrow eyes so dark they were almost black.

I whirled around and tensed.

"Doyle," he said.

"You have the advantage of me," I said.

He blinked. "What's that mean?" London accent. East End. Not a lot of education. In contrast to his head, his hands were matted with black hair. Those hands were large and rough; an old burn scar crossed the back of the right. He smelled of tobacco, cheap aftershave applied far too liberally, and the beer he'd enjoyed at lunch.

"You know who I am," I said. "Who are you?"

"That doesn't matter, does it?"

"It matters to me." Behind him, I could hear the low buzz of conversation. People were leaving the lobby, heading for the two-thirty panels and my talk. No one came our way. The man filled the hallway with his bulk. I carried nothing but a small over-the-shoulder red leather handbag containing my phone, some cash, a credit card, and my room key. The key, unlike those of old, wasn't a heavy metal thing, just a thin piece of plastic. Good for opening doors, not so good for defending oneself. The streets were dry, with no rain or snow in the forecast, so I'd worn a pair of ballet flats and wasn't carrying an umbrella.

"Whatever," he said. "You tell your uncle my people want what's theirs."

That took me by surprise. I stopped mentally inventorying the contents of my bag. "What? I don't even know who you're talking about."

"You know. We saw you talking to him earlier, so we figured you'd be a good one to deliver the message. Tell him." He turned to go. I let out a long breath. He swung around. "I'm looking forward to your talk. I think Jeremy Brett was the best Holmes, don't you?" He nodded politely and then walked away.

What on earth?

I needed to find my dad, and right now.

A small figure appeared at the entrance to the hall. The man who'd spoken to me slipped past her and disappeared.

"I knew I'd find you hiding in some dark corner," Jayne said. "You're late. Your fans are getting restless."

"That man . . ." I said.

"What man?"

"The one who passed you just now."

She shrugged. "I didn't see anyone. Are you ready?"

"What time is it?"

"Two thirty-five. You're late. It's okay to be nervous, Gemma, but you can't not show up."

"I'm not nervous."

She placed a hand lightly on my arm. "I understand."

"Is my dad there?"

"Yes, and your mom too. They sent me to look for you."

We headed for the meeting rooms at the back of the hotel. The lobby and corridors were mostly empty now. I swerved as we passed the exhibit hall. The vendors relaxed and chatted to each other in the absence of browsing customers. No one was at my Uncle Randolph's booth.

Jayne grabbed my arm. "No you don't. This way." I allowed her to lead me on.

To my surprise, the room was packed. People, Ryan among them, lined the walls.

I'd thought a handful of people from the Sherlock tourist industry, if there is such a thing and there probably is, would be interested in my tales of owning a Holmes-themed shop, but no one else.

I walked up the center aisle with Jayne. A podium with a microphone and a glass of water was at the front. A projector sat on a table and a big white screen hung on the wall. Only now did it occur to me that I should have prepared some sort of slide show to illustrate my talk with pictures of things I sold at the Emporium.

Not only did I not have a slide show, at this moment I didn't even have a speech.

"Knock 'em dead," Jayne whispered to me after giving my arm one last squeeze before releasing her grip. She took a seat in the second row. I climbed the two steps to the podium and turned to face the crowd.

My parents sat together in the front row. They smiled broadly, and Mum gave me a small wave. It reminded me of when I'd had the role of Gwendolen in my school's production of *The Importance of Being Earnest* when I was in fourth form. The only reason I, who had no interest whatsoever in theater, got the part was because both the lead and the understudy took ill and I was the only one in the class who knew the lines. I'd been roped unwillingly into helping to build the sets and had overheard most of the rehearsals.

I glanced at Ryan. He gave me a big thumbs-up. I studied the crowd. Grant sat next to Pippa. Donald had found a group of the like-minded, all of them wearing Inverness capes, ulsters, or tweed suits.

I did not see the man who'd accosted me in the kitchen hallway, nor did I see my Uncle Randolph.

"Good afternoon," I said. "My name is Gemma Doyle, and I own the Sherlock Holmes Bookshop and Emporium at 222 Baker Street in West London, Massachusetts."

Chapter Four

"Excellent speech, Gemma," Donald Morris said. "Glad you approve," I said.

"Good job, darling," my mother said.

"Imagine," Pippa said, "you managed to make a dead fictional character sound interesting. Although I fear no one can make him believable."

"I wouldn't say that too loudly if I were you," Grant said.

My sister gave him a smile.

We stood outside the lecture room. People crowded around, not only my family and friends, but others wanting to press their business cards on me or tell me about the must-have merchandise I needed to come and see *right now*.

Ryan put his arm around my shoulders. "They liked your jokes too."

"I told jokes? Dad, I need to talk to you in private."

"I'm thinking a celebratory drink would be nice," Pippa said.

"I'm in," Grant said.

"You'll have to go without me," Donald said. "I want to hear the panel on the importance of Watson. Oh, Jayne, I've arranged for us to go to the Sherlock

Holmes Museum at noon tomorrow. I don't think I can wait until Monday."

"I don't . . ." Jayne said, as Donald wandered off.

"Dad," I said. "I need . . ."

"Is this a private party or can anyone join?" Randolph Denhaugh pushed himself into the circle.

My father instantly went into full cop mode. Straight shoulders, head up, back stiff, knees slightly bent, fingers flexed. Ryan noticed and did the same.

My mother stared at the newcomer. He grinned at her.

"Get lost," Dad said.

Randy ignored him. "Anne. It's been a while."

Mum's mouth hung open, but she quickly recovered her wits and said in a low voice, "Randolph? Randy? Is that you?"

"The one and only." He opened his arms and stepped toward her. Dad pushed himself between them. "I said, get lost."

"It's all right, Henry." Mum made no move to enter her brother's hug, and he dropped his arms. "I'm surprised to see you here, Randy. Have you gone straight at last?"

Grant threw a questioning look at Pippa.

"I have," Randy said. "Straight as an arrow. I heard someone mention a drink. Sounds like a grand idea to me."

"You are not invited," Dad said.

"Come on, Henry. Be nice. For old times' sake." Randy looked at my sister, who didn't appear all that surprised to see him. He smiled, but there was something deep and unpleasant behind the smile. "I'm sure you know everything there is to know about me,

Phillipa Doyle. In return, I'd like to hear what you've been up to all these years. The parts you can talk about, anyway."

"This is hardly the place," Pippa said. "If you want to come to my office one day next week, I know people who'd like to have a chat with you."

"I've nothing to say to anyone in your office, love. I'm out of the loop these days. How about that drink, Anne? We can talk about the old times and how close we were as children." He reached out a hand to my mother. My father knocked it aside.

Randolph turned to face him. All the charm and fake friendliness fled in an instant. "Keep your hands off me, Henry. Don't you dare touch me again." He almost spat out the words.

Ryan stepped closer to Dad. Randy glanced at Ryan. He might not have been afraid of my father, but the much younger, six-foot-three, well-muscled American was another matter.

"Stay away from my family," my father said.

We were starting to attract a crowd. People hesitated as they passed us, some giving us questioning looks.

Randolph let all the air out of his chest, and he shrugged. "You never did like me, Henry. That's okay, because I never did like you. Working-class ingrate, thinking you were good enough for my sister."

"That's enough." Mum's voice was low but full of command. As one of the top barristers in the city, she knew how to take control of a room with not much more than a whisper. "Randy, I'd like to say it's nice to see you, but you didn't need to ambush me in front of my family and in a public place. Which, I've no doubt, you did in a desire to attract as much attention as possible. In that at least, you haven't changed a bit. My daughter's here for a few days and I want to spend what free time I have with her. Please call my chambers next week and we can have lunch."

"I don't think—" Dad said.

"We can have lunch," Mum said, "and at that time you can tell me what you want from me."

"I don't want anything, Anne," Randy said.

"That," she said, "I do not believe."

Memories crossed his face, memory and emotion, and I guessed he was thinking about how brother and sister had been close once, when they were children. "Believe it or not, Anne," he said in a low voice, "people can change. If they really want to. Maybe it's my time." He blinked and the traces of emotion fled. "If you change your mind, I'll be around all weekend. I'm an honest man, here to earn an honest living. Come and see me in the exhibit hall. I'll offer you a discount on a picture." He turned to me. "You and I can talk about stocking my drawings in your store."

"They won't appeal to my customers."

"Then I can do something that will appeal. Your talk was interesting."

"I didn't see you there," I said.

"I didn't intend that you should."

I didn't believe him. He hadn't been in the room. I didn't remember much about what I had to say, although I seemed to have filled the hour and even told jokes and took questions. I'd been watching everyone in there, observing who was coming and going, thinking about the big man who liked Jeremy Brett and did not like Randolph Denhaugh. He knew Randolph was my uncle, and I wondered how. I hadn't known that myself until last night.

He hadn't come to hear me either.

"Anne will not be changing her mind," Dad said. "And I certainly won't. I'm glad you claim to be on the right side of the law these days, but nothing can change the past."

"My business is with my family," Randy said. "With Anne and my nieces. Not with you, Henry."

"I'm going to have a drink with *my* family," Mum said. "Which no longer includes you, Randolph. That was your choice, not mine. I'd give you my card, but you seem to be well informed about our doings. If you want to talk privately, you can call me." She took Jayne's arm. "I suggested to Gemma that we have a little trip to Harrods tomorrow for lunch and some shopping. Would you like to join us?"

"Oh yes. That would be fun." They walked away, heads close, chatting in light voices.

Pippa gave Randy a glare, and then she followed them. Grant hurried after her.

"What did he mean, people in your office?" I heard Grant ask my sister. "I thought you worked for the Department of Transport?"

"He's not as well informed as he thinks he is," Pippa replied.

Dad, Ryan, and I were left with Randy. A tense group in a big crowd.

"As pleasant as this has been," I said. "I'll go with Mum. Come on, Dad."

Randy stared at my father. A vein pulsed in his neck. Dad stood his ground. They were close in age, Randy a fraction taller, although he carried a lot more weight on his belly and around his chin.

Ryan remained braced to intervene.

Dad broke the silence. "Stay away from my wife."

"Or what?" Randy said.

"I still have contacts at the Met," Dad said, meaning the Metropolitan Police.

"I'm sure you do. Then again, I have friends also."

I threw a look at Ryan. This was escalating far too fast.

"Yeah, well, as for me," Ryan said, "I don't know a single person in this city who's not in this hotel right now, but I've heard a lot about your English beer. Anything you'd recommend I try, Henry?"

"I'm warning you . . ." Dad said.

"Is everything all right here?" The female security guard pushed herself into our space. The radio at her shoulder spat static. "It sounds rather tense. Perhaps you gentlemen can continue your conversation elsewhere."

Like a light being switched off, the fight went out of Randy's face and body. "Nothing to worry about. We're locked in a bitter discussion of who's the best Holmes. My friend here"—he indicated Ryan—"likes Robert Downey, but I insist no American can properly portray the Great Detective." He gave the guard his big warm smile. "I'm sure you'll agree."

She tried not to smile back. She was in her late fifties, rough around the edges. Despite her job, she was the right age to be charmed by my uncle. "Not a Holmes fan myself. See you don't get too enthusiastic about this *discussion*. People are becoming alarmed."

A small crowd milled around us. They pretended to be minding their own business, but ears were definitely flapping.

"I have to get back to my booth," Randy said. "I've left it unattended for too long. Catch you all later." He walked away, followed by the security guard.

Ryan let out a long breath. "That's not good, Henry."

"Thanks for backing me up. It wouldn't have come to a fight. He's not the type."

"Sounds like you haven't seen him for a long time," Ryan said. "Maybe he's the type now."

"Maybe," Dad said. "Shall we join the ladies?"

* * *

We found Jayne and my mother in the lobby, using their mobile phones to exchange scone recipes. My mother was by no stretch of the imagination a baker—she found boiling an egg a challenge—but I appreciated that she was trying to make Jayne comfortable.

"Where's Pippa?" I asked.

"She and Grant seem to have left without us," Mum said. "Is everything okay, darling?" she asked Dad.

"For now."

"Imagine, after all these years, Randolph shows up out of the blue."

"He's got a booth in the exhibit hall where he's selling sketches from the Canon," I said.

"He's making art out of artillery pieces?"

"Not cannons. The Canon. C-A-N-O-N."

"What canon?"

"Sherlock Holmes. That's why we're here, Mum. Remember?"

"Are you all right, Anne?" Dad asked.

She shook her head. "No. I'm not. It came as such a shock. So like Randy to pop out of the woodwork like that. If he'd wanted to meet with me, he should have called or sent a letter." She took my hands in hers. "I hope you don't mind, dear, but I'd like to go home.

I did enjoy your lecture. I'll call you first thing tomorrow to make arrangements for the shopping expedition."

I gave her a hug and felt the fragile bones beneath the thin frame. "Sure."

Dad took her arm and they walked away. I thought they looked very old as they made their way across the hotel lobby.

"That's real British stiff upper lip," Ryan said. "My mom would have thrown things."

"She'll wait until she gets home to do that. What's next on the agenda?" I asked Jayne.

"Count me out," Ryan said. "The time change is killing me, so I'm going to the hotel to put my feet up and see what I can get on TV. What are we doing for dinner?"

"Let's coordinate by text," I said. "Tonight we're free, but tomorrow's the banquet."

Ryan gave me a kiss on the cheek and left.

"I'm wanting to hear the panel on Basil Rathbone and other old-time Sherlock movies," Jayne said. "Are you coming?"

"I'd planned on taking another pass through the exhibit room. I saw some interesting things this morning I want to find out more about. Now I'm rather afraid to. I don't want to run into Randy again."

"That is so weird, your mom having a brother she hasn't seen in your whole lifetime."

"It is that," I said.

"Catch you later," Jayne said. "I'll text you when I get out of the panel to find out what's going on."

I decided to gather my courage around me and venture back into the exhibit hall. That was why I'd come, and I couldn't allow some long-lost relative to scare me off. There were things I wanted to see and people I wanted to meet. I'd simply have to try to stay as far away as I could from Randolph Denhaugh, black sheep.

I spent a productive hour browsing and chatting, accepting compliments on my speech, and collecting business cards and brochures. Importing things into America to sell at the Emporium might present a problem, but some of the vendors already had contacts on the other side of the pond I could tap into.

I would have liked to have a closer look at Randy's art. His sketches weren't suitable for my store—too dark in mood—but I'd enjoyed them. Instead, I took care not to get too near. If he noticed me in the area, he also chose to keep his distance.

At ten to five my phone buzzed with a text from Jayne: FINISHED HERE. DRINK?

ME: ON MY WAY

We met outside the doors of the exhibit hall and went to the hotel lobby bar. The room was packed, but we spotted a small unoccupied table by the windows and pushed our way through the crowd. Jayne took the seat facing into the room, leaving me to look out the window. The view overlooked a laneway and the solid brick wall of the building behind.

A young woman approached our table and asked what we wanted to drink. We both ordered a glass of white wine.

"In the books I read, in England you have to order at the bar and carry your own drinks to the table," Jayne said. "The characters are always jumping up and down fetching drinks. Isn't that right?"

"Depends on licensing," I said. "It's like that in pubs."

Jayne sucked in a breath.

"I hope you're not too disappointed," I said. "Maybe we can go to a pub for dinner tonight. I've been saving a special place to take Donald."

"It's not that." She nodded to the room behind me. "Don't look now, but your uncle Randy's coming in."

I doubt there's a phrase in the English language more inclined to make people instantly turn around than *don't look now*. I refrained from doing so. "Is he alone?"

"No. He's with a woman. They're looking for a place to sit. Oh, a group is getting up. Randy's snagged two seats at the bar."

"Tell me about the woman."

"What do you want to know?"

"Everything," I said. "Start with describing her. How old?"

"Older than us. Fifty-five, maybe."

"The right age to be a wife or girlfriend. Does their attitude to each other indicate that?"

"I'm not sure. They're not hugging or anything."

"Are they sitting close?"

"Not particularly."

Lights shone on the alleyway outside the window, so nothing inside the room reflected back at me. I started to turn around.

"Duck!" Jayne yelled.

I didn't duck, but I didn't complete the turn either.

"He's casing the joint. I mean he's looking around to see who's here. I don't think he saw us. He might not recognize me. I don't think he looked at me once with all the drama swirling around."

"Don't count on it," I said. "I suspect he's very perceptive, and you were with me when we first stopped at his booth." Never mind that Jayne—tiny, blonde, fair-skinned, heart-shaped face—attracted men's attention wherever she went.

"Okay, the bartender's asking what they want. You can look if you're quick about it."

I turned in my chair. The woman was, as Jayne had guessed, in her midfifties, short and slim with chestnut hair swirling around her shoulders, dressed in tight jeans with rows of rhinestones lining the seams. The jeans were tucked into calf-high leather boots with stiletto heels. A black shirt with a deeply plunging neckline was worn under a bubble-gum-pink jacket with elbow-length sleeves. A conference lanyard hung around her neck.

While Randy placed their order, his companion surveyed the room. I'd seen her in the exhibit hall earlier, staffing a booth selling Sherlock-themed jewelry. I'd paused to look, but nothing in the collection had struck me as original or good enough to be worth bothering with. She lifted her hand to tuck a lock of hair back, and I could see a big stone shining on the third finger of her left hand.

Randy swung around in his stool and I quickly turned away.

"She does not look at all happy," I said to Jayne.

"Even I can see that."

Not happy was an understatement. The woman was furious.

"Tell me what's happening," I said to Jayne.

"They're having champagne. He's raising his glass to her. She isn't returning the toast. Wow, she downed that mighty fast."

I absolutely hated observing events secondhand, but I was afraid if I turned, Randy would notice me and then he'd come over. I had absolutely no desire to talk to him.

Our waiter placed our drinks on the table. "Can I get you ladies anything else?"

"No, thank you," Jayne said.

Jayne and I clinked glasses and took our first sips.

"I looked Harrods up on the map," Jayne said. "The Victoria and Albert Museum isn't far from there. I'm thinking of doing the museum in the morning, and then meeting you and your mother for lunch."

"Hard to do the V&A in a morning," I said. "It's huge and everything in it is worth seeing."

"But that's all the time I have. I want to see so much. That's if I can sneak away without running into Donald and being dragged on his expedition to Baker Street."

"I'll run interference for you. I'll tell him I need your help in the morning."

"What have you got to do that I'd be any help with?"

"I'll think of something. Go shopping for bras maybe. That'll scare him off."

Jayne laughed. We sipped our wine and talked about what we'd seen and done at the conference today. When our glasses were approaching empty, Jayne glanced around the room, wanting to beckon the waiter to bring the bill. "Don't look now, but she's standing up. She looks mighty angry. He's lifting his hands. He's trying to placate her." A gasp. "She knocked his hand away."

I turned fully in my seat in time to hear the woman yell, with a trace of a Polish accent, "You really are a coldhearted creature, aren't you?"

Conversation in the bar momentarily died. The woman's face was bright red, her lips tight with anger, and her eyes blazed fire. In contrast, Randy grinned his self-satisfied, smug grin. "Takes one to know one, Arianna," he said. "You were pretty quick off the mark to check out the value, weren't you? Not a whole lot of trust toward your intended."

She threw the contents of her glass in his face. Then she turned on her heel and marched out of the bar. Everyone in the room watched her go.

Everyone except me. I kept my eyes on Randy. He scooped a napkin off the counter and wiped causally at the liquid dripping down his face. "Good thing," he said in a voice designed to carry, "I didn't buy her the good stuff."

A man at the table next to us laughed. The woman with him threw him a poisonous look, and he quickly took a gulp of his beer.

"Waiter!" Randy called. "I'll have another. And this time, I will have the good stuff." He looked directly at me and lifted his glass in a toast. *So much for trying not to be seen.*

A group of people walked between us, and when they'd passed, my uncle had turned back to the bar and was consulting with the waiter.

"I wonder what that was about," Jayne said as we gathered our things and left.

I didn't reply. The man who'd accosted me in the kitchen hallway earlier, the one who liked Jeremy Brett, was leaning against a wall near the exit. He stood in a circle of laughing men, holding a glass of beer in his hand, but he was not part of the group, and he was not enjoying himself along with them. His dark narrow eyes were fixed on Randolph Denhaugh.

Chapter Five

As I'd said to Jayne, I had a special treat in mind for Donald tonight.

After our drink, Jayne and I went back to the Bentley to meet the others. We didn't bother to change to go to dinner, and we were on our way shortly after six. Early enough, I hoped, to get a nice table in the Hereford Arms.

We were in luck and a big table near the fireplace was vacant. The pub was all brick walls and old wooden floors and scarred tables. The fireplace was real, making the room warm and cozy, and candles burned in hurricane lamps on the mantel. People, many of them from the conference, surrounded the bar and kept the bartenders hopping.

"In true English fashion," Ryan said, "I'll get the first round. Grant, give me a hand. What does everyone want?"

We placed our orders, and they pushed their way to the bar. "What'll you have, mate?" asked the bartender in a strong Australian accent. Donald, Jayne, and I shrugged off our coats and divested ourselves of scarves and gloves.

Donald dropped into a seat with a happy grin. "Exactly like the sort of pub Holmes and Watson might frequent," he said.

"It's more than that." I took his hand and helped him to stand. "Come with me."

A series of framed typed statements hung on the fireplace wall. I showed Donald the last one. He gasped.

According to the sign, Sir Arthur Conan Doyle had been a regular at this very pub when he was president of the College of Psychic Studies.

I left Donald staring openmouthed at the wall and went back to our table in time to accept a glass of wine from Ryan. Grant threw menus onto the table. Pippa had planned to join us tonight, but Grant told us she'd had to cancel at the last minute.

"What do you think she does as an admin assistant," he asked me, "that she'd get an emergency call to come into work on a Friday evening?"

"No idea," I said. And that was true. I had no idea what Pippa did. But I had my guesses. "Maybe her boss needed someone to take the minutes."

"I guess that's it," he said. "She's going to try to get to the banquet tomorrow night. I bought a ticket for her, just in case."

"Step carefully, Grant," I said.

He gave me a quizzical look. "What does that mean?"

I bit my tongue. I'd once told a woman that, based on my observations, her fiancé was interested in her only for her potential inheritance. She had not taken my kindly meant interference well. I seemed to remember a door slamming in my face. I didn't want that to happen between Grant and me.

"My parents were planning to come tomorrow," I said. "I'm not sure if they'll still want to after running into Randy."

"What's the story there?" Grant asked.

I told him what little I knew, and then we went on to talk about other things.

*   *   *

Saturday morning Jayne and I were on the steps of the Victoria and Albert Museum when it opened. I tried to show her my favorite things in the short time we had, but before I knew it, it was time to hurry to Harrods to meet Mum.

My idea of heaven is the sculpture hall in the V&A; Jayne's is the food hall in Harrods. I swear she must have had them open every large red tin of tea leaves so she could drink in the aroma of each one.

Once she'd loaded herself with various boxes of tea to take home, instead of going to the restaurant for our lunch we perched on stools at the fish counter, nibbled on oysters, sipped champagne, and watched the world go by.

Then we went upstairs to shop. While Jayne gagged at the prices, Mum tried on clothes for work—gray or black suits and starched white blouses, of course—and shoes for country weekends. Jayne bought a selection of scented soaps for her mother and a silk scarf for herself.

Dusk was falling when we staggered out of the store, Mum and Jayne laden with parcels. I emerged empty-handed.

"I need to get home and change. We can share a cab." Mum asked the doorman to fetch us a taxi. "Your event starts at seven, dear?"

"You're still coming?" I asked.

One of the iconic London black cabs screeched to a halt in front of us. The doorman opened the door and bowed us in. Mum pressed a coin into his hand. We climbed in. Mum and Jayne took the bench seats and I pulled down one facing them. Jayne bounced in her seat. "This is so cool. Just like in the *Sherlock* TV show."

Mum smiled at her. "As long as we don't get into a car chase." I was delighted they were getting on so well. My parents live in a row house on Stanhope Gardens, not far from the Bentley Hotel. The cab dropped Mum off first.

"I'm assuming," she said before she got out, "dress is not too formal?"

"Only if you plan on coming in a full Victorian gown. Corset and bustle and all."

"Perish the thought."

"That's the house you grew up in?" Jayne asked as the cab pulled back into traffic.

"Yes."

"The whole house?"

"Yes."

"I was looking at pictures in the window of the realtor's office last night. Even apartments in buildings like that cost a couple of million pounds."

"Forty years ago property in South Kensington was a lot cheaper than it is now," I said. My parents' house was in the center of the row. The houses on this street were typical of Kensington and similar neighborhoods in the West End. Three stories tall, painted white with a black door, white pillars on either side of the entrance, black-and-white-check tiles on the stairs and landing, black iron railings around a set of steep stairs leading belowground to what used to be the kitchen staff door. The second-floor balcony wasn't large enough for anything more than a few plant pots, and once my father had built his woodworking studio in the back garden, there hadn't been room for anything else. On the other side of the street an enclosed and locked square-block-sized private garden was provided for the enjoyment of residents of the street.

It had been a nice area in which to grow up. The house had belonged to my mother's parents, and they'd lived with us until they died within a year of each other when I was in fourth form, the equivalent to American grade ten. The house had been one of the few things of value my grandparents had. After, I'd learned yesterday, their son had absconded with their most valuable possession.

I'd always believed my mother was their only child. Every family picture I'd ever seen had shown my grandparents with just my mother. I remembered seeing a couple of snaps of Mum as a schoolgirl standing with a younger boy. A family friend, I'd been told, before the pages of the album were hastily turned.

"It looks like 221B Baker Street," Jayne said.

"A good deal more upscale," I said. "Did you know that when Conan Doyle wrote the Holmes stories, there was no such number as 221 on Baker Street?"

"You mean it was a fictional address?"

"Yes. The street has grown, as has London, since then."

It was almost six when we got back to the hotel, giving us not a lot of time to get ready for our night out.

My suitcase and I had been joyfully reunited yesterday. I changed into a black-and-white linen dress with a matching black jacket, opaque black leggings, and ankle-high boots. I put large silver hoops through my ears and a silver chain around my neck.

Jayne looked delightful in a slim-fitting raspberry dress and red heels. Then again, Jayne always looked delightful, even in the back of Mrs. Hudson's Tea Room in a hairnet with flour on her nose.

"The belles of the ball," I said as we studied ourselves in the mirror.

She gave me a spontaneous hug. "This is so great. I'm glad I came."

"I'm glad you came too. Next time we'll have to plan on staying longer."

"Your mother's taking me to the National Gallery and the Portrait Gallery tomorrow. Want to come?"

"No time. I need to do another round of the vendors and make contact with the ones I'm interested in."

Our hotel room was large enough for a desk with chair, a gold-brocade couch with two side tables, and a coffee table. Jayne's shopping bags were strewn everywhere, and almost every surface was covered by discarded clothes, scarves and gloves, suitcases, purses, guidebooks, conference programs, electronic cables and chargers, and advertising information. The two beds, dressed during the day in rich blue duvets and mounds of matching pillows, had been turned down while we were out. Right now, my bed looked far more inviting than attendance at a stodgy formal dinner.

"Have you called Mrs. Hudson's?" I asked Jayne as I surveyed the chaos of our room, hoping I wasn't leaving anything I needed behind.

"I did earlier. I spoke to Fiona. She said every elderly lady in West London has been in. The widowed and divorced network of women of advanced years has established a schedule of rotation for having your Uncle Arthur to dinner while you're out of town."

I laughed. "Who knew there's such a network? Little do they know Arthur's the cook in our house, not me."

"From what I hear, he's in no hurry to enlighten them," Jayne said.

We went downstairs to meet the men, waiting for us in the lobby.

Donald, as could be expected, was in full nineteenth-century men's formal wear: stiff white shirt with high collar, black frock coat, shoes polished to a high gloss, dark-gray suit with waistcoat. Even a pocket watch on a chain and a tall hat tucked under his arm. Holmes himself would not have looked better heading off to a concert at Covent Garden, dinner at Mancini's, or even to accept his emerald tie pin from "a certain gracious lady."

"You look marvelous, Donald," I said, and he preened.

Grant and Ryan looked very plain next to him in their twenty-first-century business suits. Plainly dressed, but so very handsome. I slipped one hand through each of their arms. "Shall we go?"

A light rain was falling, but we didn't have far to go. The wet streets reflected the glow of streetlamps and the headlights of passing cars. Donald struggled with the small foldable umbrella he'd brought from home. Eventually he gave up trying to get it to open and hurried ahead of us. He reached an intersection and looked left before stepping off the curb.

Ryan grabbed his arm as a car sped past in a spray of rainwater, coming fast from our right. "Watch it there, Donald. Remember, they're driving on the wrong side of the road."

"We call it the correct side," I said. "You need to consciously look down and check the directions before crossing." Whether for the aid of tourists or not, in London most intersections are clearly marked LOOK LEFT or LOOK RIGHT, with arrows pointing in the appropriate direction.

Inside the hotel we divested ourselves of coats and umbrellas and followed the hum of conversation. The hallway was wide and thickly carpeted, with banqueting rooms leading off one side and smaller meeting rooms at the end. A portrait of the Queen was prominently placed high on the center wall. The doors to the banquet room hadn't been opened yet, but a bar was set up in the hallway outside. More than a few of the guests, women as well as men, wore formal Victorian attire ranging from the hastily put together to outfits that could appear on stage or in a movie. I saw lush gowns, plumes of ostrich feathers, and rows of glittering diamonds, fake or otherwise, as well as plenty of pasted-on whiskers, top hats, and pocket watches.

"Excellent." Donald rubbed his hands together in glee and plunged into the crowd. He stopped to give his compliments to a short man with a big round belly wearing Victorian men's formal wear and a fake black beard that covered the bottom of his face halfway down his neck. He held his head so high and his chin so stiff, he looked as though he was peering down at the world beneath him. I grinned to myself, thinking the Victorian mannerism was perfect but he was in danger of straining his neck.

"Can I get you a drink, Gemma, Jayne?" Ryan said.

We both said yes, and he headed for the bar as Grant called, "I'll have a beer, thanks."

Grant searched the room, peering into corners and trying to see past pillars.

"Expecting anyone in particular?" I asked.

"No," he said too quickly. "Pippa told me your parents are coming tonight. Holmes lovers, are they?"

"Dad likes the stories and the modern adaptions. Mum couldn't care less. They're coming to support me and see me accept Arthur's award. As for Pippa, she's never shown any interest in Holmes." *Or in me, for that matter.* I didn't say that out loud.

"I see someone I want to say hi to," Jayne said. "I sat next to her at one of the panels, and she was telling me about a Sherlock Holmes–themed tea at the Taj Hotel in Westminster. I probably don't have time to go myself and check it out, but I'd like to hear more. Maybe she has some ideas we can use at Mrs. Hudson's." Jayne wandered away.

"About Pippa . . ." I said.

Grant turned and faced me. "What about Pippa?" His voice was eager, his face open, like a puppy hoping for another treat.

I sighed.

"She isn't . . . uh . . . married or anything, is she?" Grant asked.

"Married to her job, I'd say."

"Her job. You mean as an admin assistant?"

Time to change the subject. "Have you purchased any books yet?"

"Books?"

"Yes, books. The reason you're here. Remember?"

"Oh, right," he said. "Books. I haven't bought any yet, but I have my eye on a couple of Conan Doyle first editions I have buyers for back in the States."

I caught sight of Ryan, attempting to weave his way through the crowd with two glasses of wine and two beers. "Our personal waiter needs help," I said to Grant, who hurried to relieve Ryan of some of his burden.

Ryan handed me a glass. "Where's Jayne?"

"She went to talk to someone." I took the extra drink from him. "I'll hold on to this."

"Your parents have come in," he said.

I turned. My mother was lovely and elegant in a black cocktail dress with restrained gold jewelry, and Dad wore a gray business suit about twenty years out of date. They spotted us and headed our way. I handed Mum the spare glass of wine.

"That's excellent service," she said. "Thank you." She took a sip and studied the room. "Good heavens, I do believe that's Marian Forrester over there. Henry, isn't that Marian? What on earth is she wearing? I never would have taken Her Ladyship for a Sherlock fanatic. I have to go and say hello."

Mum hurried off.

"Is . . . uh . . . Pippa coming?" Grant asked, trying not to sound too hopeful.

"She's taking care of the coats," Dad said.

At that moment Grant's entire face lit up, and I didn't have to turn around to know my sister had arrived. She wore an electric-blue dress with a deeply cut curved neckline, fitting snugly at the top and flaring abruptly at the waist in a spray of stiff satin. Her shoes had sharp heels and she carried a small, plain blue bag over her shoulder. The bag was similar to mine. Like me, Pippa didn't like to have her hands occupied with a clutch purse. Grant hurried toward her without a word of goodbye, leaving me between Dad and Ryan. Pippa smiled when she spotted Grant.

"I've been wanting to ask you," Dad said to Ryan, "are you getting much anti-terrorism training in your department?"

I left them to talk shop. It was after seven. The doors were late opening. I stood against a wall, looking out over the crowd. I spotted Randy, close to the bar, glass of smoky liquid in hand. He was with a large group of people, talking and waving his hands in the air. He lifted the glass to his mouth and took a drink. He looked over the sea of heads between us, caught my eye, and gave me a nod. I didn't return it. He was drinking, as was almost everyone here, and I didn't know if he got aggressive when he drank. More aggressive, I should say. It might not have been a good idea for my parents to come tonight, but I hadn't said anything, thinking my dad knew what he was doing.

The woman I'd seen with Randy in the bar, the one who'd thrown her drink in his face, was on the far side of the room. She sipped from a glass of wine and laughed uproariously at whatever her companions said. She so pointedly didn't look in Randy's direction I knew she was fully aware of exactly where he was and what he was doing.

Randy's companions moved on, and he was left standing alone. He was now watching my mother, chatting to a woman dressed in an elaborate scarlet dress of the sort seen on the cover of the historical mysteries I sell at the Emporium. Mum's back was to her brother, and I hoped she hadn't seen him.

He made no move to approach her, and so my gaze traveled on. The man who'd accosted me in the hallway was here, dressed in an expensive suit that fit him well but didn't look like the sort of thing he was comfortable in. He was facing away from me, but I recognized that bald, bullet-shaped head and thick neck. He did not have a drink in hand and didn't appear to be with anyone.

My father continued chatting with Ryan, but his gaze moved constantly between his wife and her estranged brother.

The small dreadlocked woman who'd accused Randy of stealing her ideas headed his way. He saw her coming, and his face darkened. He slipped into the safety of the crowd and disappeared from my view.

The horde was getting restless, and I was debating finding myself another glass of wine when I saw the bullet-headed man moving. He crossed the room as fast as he could, almost pushing people out of his way. The moment I realized where he was heading, I also moved. Unfortunately, at that blasted moment, the doors of the banquet room were thrown open and the crowd surged forward. I fought my way through the mass of hungry people, feeling like a salmon swimming upstream.

"Gemma, I'm glad I ran into you. I own a small souvenir store in Edinburgh, and we stock a lot of Conan Doyle items, but I'm thinking of . . ."

"Sorry, no time. Gotta run. Talk later." I pushed my way past the man from Edinburgh, who said to his companion, "That was rude."

By the time I reached my mother, she stood alone. Her perfectly made-up face was pale. "There you are, dear. I've just had the strangest encounter."

"What did he want?"

"I scarcely know. He told me people had sent him here. I assumed, at first, he represented someone on the opposing side in a legal case I'd won. That does happen sometimes. Don't tell your father."

"That wasn't it this time?"

"No. He told me to tell my brother to watch his step. I have absolutely no idea what that means, and I have no intention of telling my brother anything. I attempted to tell him so, but he walked away."

"Did you sense a threat from him?"

"Not directed at me, no. He was simply delivering a message. A message I failed to understand. Do you know something about this?"

I shook my head. "He said much the same to me earlier."

Except for the bartenders at their station and a couple of men getting themselves another drink, the hallway was empty. Everyone had gone into dinner. "Are you going to tell Dad?"

"This time, yes, I am. Randy's problems are not ours, but if they threaten to become so, Henry needs to know." She slipped her arm through mine. "Shall we go in?"

Fortunately, the seating was preassigned, so I didn't have to worry about Randy trying to push himself into our group. The big round cloth-covered tables seated ten. The eight of us—Grant, Donald, Ryan, Jayne, Mum, Dad, Pippa, and me—and a German couple dressed as Sherlock Holmes and Irene Adler. Donald immediately recognized kindred spirits and fell into intense debate as to whether or not Irene Adler, had she not just hastily married Geoffrey Norton, would have remained in London to be with Sherlock.

Dad explained to Ryan, in great detail, the organization of police forces in the United Kingdom. Mum and Jayne chatted about shopping and afternoon tea opportunities in London, Donald and his new friends went on to discuss Sir Arthur Conan Doyle's interest in spiritualism, and Grant remained enraptured in every word that came out of Pippa's perfectly lipsticked mouth.

I was left to my own devices. I couldn't see much, as I was sitting down and the room was full. Forty tables with ten chairs at each, and all the seats were taken. Conversation filled the air, and people had to shout into their neighbor's ear to be heard. The waiters began to serve the first course—an insipid green salad—and the clamor of dishes and cutlery added to the cacophony.

The room, as well as the meal of tough chicken and overdone roast potatoes followed by a chocolate cake so dry it had me longing for the delights of Mrs. Hudson's Tea Room, could have been in any hotel in the Western world.

At last the meal was over, plates were cleared, coffee and tea served, and the program of speeches began.

I was called upon to be the first speaker. The host announced the award and mentioned that Arthur Doyle was not able to accept it in person but I, as his partner in the business, would do so on his behalf.

I made my way to the front to polite applause. The host shook my hand and gave me the foot-high glass statue of the Great Detective, complete with pipe and deerstalker, which was Arthur's award. We posed for a picture and then I began my speech. I kept my remarks short and to the point. I thanked the committee, on Arthur's behalf, for the honor. I told them, to murmured approval, about my attempts to ensure that a proper cup of tea was served in Mrs. Hudson's Tea Room. I invited everyone here present to visit the

Sherlock Holmes Bookshop and Emporium on their next visit to the United States.

As I babbled on, I took note of what was happening in the room.

Randy sat with a group consisting mainly of vendors from the dealers' room. The woman who'd thrown cheap champagne into his face was at his table, but seated on the opposite side. She pointedly avoided looking at him. I suspected they'd been assigned their seats before the spat and she hadn't been able to change her table at the last minute.

The dreadlocked woman was at a table shoved into the back corner, next to the kitchen. I didn't see the bullet-headed man anywhere. It was possible he didn't have a ticket for the dinner. Anyone could wander into the reception, but not to the dinner itself.

I thanked everyone once again and left the podium, to another round of polite applause. Rather than me, they'd hoped Martin Freeman would appear tonight, as had been rumored, but he hadn't. Even I was disappointed at that.

Ryan, Grant, Dad, and Donald stood up when I approached our table. "Well done," my father said. I put the statue in the center of the table.

"Good job," Ryan said, before excusing himself and leaving the room. A minute later, I felt my bag vibrate. I checked my phone. A text from Ryan: CAN WE BLOW THIS POP STAND?

I didn't know what a pop stand was, other than a place to purchase soda drinks, but I got the reference. SOON.

I put my phone away and looked up to see my sister watching me. *Naughty, naughty*, she mouthed.

Mum's friend was the next speaker. She talked at length, with detailed references to the Canon, about Holmes's occasional tendency to skirt the finer points of the law. As a judge, she didn't approve. She droned on and on in a relentless monotone as though she were delivering instructions to the jury in a shoplifting case. I felt my eyes getting heavy. Jayne yawned.

Ryan came back, and my dad was next to excuse himself, digging in his pocket for his phone before he'd finished pushing back his chair.

Jayne leaned across Ryan and whispered to me, "Want to come to the ladies' room?"

"Anything to get out of here," I said.

"We're not leaving yet, are we?" Donald asked. "This is so fascinating."

"We'll be back in a minute," I said.

Ryan, who'd been ready to eagerly leap to his feet, sank back into his chair.

Jayne and I made our way between the tables. I noticed my Uncle Randy's chair was empty.

"I think Grant has a crush on your sister," Jayne said.

"It would appear so. Good thing he's coming home with us on Tuesday."

"Why's that a good thing? She's a couple of years older than him, but that doesn't matter these days."

"No reason," I said.

"After all, you ditched him for Ryan. Which I still maintain was the right thing to do. Grant's searching for solace elsewhere."

"I didn't ditch anyone. Grant and I were never officially dating."

"No, but he wanted you to be," Jayne said.

In the hallway, the bartenders were clearing up, and a handful of people chatted over a last drink.

On our way into the ladies' room we passed the dreadlocked woman coming out, drying her hands on the seat of her skirt. Her face was set into a deep frown, and she pushed briskly past us without giving us a glance.

Jayne and I lingered at the sinks as long as we thought polite and then went back to our seats. As we came in, Mum's friend finished, to relieved applause. Next up was the conference organizer. He pulled out, to almost audible groans, a sheaf of papers and began to read. A few people started to gather up their belongings and say their goodbyes, but most were too polite to leave midspeech. Ryan's hands were under the table as his thumbs rapidly moved. My father hadn't come back. Grant smiled at Pippa and she smiled back.

At last the organizer thanked everyone for coming and his voice ground to a halt. The noise of chairs being pushed back and people leaping to their feet was deafening. I picked up the statue. It wasn't at all attractive, and I didn't think Uncle Arthur would care what we did with it. I'd make room for it on a shelf in the shop. It wasn't any more tasteless than some of the things we sold.

Before we could move, Mum's friend swept down on her. "Anne! How did you like my talk? I worked so hard on it."

"Very interesting," Mum said politely. "Marion, I don't think you've met my daughters, Phillipa and Gemma. Henry's around here somewhere."

Introductions were made, and polite chat commenced.

Finally Marion said, "We must have lunch one day soon, Anne," and left.

Mum picked her clutch bag off the table. She smiled at Ryan. "I hope you weren't too dreadfully bored."

"Not at all," he lied.

"Because I was. If I never hear the words *Sherlock Holmes* again, it will be too soon. Anyone for a night-cap? The bar here will be dreadfully crowded, but the Bentley should be lovely and quiet."

We agreed enthusiastically and headed for the doors, me lugging Uncle Arthur's award. Donald lingered to exchange email addresses with his new friends, and then he ran to catch up with us.

We stood in a circle in the hallway as all around us people made their way to the elevators or the exits. My father was nowhere to be seen. The bar had been removed and the dirty glasses and crumpled napkins cleaned up.

"I wouldn't be at all surprised," Mum said, "if your father snuck off to a nearby pub. The rat." She pulled her phone out of her bag. "I'll let him know where we're going."

We'd come out through the far doors of the banquet room, near the end of the hallway, next to the guests' business office and a couple of small meeting rooms.

"We might as well wait here for a minute," Ryan said. "Everyone and their dog will be collecting their coats."

I went to stand beside him, and I slipped my free hand into his. "Sorry we're not getting much of a chance to be together," I whispered in his ear. "I'd love to show you all my favorite places in London, but . . ."

"But you brought half of West London with you on this trip," he said. "Not a problem. Plenty of years yet to come back to London together."

My heart dropped to my shoes. Was Ryan suggesting we were now back on a permanent basis? That we had a future together?

We'd been a couple once before, on the verge of getting formally engaged. The relationship had not ended well, all of which was my fault, and he'd left to take a job in Boston. Now he was living and working in West London again and we were together again. I was taking things as they came. Taking it slowly.

Did he have other ideas?

Did I mind if he did?

I looked away to see my sister watching us. She wiggled her eyebrows in amusement.

The hallway was steadily clearing out. Only about twenty people were left milling around, and Mum said, "It should be safe to go for the coats now."

A woman barely out of her teens, dressed in the uniform of the hotel's waitstaff, approached the door to one of the meeting rooms. She carried a large empty tray, and Grant held the door open for her. She muttered her thanks and went inside. He let go of the door and it swung shut behind her.

Seconds later the door flew open with such force it hit the wall and the waitress ran out. Her eyes were round and wild and she gasped for breath. She glanced around the room, rapidly emptying out as everyone headed for their rooms, the bar, or the coatroom. My group was the closest to her.

Ryan took one look at her face and said, "What's the matter?"

She gasped and her legs gave way beneath her. As she fell, she called, "Help. Someone call 999!"

Ryan grabbed her before she hit the floor.

"What? Where?" Pippa said.

The waitress lifted a shaking hand. "In there . . . He's . . . I think he's dead."

Pippa wrenched open the door. I shoved the glass statue at Jayne, not stopping to notice if she caught it or not, and Pippa and I ran into the room, leaving Ryan holding the waitress.

My uncle Randolph, black sheep of the Denhaugh family, lay on the floor faceup, beneath a painting of sheep grazing in a meadow. A length of rope was tied tightly around his neck, his head lolled to one side, and his eyes bulged. He did not move.

My father knelt beside him. A lamp with a heavy orange base lay on the floor next to him, and his hands were on the rope.

Chapter Six

M y father groaned and swayed. He took his hand off the rope and put it against the floor for support.

Pippa flew across the room and grabbed his arm. "Steady there. Can you stand?"

"Pippa?" he said, blinking rapidly. "What's happening?"

"I need you to come with me," she said. She put her arm under his left shoulder and helped him to his feet, and then she led him away. His steps were hesitant, and he would have fallen had she not been supporting him. As they passed me, she gave me a nod. I nodded in acknowledgment. She'd asked me to stay, to figure out what I could of what had gone on here in the short time before the authorities arrived.

"Henry!" I heard my mother cry. "What's happened?"

"He needs to sit down," Pippa said. "Has someone called 999?"

"I did," Grant said.

"Gemma?" Ryan called.

Pippa snapped out orders. "Ryan, help that woman to a chair. Grant, check on the man in there. Everyone else step back."

Grant ran past me. He dropped to his knees next to Uncle Randolph. He tore at the rope around Randy's neck, but he couldn't loosen it. He put his fingers on the man's neck, looked up, and gave me a shake of his head.

I stood perfectly still, taking in everything I could of my surroundings.

The room was furnished in a retro style, with a thick cream shag carpet, orange sofa, and two matching chairs around a large coffee table. A bookcase, with books so perfectly aligned it was obvious no one ever read them, filled one wall. The mass-produced, but tasteful, paintings on the walls showed English pastoral scenes. The room had no windows, and light came from a wide-bottomed orange lamp on the far side of the couch. The lamp was one of a pair—its mate was now lying on the floor with its electrical cord yanked out of the socket.

Eight dirty glasses holding the residue of red wine, beer, and whiskey were on the center table, but otherwise everything appeared to be in order, except for an overturned side table and the lamp on the floor. I touched the base of the lamp with my toe. It was solid and heavier than it looked. The bland scent of cleaning products lay over everything, but that was being overtaken by the smell of death. This room had no windows, thus no drapes. No side door and no closets. The table didn't have a tablecloth over it; the couch and the bookcase were pushed up against the wall. No place to conceal anyone larger than a mouse.

My uncle Randolph lay on the floor faceup, staring at the celling. The rope around his neck appeared to be quite ordinary, a beige rope, about three feet long, of the sort everyone had in their home for tying down garden furniture, wrapping burlap around plants, or securing heavy parcels. The ends were rough and shredded as though they'd been cut from a larger piece with a not-very-sharp knife or ordinary kitchen scissors.

Behind me, coming from the hallway, I heard the increasing buzz of conversation as everyone asked everyone else what was going on. Pippa told Ryan to keep everyone out of the room, and I heard him politely telling people to mind their own business.

"Use a handkerchief or the edge of your jacket," I said to Grant. "Get his phone and hand it to me, but don't put your prints on it. Quickly. They'll be here in a minute."

Grant patted Randy's pockets. "He doesn't seem to have one."

Everyone has one. That Randy didn't meant whoever had been in this room with him had taken it.

I heard a shout, and Ryan said, "In there." The security guard I'd encountered earlier ran into the room. "Oh my gosh," she said. "Is he . . . ?"

"I'm afraid so," Grant said.

She bent over, rested her hands on her thighs, and her back heaved.

"Don't do it," I said. "You don't want to mess up the scene. Take a deep breath. Slowly, mindfully. In and out. In and out. There you go."

She breathed once, and then she straightened and looked at me. "Are you the police?"

I considered saying yes, but I'd seen all I could see for the moment. "Not exactly."

"Then get out of here. What about you?" she asked Grant.

"An innocent bystander."

"In here," Ryan said, and two paramedics came into the room. Grant pushed himself to his feet and got out of their way. He and I slipped into the hallway.

A male security guard stood at the entrance to the banqueting area. His arms were crossed over his chest and he no doubt thought he looked very formidable. It would have helped with his image if he'd been old enough to shave. "No one moves until the police get here," he announced.

My father sat in a chair; my mother stood beside him, her face grim, her hand on his shoulder. Pippa crouched in front of him. I went to join them.

"Don't remember." Dad shook his head. "I remember leaving our table thinking I'd check the football scores. Next thing I knew, you and Gemma were in the room and Randy . . . Randy was on the floor."

"Let me have a look at you, sir." Another paramedic approached my father. A uniformed police officer followed him.

"I'm okay," Dad said.

"You certainly are not," Mum said. "He can't remember the last fifteen or twenty minutes."

Dad turned slightly to let the medic have a look, and I noticed a patch of matted hair and a wet spot on the back of his head. I sucked in a breath.

The medic saw it too. "You've had a blow to the head, sir. We'll get you to hospital, have that checked out."

"I don't need . . ." Dad began.

"Yes, you do," Mum said.

Pippa drew me aside. "Anything?" She meant, I knew, had I noticed anything out of place.

"No. There's no other exit to that room and no possible hiding places."

"I don't want to be involved. I'll go with Mum and Dad to the hospital. You stay here in case the police have questions."

"Of course they'll have questions," I said. "That was no accident."

"Even you and I don't know that yet."

We kept our voices low and almost instinctively moved away from our parents and the people hovering around them. "Don't be ridiculous," I said. "Dad didn't hit himself over the head."

Ryan came up behind me and put his arms around me. "You okay, Gemma?"

"I'm fine," I said. "How's everyone else?"

Jayne and Donald were sitting together. Their faces were pale and they were not talking. Arthur's award lay on the floor at Jayne's feet. Grant dropped into a chair next to Jayne and put his head in his hands.

More police were arriving. One guarded the door, another went into the meeting room, while one questioned the young waitress.

"I'll get you a stretcher," the paramedic said to my father. "And we'll be on our way."

"Not so fast." A man crossed the room, heading for my parents. He wore a cheap, ill-fitting suit and a tie with a coffee stain on it. The laces on his right shoe flapped behind him. His head was covered in a few greasy stands of hair and his shoulders were sprinkled with dandruff. His narrow eyes passed over Pippa and me, lingered a brief moment on my mother, and then settled on my father. "Henry Doyle. What have you gotten yourself into now?"

My dad looked up. His jaw clenched. "Sam Morrison. Still an inspector, are you? Not demoted yet?"

"I wouldn't give you the satisfaction, Henry. What's happened here?"

"A man is dead in that room," Pippa said. "My family and I happened to be the ones nearest when he was discovered, and we attempted to help."

Grant got to his feet and stood next to Pippa. Sam Morrison looked at him for a long time. Next he turned his suspicious gaze onto Ryan.

I realized Morrison was paying attention only to the men in our circle. That was quite the mistake. And one I could take advantage of.

"I . . . I . . . went into the room. I wanted to help, if I could." My voice quavered with emotion. Ryan glanced at me in surprise. "My father needs to go to hospital. Please. You can follow us there."

"I'm sorry, Miss," Inspector Morrison said to me in a kindly voice that put my back teeth on edge. "Your father looks well enough to answer some questions first. I need you people to stay here while I check the scene." He turned to the uniformed officer who'd followed him. "Start taking names and addresses of everyone here, but no one's to leave until I say so. I'll handle this group myself."

She nodded and walked away.

"There was a banquet here tonight," Ryan said. "Must have been three hundred people . . ."

"Four hundred," Pippa and I said in unison. "Plus the staff."

"Uh, okay," Ryan said, "four hundred people. Most of them left before this was discovered. We were lingering to let the crowd disperse, that's all."

"American, are you?" Morrison said. "What brings you here, and why you do think you can tell me how to do my job?"

"My name's Ryan Ashburton. I'm a police officer. A detective in West London, Massachusetts. But that's not why I'm here. I'm attending the conference."

"Is that so? They tell me this was a Sherlock Holmes convention. About the last thing I need. First a bunch of Holmes wannabes and now an American hotshot. Don't any of you move. I'll be back."

He went into the meeting room. Behind Morrison's back, Ryan rolled his eyes. I would have followed the inspector, but the stern-faced officer guarding the door held up his hand.

"I'm all right," Dad said to the hovering medic. "Bit of a sore spot on the noggin but nothing more serious. I don't need to go to hospital. My wife will stay with me all night, and if there are any problems we'll go straight to casualty."

"If you're sure, sir."

"I am. Thank you."

The medic left, and we were momentarily alone.

"What happened, Henry?" Ryan kept his voice low. "Do you really not remember?"

"Not here," Pippa snapped.

"Randy?" my mother said. "He's dead?"

"I'm afraid so, Mum," I said. That the medics had not come rushing out, bearing my uncle on a stretcher, confirmed what Grant and I had observed.

"How?" Mum said.

"That's a matter for the police," I said.

"You were lucky, Henry," Grant said. "Looks like someone was after Randy and you got in the way."

I kept my questions to myself. If Dad had gone into the room with Randy, it would not have been to enjoy a chat about the old days over brandy and cigars. I believed my dad when he said he didn't remember how he got into that room, or why, or what happened in there.

I believed him, but his failure to remember was going to complicate things badly.

Morrison returned, pulling off thin blue gloves. The officer who'd been with the waitress came up to him and whispered into his ear. Morrison went to speak to the waitress. I edged closer in a blatant attempt to hear what she had to say.

"Why don't you remain where you are, Miss?" the officer assigned to watch over us said.

"Getting a cramp in my foot," I said. "It helps to move around."

The young waitress was huddled into herself in an armchair. Her shoulders shook and she wept as she spoke. She mumbled a few sentences I couldn't hear, and then she lifted her head and pointed directly at my father. "Him!" she said. "He was kneeling right beside him, tightening the rope. I saw it! I'm lucky he didn't kill me too!"

Morrison's back was to me, so I didn't hear his reply, but he must have told her she could go, and the medic guided her to her feet.

She threw a panicked look at my father and allowed the paramedic to take her away. The few onlookers, trapped in the hallway, murmured their sympathy as she passed.

Morrison walked slowly and deliberately back to my parents. He kept his face impassive and his eyes steady, but I detected a slight upturn at the corners of his mouth. I put my arm around my mother.

"Well, well, Henry Doyle," Morrison said. "Looks like you've stepped into it this time."

"I have no idea—" Dad began. His color was not looking good, and I didn't like the way his eyes seemed not to be focusing. He needed to get out of here and lie down.

"My husband has no recollection of events of this evening," Mum said in her best barrister tone. "He will contact you in the morning, after he's rested, to make a statement."

Morrison ignored her. "Did you know the dead man, Henry?"

Dad said nothing.

"Do you know him, Mrs. Doyle?" Morrison asked Mum.

"I haven't been in that room, so I haven't seen anything for myself," she said, neatly avoiding the question.

He turned to me. "What about you?"

I hesitated. Everyone watched me. I couldn't out-and-out lie and say I didn't know him. Plenty of people had seen me talking to him. "His name's Randolph Denhaugh. I'd never met him before this week."

Morrison nodded. "That's what his driver's license says. What's this Denhaugh to you or your father?"

I said nothing. Pippa broke the silence. "Randolph Denhaugh is . . . was my uncle. My mother's brother. They have been estranged for some time."

Morrison couldn't contain the smug grin that crossed his face. "Is that so? You didn't just happen upon the victim of a random attack then, Henry. The young lady who found the body says you were beside him, tightening that rope. What do you have to say about that?"

Dad said nothing. That he hadn't leapt to his feet and defended himself was not a good sign.

"She truthfully reported what she saw," Pippa said, "but she is mistaken in her interpretation. It's natural enough for anyone coming upon such a scene to immediately try to help the . . . person in distress. Obviously that is what my father did."

"That's right," Grant said. "I did the same myself. I tried to loosen the rope, but it was too tight. If I had a knife on me, I would have cut it off. But I don't. I'm sure Henry was only trying to do the same."

Morrison ignored him. "You look okay to me," he said to Dad. "Constable Jones, take Mr. Doyle here to the station. I'll be along later to talk to him." The policewoman took a step forward.

"You can't do that," my mother said. "My husband is clearly unwell. He needs to be seen by a doctor."

"I heard him tell the medics he didn't need their help," Morrison said. "If you won't come willingly, Henry, we'll put the cuffs on."

Dad still said nothing.

Pippa pulled her phone out of her bag. "This has gone far enough. A word, Inspector."

"Who are you?"

"Phillipa Doyle." She pushed buttons on her phone. Someone must have answered immediately, and she said, "Hold on one moment, please. Inspector, you'll want to take this call."

"I'm not wasting my time nattering to one of your boyfriends. If he's a lawyer, tell him to come down to the station."

"You will want to take this call," Pippa repeated. She walked into the center of the room. If the floor had not been covered in industrial carpet, her heels would have beat a furious rhythm. She didn't so much as glance over her shoulder to see if Morrison followed her.

But he did.

She handed him the phone. He looked at her. He looked back at us. He took the phone.

He said, "Hello?" and listened for no more than a second before all the blood drained out of his face. He nodded and shoved the phone at Pippa. She didn't smile as she put it away.

Morrison marched back to our little group. The smirk had been wiped off his face and something dark and unpleasant lurked behind his eyes.

"You can take your husband home, Mrs. Doyle," he said to Mum. "Go straight to your house and ensure he remains there. I'll pay a call in the morning. I'll decide at that time if charges are to be laid."

"Thank you," Mum said.

"Give Constable Jones your address. The rest of you are not yet free to go. Do you understand me?"

We chorused yes.

"I'll assist my mother," Pippa said.

"You do that," Morrison said. The look he gave her was not friendly. It was also, I thought, tinged with fear. He went into the meeting room. Forensics officers had started to arrive.

Mum and Pippa helped Dad to stand. He gave me a smile that, although it was weak, I was glad to see. I was also glad to see that the bleeding on his head seemed to have stopped.

They crossed the room slowly, Mum and Pippa supporting Dad. Everyone, police officers and medics included, stopped what they were doing to watch them go.

When they were out of sight, Ryan whirled around. "What the heck was that about?"

"Who did Pippa call?" Jayne asked.

"Did she phone her boss and ask for help?" Grant asked.

"I don't entirely know what Pippa does," I said, "but I suspect she doesn't actually have a boss. Except for maybe . . ." I let my voice trail off as I turned to glance at the portrait of Her Imperial Majesty staring out over the room.

Donald gasped. "You don't mean . . ."

"As I said, I don't know."

"I don't get it," Ryan said.

Donald winked at me. "Mycroft Holmes, Sherlock's older brother, didn't work *for* the British government. According to Dr. John Watson, Mycroft *was* the British government."

"Geez, Donald," Grant said, "as interesting as that is, I don't know that we want to get into a discussion of Holmes' family situation right now."

"If you will come with me please, madam," Constable Jones said to me. "The inspector will talk to you now. The rest of you, please wait your turn."

I followed her. The business office had been set up as an impromptu police headquarters. When I'd glanced in there yesterday, idly exploring the hotel venue, the three desks and chairs had been set into a row, all of them facing the wall. Now, one of the desks had been moved so it was perpendicular to the others. The intent had been to create a more formal space to allow Morrison to sit behind the desk looking authoritative and glare at the person he was talking to.

He glared now, as I came in. I was in a bit of a pickle here. I wanted to help the police as much as possible, let them know everything I'd learned or observed around Randy, but I didn't trust Morrison. Obviously he and Dad had a history, and equally obviously they were not friends. My initial impression of Morrison was that he wasn't all that bright, and he was likely the sort who leapt to conclusions and couldn't later back down in the face of fresh evidence.

I kept my expression impassive and sat down. I tucked my hands neatly into my lap.

Morrison stared at me. If the stare was supposed to be intimidating, it failed, but I made the attempt to appear suitably intimidated. I twisted my hands together and gave him a tight nervous smile.

"Name?" he snapped.

"Gemma Doyle."

"Is that so? Henry's daughter?"

"Yes, I'm the younger one."

"What do you do for a living, Ms. Doyle?"

"I own a bookshop."

His eyebrows rose. Clearly he'd been expecting me to say that I organized the movements of Her Majesty's navy, or some such thing. Instead, a lowly bookstore owner.

"How many stores do you have?"

"One. And a half interest in the tearoom next door. In Massachusetts, in the United States, where I now live. I'm here for this conference."

He leaned back in his chair, visibly relaxed. I wasn't even a bookshop tycoon. He then asked me the standard questions about my uncle Randolph, and I answered honestly. I'd never met the man before this week. He'd left the family many years ago and he'd had no contact with them since. I said nothing about Randy's past as a forger of fine art. If he had a police record and had spent time in prison, even Morrison should be able to find it.

"When the security guard arrived on the scene, she found you and one of your American friends in the room. What were you doing there?"

"We'd been at the banquet and were waiting for the crowd to disperse before collecting our coats and going back to our hotel, as my friend told you. The waitress went into the room to clean and she immediately ran back out, clearly in some distress. Naturally, we went to see if we could help." I'd gone into the room with Pippa, who'd then sent Grant to see to Randy. I didn't bother to mention that. "There was," my voice broke, "nothing we could do. My father had obviously been attacked as well." Tears welled up in my eyes. I swallowed heavily.

"Perhaps," Morrison said. He didn't ask the most obvious questions: had I seen anyone else in the room, had I moved or removed anything, had I touched anything, had Randy been dead or alive when I found him and had he said anything to me. Had I vacuumed the floor and dusted off the countertops. He didn't even ask if I'd removed Randy's phone from the body. "Thank you for your time, Ms. Doyle," he said at last. "When are you scheduled to go back to America?"

"Tuesday."

"I see no reason for you to change your plans, as long as you give us your contact information in case I have further questions."

"There are one or two things I'm thinking might be important."

"What's that?"

"On Friday Mr. Denhaugh had an argument with a woman in the dealers' room. She accused him of stealing her ideas."

"What sort of ideas?"

"He was selling sketches of scenes from the Sherlock Holmes books and stories. She said that was her idea, and he'd stolen it."

Morrison gave me such a patronizing smile, I was surprised he didn't get up and pat me on the head. "I'm sure that's nothing. Some drawings of Sherlock Holmes are hardly anything to kill a man over."

"I guess not." I'd been about to tell him about the argument I'd seen in the bar, but I decided not to. I didn't need another pat on the head. "Something else happened that you might be interested in. On Friday afternoon, a man came up to me when I was alone, preparing to deliver a lecture. He told me he had a message for Randolph."

"What sort of message?"

"He said something about people sending him to get back what belonged to them. I had no idea what he was talking about and told him so. That man later—"

"Don't lie to me, Ms. Doyle."

"What?"

"You're trying to protect your father. I can understand that, but you don't want to get yourself in trouble by making up stories about some mysterious man lurking in dark corners."

"Now see here, Inspector, that is—"

"That'll be all, thank you." He nodded to Constable Jones, who'd been standing next to the door with her arms crossed over her thin chest. I hesitated, considering giving Morrison my opinion on overzealous police officers who disregarded witness testimony if it didn't suit their preconceived conclusions.

"Thank you for your time, Ms. Doyle." A smile touched the edges of his mouth. If anything, it made him look even less attractive than when he was frowning.

I got to my feet. "You are making a mistake." I walked out, followed by Constable Jones, who then asked Jayne to come with her.

I joined Donald, Grant, and Ryan. Other than the police officers and a hotel manager, everyone else had gone.

"The police took people's statements and let them leave," Ryan said. "Seems we're the only ones the Inspector wants to interview himself."

"Because of Dad," I said.

"Yup."

Chapter Seven

None of my friends were questioned by Morrison for long. When Ryan came out, he whispered to me, "Are all English police detectives idiots?"

"Not at all. It seems we got the bottom of the barrel. One who, unfortunately, appears to have a history with my father."

Interviews done, statements made, and contact information collected, we were at last allowed to leave. When I went to pick Uncle Arthur's award off the floor, an officer told me to leave it. I didn't argue.

Dead tired, we staggered down the quiet dark street back to the Bentley. Ryan and I lingered in the lobby after everyone had said their good nights and gone upstairs. In a back room a vacuum cleaner purred. Ryan pulled me close, and I buried my head in his chest with a contented murmur. "What do you think happened tonight?" he asked.

"I have no idea. All I know is that Randy was not a man who made friends easily. The dinner was for ticketed quests only, but anyone could have wandered into the hotel. Maybe he or she called Randy and asked to meet. It's interesting that he didn't have a phone on him."

Ryan leaned back and looked into my face. "How do you know that?"

"I had Grant search the body before the security guard arrived, of course."

He shook his head. "Of course."

"I was interested in any recent calls Randy had received or made. That the killer must have taken his phone proves my point. I don't see what I can do here, as I don't know the people involved, but unless this is cleared up fast and my father proved to be innocent, I'm not going home on Tuesday."

"I figured you'd say that. I'll stay too."

"You don't have to."

"No. But I will."

The stubble on his face was coming in thick and dark. I ran my fingers over it. "I'm thinking," he said, "that your dad saw Randy go into that room and decided it was a good time to have a chat. He walked in on an argument and got a bash in the head for his pains."

"Agreed." I snuggled back into Ryan's chest. "How's Donald working out as a roommate?"

"An absolute nightmare. I can't tell if he's snoring or if a train track runs through our room. I'm barely able to get a wink of sleep."

"Speaking of sleep," I said.

He pushed me away. "We'd better try to get some."

"Hold on a moment. I need to check in with Pippa."

"Isn't it late to be calling?"

"She'll be up."

And she was. She was at the house on Stanhope Gardens, she told me. Dad had gone straight to bed, and she and Mum would check on him throughout the night. He hadn't remembered anything more about what happened earlier. "In the morning, I'll have my office check into DI Morrison," she said. "I don't like that he and Dad appear not to like each other. I'll try to have him replaced."

"So much for not getting involved," I said.

Her sigh came down the line. "Can't be helped. I couldn't have him arresting Dad."

"I'm going to cancel my flight home. I'll stay as long as needed."

"That's good," she said. "Come to the house in the morning. If Dad hasn't remembered what he saw, we might need to talk it all through. We can try to jog his memory."

"Call me if anything happens." I put my phone away.

Ryan pressed the button for the elevator. It arrived immediately and we got in. He pushed the button for the third floor. As the doors swooshed shut, he gathered me into his arms and kissed me, long and deep. The door pinged open but we didn't separate. The doors shut and we headed back down.

Ryan reached behind him and pressed the button again.

Up we went again.

"We could ride the elevator all night," I murmured.

"And wouldn't I like to. Better than listening to Donald snore."

"But other hotel guests might object." I pulled myself out of his embrace, very reluctantly, and waved my arm in the doorway before it could close again.

"Good night, Gemma," he said.

* * *

I'd intended to get up early and go to my parents' house without waking Jayne or even stopping for a cup of tea, but by the time I woke, surprisingly late, I found Jayne up and dressed and making herself coffee. The first rays of sunlight touched the edges of the thick drapes.

"Good morning," she said. "Have your shower and get dressed and we'll go."

"Where are we going?"

"Ryan texted me last night when he got in. He said you're going to your parents to talk things over, and I'm to call him as soon as you're up. I did that just now when you started to stir. He'll meet us downstairs in ten minutes."

"Us? You don't have to come, Jayne. You wanted to see more of the city today."

"The city can wait."

This time the tears that threatened to fall were genuine. I swallowed heavily and headed for the shower.

Not only Ryan was waiting for us in the lobby, but Donald and Grant also.

"What's happening?" I said.

"We're going with you, of course," Donald said. "You need our support."

"What about the conference? Today's the last day."

"There will be other conferences." He pointed toward the door with his useless little umbrella.

"Let's go, then," Grant said. "Do we need a cab?"

"It's close enough to walk," I said.

We passed the conference hotel on our way to Stanhope Gardens. A blue-and-yellow police car was parked outside, and I wondered if the conference's scheduled programming would continue.

It was a Sunday morning, the air cool and crisp, the clouds overhead gray and heavy.

Kensington is a very affluent neighborhood— Kensington Palace itself is situated at the end of the road—of stately white Georgian townhouses and enclosed private gardens, but also bustling streets of local pubs, good restaurants and trendy cafés, and funky shops. On a crisp morning in January, the trees were bare and the flowerpots empty. We were out early enough that the restaurants on Gloucester Road were just starting to open, but the streets were already busy with dog walkers and cyclists, the occasional jogger, and people in search of Sunday morning coffee.

As Stanhope Gardens came into view, I quickened my pace. I was afraid I'd see a police car parked outside the house in the middle of the row, but if one was there, it wasn't marked.

Pippa answered the door to my ring. Pippa and a big black dog.

Jayne immediately dropped to her haunches to greet him.

"What on earth?" I said.

Pippa's mouth pinched in disapproval. "This is Horace. He belongs to Dad. I cannot imagine what Mother was thinking to allow it." My sister had on the same dress she'd worn last night, but in true Pippa fashion, she still managed to look fresh and bright.

"A schnauzer," Grant said. "And a big one. Nice-looking animal."

I held out my hand. Horace gave it a quick sniff before studying me through his intelligent brown eyes. He was solid black, with dense wiry fur, a beard, and small erect ears. He stood about two feet tall and weighed sixty or seventy pounds. He went on to sniff at my trouser legs, and I wondered if he could sense traces of Violet.

"What about Mum's allergies?" I asked.

"When Dad retired," Pippa said, "he insisted he needed a companion while Mum's at work all day. This

breed is supposedly good for people with severe allergies, and Dad promised to keep him clean and well-
groomed and away from her office and the bedrooms."

"I think he's beautiful." Jayne gave Horace a hearty
slap on the rump and then pushed herself to her feet.

"Are we going to stand on the front step all day?"
Donald asked.

Pippa stood back and we filed into the house.

"Horace Walpole?" I asked Pippa.

"Of course," she replied. The dog had been named
for the eighteenth-century English novelist and politi-
cian, one of my father's favorite historical figures.

While Pippa helped us with our coats, the dog
danced around our feet, thrilled to have visitors.

I turned to see Jayne's mouth hanging open, and
I hid a grin. I thought she'd be impressed. When my
grandparents owned this house, it had been gradually falling into genteel disrepair, but over the years
Mum and Dad fixed what needed fixing and upgraded
it as needed. The entrance hall was large and grand,
with off-white paint on the walls and white tiles on
the floor. The furniture consisted of a chaise longue
in soft cream and a glass-topped table on which sat a
gold reproduction-antique clock. A sweeping staircase with an oak banister led upstairs, and a portrait
of my mother, young and beautiful, painted when
she was first called to the bar, hung on the wall.

"Mum and Dad are in the library," Pippa said.

"Library?" Jayne squeaked. "You have a library?"

"How's Dad?" I asked.

"He slept well, despite us constantly checking on
him, and says he feels fine this morning," Pippa said.
"Although he has a slight headache. He hasn't remembered anything more about last night."

"Have you heard from Inspector Morrison this morning?" Ryan asked.

"He just left. Dad had nothing further to tell him. Morrison wasn't happy about that."

"What's the story there?" Ryan asked. "It's obvious they know each other."

"I'll let Dad explain, if he wants to." Pippa led the way down the hallway. Jayne kept tripping over her own feet as she studied the paintings on the walls and peeked into the rooms we passed as Horace bounded on ahead.

The library is Dad's room. Whereas the entrance hall is decorated to Mum's taste, all shades of white and elegance, Dad chose the colors in here. Blue, blue, and more blue. The carpet was a deep navy, the walls periwinkle, the bookshelves cobalt, the chairs upholstered in some combination of blues and whites. Jayne, in a blue sweater and dark jeans, almost faded into the walls.

Dad sat in his favorite wingback chair next to the fireplace. He was dressed in casual trousers and a brown-and-orange cardigan, and I was pleased to see his color was almost normal. A discreet white bandage had been applied to the back of his head. As we came in, he started to struggle to his feet, but Ryan put up a hand. "No need to get up, Henry. You need to rest."

Dad fell back into his chair. Horace ran to his side, and my father rubbed absentmindedly at the dog's ears. "Good morning, Gemma, my dear. Nice of you to bring your friends."

"I've been worried about you." I gave him a kiss on the top of the head, taking care to avoid the bandage.

"Dr. McMaster came by last night to have a look at him," Pippa explained.

"Your doctor does house calls?" Jayne said. "In the middle of the night?"

"A longtime family friend." My mother came into the room. She looked elegant but casual in beige trousers with a dark-red silk blouse and gold earrings. I gave her a kiss on the cheek while my friends said good morning.

"I'm sure you'd all like tea or coffee. Jayne, would you mind giving me a hand?"

"Not at all."

Greetings over, Grant headed immediately to the bookshelves. He was going to be severely disappointed. My parents had a big library, but it contained nothing of monetary value. The books were ones they'd bought at a neighborhood bookstore because they wanted to read them.

Donald wouldn't find anything of interest here either. Neither of my parents read crime novels, and particularly not Sherlock pastiches. Dad was a retired cop and Mum a criminal defense lawyer. They said they had enough of crime in their real lives. Dad read history mostly, and Mum had a surprising weakness for gaudy historical romance, the more bodice-ripping the better.

Pippa spoke to me quietly. "Did you have to bring everyone?"

"You try and keep them away."

Mum came in carrying a large tray bearing a teapot, coffee carafe, jugs of milk and cream, and a bowl of sugar with a small silver spoon. Jayne followed with cups and mugs. "Wow!" she said, "that's a heck of a kitchen." While she asked everyone what they wanted and poured the drinks, Mum went back for another load and reappeared with plates of fresh croissants and jars of strawberry jam and butter.

We took seats, balanced cups and plates on our laps, and dug in. Horace seemed to be well trained and didn't try to snatch the pastries off anyone's plate, but he did sit close to Dad with an expectant look on his face.

"Oh my gosh." Jayne wiped flakes of pastry off her blouse. "This has got to be the best croissant I've ever had."

"And that's saying a lot," I said.

"Mmmmuummm," said Donald.

"They're from Paul's Boulangerie," Mum said. "I made a run this morning. I cowardly ducked out the back door, leaving Pippa to answer the knock from the police at the front."

"What's the story between you and DI Morrison?" I asked my father.

Dad could be blunt when he wanted to be. He wanted to be now. "He's a fool. Do you get completely incompetent and slightly crooked cops in America, Ryan?"

"Now and again," Ryan said.

"Incompetent was immediately obvious," I said. "But not crooked."

"He's been known to turn a blind eye in return for a monetary favor," Dad said. "All minor stuff, so somehow he seems to get away with it without coming to anyone's attention. As you surmised, Gemma, he and I have clashed before. More than once. We started on the force around the same time, and were assigned to the same station. Even back then, I thought he was sloppy and lazy. I rose through the ranks far faster than he did, and he never forgave me for it. As I recall, he didn't come to my retirement party."

"Would he frame you?" Pippa asked.

Dad sipped his coffee and thought about that. "I'd say no. If I was still on the force, maybe. But I'm no threat to him now. No, what we have to worry about with Sam Morrison is that he'll be too lazy to do much more than follow obvious clues."

"And you're the most obvious clue," Ryan said.

"'There is nothing more deceptive than an obvious fact,'" Donald said solemnly. "*The Boscombe Valley Mystery.*"

"Thank you, Donald," Grant said.

"You still don't remember anything, Henry?" Ryan asked.

Dad shook his head. "I've been racking my brains, but nothing helps. It's all a fog."

"Don't try so hard to remember," Mum said. "It'll come to you when you least expect it."

"Hard not to," Dad said.

"So," Jayne said. "What are we doing to do?"

"*We*," I said, "are going to do nothing. We don't know the people involved in this. It's not like back in West London where I can ask around of people I know, and half the people in town know the business of the other half."

Jayne's pretty face fell. "You mean we have to sit and wait for something to happen?"

"Gemma's dad didn't kill Randy," Grant said. "Maybe this Morrison is an idiot, but the rest of the Metropolitan Police are not. They'll find Randy's killer soon enough." He was looking around the room, but he was speaking to Pippa. He still seemed to be under the impression she could be comforted by platitudes.

"Grant's right," Pippa said, appearing to be comforted. "We'll let the police take care of it. Dad, you have plenty of contacts in the Met. Tap into them and find out what's going on. Maybe drop a word or two into friendly ears that you don't trust Morrison."

"I can do that," Dad said.

"Excellent plan." Donald reached for another croissant. "Even the Great Detective himself was not averse to asking for help when he needed it."

"Not everyone who goes to a Holmes convention," Grant said to Pippa, "thinks everything in life has to be done according to Sherlock."

She gave him a warm smile as she stood up. Horace scrambled to his feet. "I don't know about you," Pippa said, "but before I do anything more, I have to get home and out of these clothes. I must look a total mess."

"Not at all," Grant said.

He was rewarded by another smile. I caught Ryan trying to smother a laugh.

"Gemma," Pippa said, "help me with the dishes, will you? Mum, I think Dad can be left alone for a few hours today as long as you keep your phone close. Perhaps you could take Jayne to see some of the sights."

"Would you like that, Jayne?" Mum asked.

"If you're sure I can't do anything to help. There's nothing like a local guide." Jayne's phone rang, and she checked the screen. "I'm sorry, but I have to get this." She hurried out of the room.

"How about a visit to the Sherlock Holmes Museum on Baker Street?" Donald said.

As a barrister, Mum had to be a competent actor. It required all her skills not to look completely horrified at the suggestion.

I gathered cups and plates, indicated to Ryan to stay where he was, and followed Pippa down the hall and into the kitchen. Horace followed me.

The kitchen was at the back of the house, overlooking the small garden, neatly put away for the winter, and Dad's workshop. We were a good distance from the library, but I kept my voice low. "What do you want me to do?"

Horace went to his water bowl and began slurping.

"Unlike your extremely handsome and overly optimistic friend—and when we have time, I want to hear the story there—I do not trust the Met to always get the right person. My office cannot be involved in any of this. The conflict of interest is simply too great."

"So you want me to be involved in your place?"

"I've been kept appraised of some of your activities in West London."

"From more than Uncle Arthur, I presume."

"Did you doubt it?"

"No."

"You seem to have made a name for yourself as one who can get to the bottom of cases the police cannot."

"Ryan's a good detective," I said. "None better. I work faster because I can be pushier, that's all."

"And pushy is what we need here. I will monitor the progress of the official investigation from a distance and keep you informed. In the meantime, the best place for you to start is Randy's apartment."

"Considering I don't know where that is, I assume you do."

"The police arrived there a couple of hours ago. They've taken some items away, which may be a problem for us, but you might still be able to find out what he was up to in the way of illegalities, and if he had any enemies."

"From what I observed in two days, he did. Have enemies, I mean. I don't know about him breaking the law, although Dad tells me he had a history of doing that. Before searching his place, I'd like to go back to the conference. I saw two, three, different people arguing with him. This might have been a simple quarrel gone wrong and when I confront her, or him, she'll break down and confess."

"Stranger things have happened," Pippa said.

"If that doesn't produce any results, how am I going to get into his apartment?"

She checked her watch. "At fifteen minutes past one this afternoon, the electronic locks on the front door of the building and on his flat will be inactive for two minutes."

"Convenient."

"It is, isn't it?" She gave me an address in the East End of London. "Oh, one more thing. Do not call me at my office or on my usual phone with updates on this matter. Use this number." She rattled it off. "Actually, two more things. Ditch the entourage."

"How am I going to do that?"

"Up to you. You can't have a gaggle of Americans traipsing around London after you. Thus I suggested Mum take Jayne on an outing. If you want someone to watch your back, your boyfriend can do it."

"You'll have to distract Grant."

Something lit up in her eyes. "I've been assigned less onerous duties."

"That includes Donald."

"Oh, yes. Donald. I suspect he means well, but . . ."

"Ryan too. Jayne will come with me."

"Why?"

"I need a wingman, but that can't be Ryan. If things go pear-shaped"—such as us being arrested for break and entry—"he could be seriously compromised."

She was about to argue, but read my face and let it go.

We went back to the library, leaving the dishes undone. We found Donald examining the bookshelves, Ryan and Grant asking Dad questions such as how many officers the Met would be likely to assign to the case, and Mum and Jayne flipping through a huge glossy cookbook. I had no idea why there would be any cookbooks in my parents' house. Must have been a gift.

Pippa clapped her hands. "I've had a marvelous idea." Her voice rose two octaves from when we'd been talking in the kitchen. "Donald, you want to go to the Sherlock Holmes Museum, but I have something much, much better in mind."

Donald looked thrilled, Grant pleased, Ryan dubious.

"A private tour of Scotland Yard! You don't mind if we leave you for a while, do you, Dad? I had to pull a lot of strings to get us into the Yard on such short notice."

"I'm fine," he said. "I might have a short nap."

Donald looked like a kid who'd found the biggest and shiniest bike under the tree Christmas morning. Then again, maybe even as a child, Donald would have preferred a Junior Sherlock detective set. "Might we possibly see records from the Jack the Ripper case?"

"I'll see what I can arrange," Pippa said.

"I'll bow out, thanks," I said. "I need to go back to the conference. I arranged to meet with a vendor to talk about selling his items in my shop."

Indecision crossed Grant's face. He still had business to do at the conference, and everything shut down at three this afternoon. But on the other hand, Pippa was offering a day together.

Pippa, who'd also read Grant's face, turned her smile on him. "Please say you'll come, Grant. It wouldn't be as much fun without you."

He gulped and nodded.

"We can meet for dinner here," Pippa said. "To exchange news about our day."

"Anne and I were planning to go to the Portrait Gallery," Jayne said.

Mum started to nod, but Pippa jumped in. "On second thought, I'm not sure Dad should be left alone."

"I'm—" Dad said.

Mum could also pick up on unspoken signals. "You're right, dear. Maybe tomorrow, Jayne."

"Great," I said. "Let's go."

"I'll pass on Scotland Yard," Ryan said. "I'll go with Gemma to the conference. The people who attacked Henry and Randy might still be there, and I don't want her to be alone."

"Oh, no," Pippa said. "You're coming with me. I want to hear an American's impression of the way we do things in the UK. Gemma will have to manage without you."

"Jayne can come with me," I said. "She'll protect me, won't you, Jayne?"

"I will? Okay, I can do that, I guess."

I grabbed Jayne's arm. If I wanted to be at Randy's apartment by quarter after one and spend time at the conference first, we needed to leave now. "We'll coordinate dinner by text," I called over my shoulder. I almost dragged Jayne out of the library and down the hall. I shoved Jayne's coat into her arms and grabbed mine. I opened the front door and looked down. Horace had followed us. He stood still, simply watching me. "Guard Henry," I said to him.

I swear he nodded in reply.

"Guess who that was calling me?" Jayne said as we hurried up Stanhope Gardens.

"I have no idea."

"Jack!"

I stopped walking. "Why?"

"To check in. Wasn't that nice of him?"

"I thought he was out of the picture."

"He wants to be back in it."

Jack was Jack Templeton, whom Jayne had dated for a short while last summer. I didn't like Jack much, and I still maintain that's not because the first time we met, when he didn't know who I was, he called the Emporium pretentious and me a nutty Englishwoman. Jayne had, in my opinion, appalling taste in men. Then again, to be fair, her boyfriends probably thought she had bad taste in best friends and business partners. Jack was rich, having made his money in an Internet start-up that had been bought by a big firm. He was as snobby and, dare I say it, pretentious as only the nouveau riche can be. He'd tried to charm Jayne with expensive presents, dinners in the best restaurants, and offers of a quick run down to Bermuda on his yacht, but they soon broke up when he couldn't understand how important her job was to her and the amount of time she needed to devote to it in the summer tourist season.

Jayne might have bad taste in men, but she never took them too seriously, and she'd casually told me about the breakup over an industrial-sized mixer churning chocolate cake batter.

"I phoned him last night when we got back to the hotel, while you were still downstairs with Ryan, and told him what happened. He called me just now to ask for an update. When I said we were going to stay a while longer, he said he'll try to get away and come over to help."

"Marvelous," I said.

"Do you really think so?"

"No."

* * *

The patrol car we'd seen earlier was still parked in front of the hotel. Police officers in plain clothes as well as dark-navy uniforms and hats with black-and-white-checked bands mingled with the conference-goers, but they weren't an overwhelming presence. Most people seemed to be simply going about their business, more interested in the cases of Sherlock Holmes than the real-life drama of last night.

On the walk to the hotel, I'd told Jayne I wasn't really going back to the conference for store business.

"I wondered what you and your sister had to talk about for so long," she said. "What's up?"

"A bit of minor poking around."

"Yeah, right," she said. "You and your sister look a lot alike. You're both tall, the same brown eyes, oval-shaped face, same hair color, although hers isn't curly like yours."

"That's only because she spends an excessive amount of money and time to keep her hair under control." I flicked one of my curls off my cheek. My hair was never under control.

"There's something else different about her I can't quite put my finger on."

"Thank heavens for that."

"How much older is she than you?"

"Seven years. Enough that she always thought she could boss me around."

"She seems to like Grant."

"So she does," I'd replied.

I checked the notice board in the lobby as soon as we arrived, and all the day's planned activities seemed to be continuing. A small note had been stuck to the bottom letting us know that the small meeting rooms and business office were not available today.

Jayne and I went down the main hallway. A uniformed police officer stood outside the meeting room where we had found Randy, and blue police tape had been strung across the doors. The business office had a sign on it that said CLOSED.

We next went to the dealers' room. Randy's booth was covered in a drop cloth. Most of his sketches were probably gathering dust in a police evidence locker somewhere.

I stopped at the booth next to his. It sold clothing—Inverness capes, ulsters, deerstalker hats. I flipped through the pile of hats while Jayne pretended to be interested in the coats. "Terrible about what happened yesterday," I said when the vendor approached me.

She shivered and gave Randy's booth a sideways glance. "Yeah."

"Did you know him?"

"Not before this weekend. We sat at the same table last night at the dinner, but didn't talk except to say hello. Just goes to show, doesn't it?"

I didn't bother to ask what it went to show. "Did he seem to be bothered about anything?"

"You mean at dinner? Not that I noticed. He drank a lot, but that doesn't mean anything, does it?"

"Did he have a date?"

Her eyes narrowed. "Are you going to buy one of those hats?"

"I have a friend who'd love it." I plucked a deerstalker off the top of the pile and asked her the price. About three times what I'd pay to get a similar item into the Emporium. I pulled money out of my bag.

She took the bills and popped the hat into a plastic bag. "He was trying to make nice with a woman at our table, the Polish one who's selling the jewelry, but she was having none of it."

That would be the woman I'd seen throw her drink in his face, the one who hadn't been able to get her table changed for dinner.

"Anyone seem unduly interested in him over the last few days?"

"Are you with the police?" she asked me.

"Just curious." I hadn't put my conference pass around my neck this morning.

She turned and began to tidy a display of overly large magnifying glasses.

"Maybe I'll take a second one of these hats," I said. "My father would absolutely love it." I peeled off more bills.

"This one woman got into his face so much on Friday, security had to be called. She was babbling on and on about him stealing her ideas. He seemed to think it was dreadfully funny, and that only made her madder." She chuckled. "You don't think I came up with the design for these hats all on my own, do you?"

"Nothing original under the sun," I said.

"So true."

I took my two unwanted deerstalker hats and wished her a good day.

Jayne had been listening to the exchange. "You didn't learn anything new, did you?"

"No. The argument sounds like the incident we saw. The woman with the dreadlocks upset about him apparently stealing her ideas."

As well as Randy's, one other booth was shrouded in darkness, and dust cloths covered the jewelry made by the woman who'd thrown wine in Randy's face. I headed for it, and when we got there, I handed my bag of hats to Jayne. "Oh dear," I said. "I have a stone in my shoe." I leaned up against the cloth-draped table, right about where I'd seen the small cash box and receipt book yesterday when I checked out the booth. I kicked off my shoe and shook it with my left hand while I slid my right hand under the cloth. I felt around and soon found what I was after: the little stand propping up her business cards. I plucked a card from the stack, slipped it into my pocket, and put my shoe back on. "Much better," I said to Jayne.

We walked to the end of the row. My plan was to find the people I'd seen at Randy's table last night, most of whom were vendors here, and ask them what they'd seen or heard.

Instead I saw something that had me spinning around on my heel. The broad back of DI Sam Morrison as he talked to a man selling his own series of pastiche books. "Maybe not," I said to Jayne. "Let's go. We have an appointment."

"We do? Where?"

"Across town. Mustn't be late."

As we crossed the lobby, I spotted something I wanted at the concierge desk, and I made a quick detour.

I plucked a street map of London off the top of the display and tucked it into my handbag. I took the receipt for the hats out of the plastic bag and put it into my pocket. I was about to dump the hats into the trash, but then I decided some keen conference-goer might like them, so I placed them on a table. I could see absolutely no reason why I'd want to wear a deerstalker today and I didn't want to carry them around. It might be nice to disguise my face from CCTV cameras, but wearing a deerstalker would only attract attention to me. I'd give the receipt to Pippa and ask that her "office" reimburse me.

The doorman opened the door for us and we went outside. I stopped on the hotel steps and mentally slapped my forehead.

"What is it?" Jayne said. "You've thought of something important. I can tell."

"In West London I'm so busy trying to avoid letting Ryan and Louise know what I'm doing, I forgot that here I am not entirely without resources." Detective Louise Estrada was Ryan's partner.

I sent a text to the number Pippa had given me. CHECK CCTV FOOTAGE. I described the bullet-headed man as best I could, as well as where and when I'd seen him. I did the same for the dreadlocked woman. I didn't ask Pippa to find Randy's angry Polish girlfriend. Her business card kindly provided me not only with a name, Arianna Nowacki, but a phone number and London address.

"What's so funny?" Jayne asked.

"I'm thinking of poor Pippa trying to keep Ryan, Donald, and Grant entertained all day."

We went to Gloucester Road Tube station and took the District Line train to Westminster, where we changed to the Jubilee Line. We got off at London Bridge station. London Bridge was a long way from where we needed to go, but we were half an hour early, and I didn't want to be seen hanging around Randy's building waiting for the appointed time.

"I feel like a latte," I said to Jayne when we emerged onto the street. Aside from a few tourists, recognizable by the cameras around their necks or phones held in front of their faces, this area, close to the business district called The City, was almost deserted on a Sunday at noon.

"You do? You don't drink coffee."

"I can make an exception now and again. We're early for our appointment."

"This mysterious appointment you won't tell me about?"

"The very one."

I'd spotted a coffee shop and we went inside to be enveloped in the familiar scents of steamed milk and roasted coffee beans. We bought drinks and found seats, which wasn't difficult, as the place was empty except for one scruffy young man hunched over a laptop in a corner.

Jayne pulled out her phone and read the screen. "Text from Jack. He tried to clear his schedule for the next few days, but couldn't manage. He's not going to be able to come."

"What a disappointment," I said.

"Probably just as well," she said with a sigh. "I'm not sure I want to get back together with him. And if he came all this way, I'd . . ." her voice trailed off, and she sipped her coffee.

"Even if he did come, this will all be over soon, and he'd only have to turn around and fly back with us."

"Do you think so?"

I wanted to say "No," but I didn't.

Jayne was half finished her drink—I hadn't even touched mine—when I hopped off my stool. "Time to go."

Back we went to the underground. As Jayne swiped her pass and the turnstile opened, she said, "Is there a reason we're popping in and out of subway stations and on and off trains?" to which I replied, "Just a precaution in case someone tries to follow us."

Jayne studied the passersby.

I'd been watching, but I hadn't seen any signs of being followed. There's not much one can do if the surveillance is professional and highly coordinated, but if one or two people were watching us, I would have spotted them lurking around the quiet coffee shop.

We caught a Jubilee Line train to Canary Wharf. When we reemerged into the cold air, it was five to one. Timing things down to the second wasn't proving to be easy, not when we had to rely on public transit.

"Why are we walking so slowly?" Jayne said.

"Aren't you enjoying the view?"

"I guess."

The area known as Isle of Dogs is surrounded on three sides by the River Thames. When London was the largest and most important city in the world, the great dockyards sent ships to every corner of the earth, trading in tea, sugar, rum, textiles, and everything else imaginable. As cargo ships got bigger and bigger and their cargo was increasingly carried in containers, which the docks couldn't handle, the area fell into ruin and decay. Now, however, it's a dense development of luxury high-rise apartment buildings and exclusive office towers with fabulous views of the river and the city.

"Nice area," Jayne said.

"It is. Expensive to live here, so close to the business district."

I know London well, which I should, as I'd lived here most of my life, but I wasn't all that familiar with the East End. I didn't want to use my phone and thus leave an electronic trail, so I'd grabbed a paper map off the concierge desk at the hotel. My intention was to stay completely off the police radar. Everything I learned I'd pass on to Pippa and leave it up to her to decide what to do with the information. Hopefully, no one would have reason to check on my activities, but better safe than sorry. London's full of CCTV cameras, recording just about everywhere in public spaces. Again, I expected no one would have reason to want to track my activities, but I tried to avoid the cameras when I could see them, which I knew wasn't always the case. A cold east wind was blowing off the river bringing the threat of icy rain or snow, and before stepping out of the underground, I'd pulled my scarf up around my neck and walked with my face down. Jayne had on a black-and-white-plaid wool coat, a heavy gray scarf, and a white beret that did nothing to keep her warm but looked very cute.

We walked for less than five minutes before arriving at the address I'd been given. The streets in this area, close to the City and its giant office towers, were largely empty, it being a winter Sunday, but a few people were braving the weather, walking dogs or children or jogging along the riverside. I checked the time on my phone. Thirteen minutes after one; two minutes to go. I opened the front door and we stepped into the vestibule. I pulled out my street map and consulted it, twisting it every which way as though trying to figure out where I was, where I wanted to go, and how the heck I was going to get there. Jayne read the name plates on the wall. "Are we here to see anyone in particular?"

The sound of the electronic lock disengaging was barely audible. I pulled the handle and the door slid soundlessly open. I hadn't taken off my gloves. I slipped through, and Jayne followed.

"Did you call someone?" Jayne said. "I didn't see you doing that." She began to peel off her gloves.

"Keep those on," I said. Her blue eyes opened wide. I pushed the lift button and it arrived instantly. Jayne and I stepped inside. We wanted the fifteenth floor.

The lift rose quickly, not stopping at any other floors. The doors whooshed open and we stepped into the corridor. Number 1508 was at the end of the hallway. I walked briskly down it, aware that my time was limited.

We saw no one.

The door of 1508 opened at the slightest twist of the handle, and I stepped in. Jayne followed.

I hadn't told her what we were doing here. In case things went wrong, plausible deniability would be the best option for her.

"Gemma," she said, "I think it's time you told me what's going on."

"This is Randy's flat. I'm going to have a quick look through his things. You stand here and listen at the door. If you hear anyone outside, anyone trying to get in, come and get me."

"What I want to know is how *we* got in."

I didn't answer. Whether Randy owned it or rented, this was a mighty expensive flat. The door opened directly onto a vast living space of white walls, blond wood floors, white leather couches and chairs, and a coffee table the size of a small Caribbean island. French doors led onto a veranda with a glass railing, big enough for two lounge chairs, a teak outdoor dining table set, and even an enormous steel barbecue. London stretched into the distance. On a clear summer day, the view must be breathtaking. Contemporary art, all bright colors and slashing brushstrokes, lined the interior walls. A long low gas fireplace was set into a pit in the center of the room.

No wall separated the living space from the kitchen, and it was clearly a kitchen designed for entertaining: high-end appliances, open spaces, glass-fronted cabinets, and barstools gathered around a center island. I opened a small door to see row upon row of nicely stocked wine racks.

I could detect some evidence of the police presence. Either that or Randy wasn't very neat. Cabinet doors stood open, showing a large selection of dishes and glassware as well as tins and packages of processed food. The fridge contained bottles of beer, one open bottle of white wine, a few condiments, some quietly rotting vegetables, and not much else.

The hallway was carpeted in a thick creamy weave. Five doors led off it, and they were all open. The first was to a small linen cabinet. The sheets and towels had been rummaged through, leaving the stacks in disarray and a couple of fluffy white towels on the floor.

I went into the den. The police had been here before me. The filing cabinets were open, one with signs of the lock being forced. An empty space in the center of the giant steel and glass-topped desk showed where the computer had sat. It was, I assumed, now being searched by the police boffins. Most thoughtless of them. I'd have liked to search the hard drive myself.

Nice of the police to break the lock on the filing cabinet, though. I searched through it quickly, but there wasn't much to read, and nothing at all personal. Either the police had taken everything away or Randy didn't keep paper records. In an otherwise empty desk drawer, I found credit card statements for the previous two months in the name of Randolph Denhaugh. There were only a handful of expenses, but the numbers were eye-watering. Thousands of pounds at restaurants, some of the names I recognized as belonging to top celebrity chefs; several hundred pounds at a wine merchant.

My uncle had supposedly been down on his luck. He was, he'd told me, making his living by drawing and selling sketches of the Great Detective at a Sherlock Holmes convention. Judging by this flat, and these bills, he either had a lot more funds than he was letting on, or someone was financing his lifestyle.

I didn't find any records that would indicate the ownership of the flat and nothing in the way of utility bills or car payments. The police might have taken those. Or the bills might not have been coming directly to Randy.

The room across the hall was a guest bedroom. Nice furniture, king-sized bed. The duvet, pillows, and sheets were crumpled on the floor, the mattress off kilter, showing that the police had been here before me. The closet doors were open, and they were completely empty.

The next room was likely Randy's bedroom. This bed, even bigger than the other one, had been also been searched. Bedding lay on the floor, the mattress half off the bed. The closet didn't have many clothes— all of them men's—but some had fallen on the floor and had not been picked up.

I went through the pockets quickly. The clothes were all of good quality, from good shops, and pretty trendy. Judging by the size, they belonged to Randy.

I thought back to what he'd been wearing at the conference, and why I'd concluded he didn't have a lot of money. Either he'd been intending to deceive people, or he hadn't wanted anyone to know what he was up to these days. Or maybe he kept his life neatly divided into two separate compartments.

Two books were on the night table. Simon Schama's *The Embarrassment of Riches*, a history of art in the Dutch Golden Age, and *Red Notice* by Bill Browder, about official corruption in Russia. An interesting contrast in reading material.

The last room I went into was the true eye-opener. It faced south, the far wall a sheet of sparkling glass. Even with the gray winter skies, light poured into the space. A large, heavily scarred wooden table held an array of small pots and paintbrushes, and bare canvases of various sizes were stacked in a corner. An easel with a canvas on it was set up near the window, basking in the light. The painting was in its early stages yet, but it appeared to be a portrait of a stout woman dressed all in black. The little pots held traces of thick oily paint, but there wasn't a tube of commercially bought paint in the room.

Randy had been making his own paint.

No one today was buying paintings like this one. Not new paintings, anyway.

My Uncle Randolph was back in the art forgery business. I was surprised the police hadn't taken all this away. Perhaps they'd sent someone around who didn't recognize what this meant and didn't know Randy's history. If this was a forgery of an old master, and I was certain it must be, he had to have been working from photographs of the original, but I didn't see anything like that lying around. The police might have taken them.

I leapt out of my skin as a voice from the doorway said, "My mom paints sometimes. She'd kill for a studio like this one."

I put my hand to my heart. "Did you have to creep up on me?"

"I wasn't creeping. That carpet's thick. Forget what I said about killing for a studio. Bad choice of words. Did you find what you're looking for?"

"Considering I don't know what I'm looking for, I can't say. But this is all extremely interesting. I thought you were guarding the door."

"I got bored."

"Give me another five minutes, and we'll be out of here."

"Okay."

I stood in the center of the room and studied the studio. The police hadn't done much searching in here, probably thinking dabbling in art was the guy's hobby and of no interest to them. A long low table filled the back wall. The drawers were all closed. I opened them. I took a stack of pencil drawings out and flicked quickly through them. These appeared to be the preliminary sketches for the Holmes pen-and-ink art he'd been selling at the conference. Even these rough ideas, unfinished, were very good. He had a genuine talent. Too bad . . . I glanced at the painting on the easel and then continued to search. The next drawer contained the tools of Randy's legitimate trade. Pencils, pots of ink, pens, unused drawing paper. Another drawer had several books on the art of sketching. One of them was by Randolph Denhaugh himself. Simply because I was curious, I picked it up and flipped through it. It was intended to be a step-by-step beginner's guide for the amateur artist.

A piece of paper fluttered to the floor. I picked it up.

It was a business card from Gallery Lambert, located on the South Bank near the Tate Modern. Judging by the heavy cream paper, the ornate inlaid gold script, and the tiny logo of the gallery, this place didn't sell tubes of paint to students or mass-produced art to tourists.

I memorized the address and put the card back.

I'd once seen a sign in a public park that said, TAKE NOTHING BUT PICTURES AND LEAVE NOTHING BUT FOOTPRINTS.

I intended to leave no footprints, and I wouldn't take any pictures that might be incriminating if my phone was searched. But I was taking plenty of impressions and the memory of the name and address of that art gallery.

I walked quickly back to the entrance, checking behind me as I went to ensure I was leaving nothing, not even a depression in the carpet, behind me.

"Let's blow this pop stand," I said to Jayne.

"Happy to. Find anything?"

"I think I did. I need to check in with Pippa."

I listened at the doorway. I could hear nothing, and so I slowly opened the door. I peeked up and down the hallway, saw no one, and we left the flat as silently as we had entered.

Chapter Eight

"You need some new jewelry," I said to Jayne.

"Always, but why now?"

"Because I know just the place to go."

We were in a restaurant not far from the Tower of London. Before Jayne and I talked about what I'd discovered or I called Pippa, I wanted to get far away from Randy's neighborhood, so we'd taken the Docklands Light Railway to Tower Gateway. We wandered through the narrow winding streets near the Tower of London and eventually chose a promising-looking pub by the name of The Crutched Friar.

Even in January, the place was packed with tourists, speaking in all manner of accents and languages, but we managed to find a table for two in a comfortable alcove. Jayne ordered a beer, but I asked for tea.

"My dear long-lost Uncle Randolph appears to be back in the art forgery business," I said to Jayne when our drinks were served and the waiter had taken our lunch orders. I didn't worry about keeping my voice down. Even in this corner, I could hardly hear Jayne, sitting directly across the table from me.

"Do you think that got him killed?" she asked.

I thought of the bullet-headed man. "It might have. Big money illegally obtained means ruthless methods and ruthless business partners. But I have no evidence to that effect. I have, truth be told, no evidence of anything. That flat didn't look at all lived in, and he didn't keep a lot of possessions in it. It's possible his real home is elsewhere. In a desk drawer I found two months' worth of credit card statements. If it had been one month, I'd think he was the sort who kept the most recent bill only. But two indicates the start of a habit. That's the sort of drawer into which people stuff their bills and other papers and let them stack up until they can't get the drawer closed. So they pitch it all and start collecting all over again."

"Sounds like the state of the drawers in your office back at the Emporium."

"Precisely."

"I keep expecting that one day I'm going to find a receipt for a load of coal at the bottom of my accounts." Jayne sipped her beer.

"Coal? Why would you buy coal?"

"That's my point, Gemma. I don't buy coal. I have an electric oven. Before the electric stove, the person who lived in what's now the tearoom would have cooked over coal or wood."

"Oh, right. Anyway, that leads me to conclude Randy's been in that flat for two months. All the clothes in his closet were winter things. No summer clothes or shoes. Interesting that he bought everything new rather than just moving all his stuff. That flat is incredibly expensive, meaning he'd come into a lot of money recently so he could afford it, or someone was putting him up there. As to why, seeing the artist studio, I can only conclude he was there to paint."

"Paint what?"

"An old master. Likely seventeenth-century Dutch from the quick look I had."

"You mean like Rembrandt or Vermeer?"

"That time period, anyway. My knowledge of art history isn't extensive."

"Probably more extensive than anyone I've ever met," she said.

"I appreciate the compliment, but modesty forces me to confess I know nothing about art other than what I saw on our annual school trips to the National Gallery when I was but one in a long line of giggling, pinafore-wearing, pig-tailed girls who'd have preferred to be just about anyplace else."

The waiter arrived with our steak and ale pies, hot and fragrant and steaming.

"Ooh, this smells good," Jayne said.

We stopped talking while we enjoyed our first few bites.

"Every meal I've had in London's been great," Jayne said when she came up for air. "Except for that banquet last night, which was pretty bland. I thought the English were terrible cooks."

"A foul rumor spread by the French."

"Do you have any long-lost relatives living in Paris?"

"Not that I know of."

"Good. We can go there for our next trip."

I put down my fork. "I've ruined your vacation. I'm sorry."

She lifted her glass. "Vacations are overrated. Your father needs your help, and you need my help, and I want to give you what help I can. Although I still don't quite know what I'm doing to provide this help."

"Thanks," I said.

"Besides, I'm seeing some of the best parts of London. Things the tourists don't usually get to. Like the inside of a really expensive apartment in Canary Wharf and a really, really expensive house in Kensington." She put her glass down and took a mouthful of beef and chewed thoughtfully. "Gemma, are your folks rich? Like super-rich?"

"Not at all. They both worked hard all their lives at demanding careers. Dad's got a good pension now, and Mum's still working. The house belonged to my grandparents, and we lived with them for many years. They're both gone now. My parents are ordinary working people who happen to live in a great area without needing a mortgage. They've been talking about selling the house when they both retire. It quite likely will bring in a lot of money, so I guess they'll be rich then."

"I've seen some of those prices. Wow!"

"Wow indeed. But London's an expensive city, and I don't see them moving very far away, although I know Mum would like a country place."

"You don't have any dukes or lords in your family, do you? Your dad's pretty down-to-earth, but your mom seems the type."

I ate my pie and didn't mention my second cousin three times removed—or was it my third cousin twice removed?—who was the current earl. I returned to the original subject. "I did find one item of interest in Randy's place, but I'm going to follow that trail later. I have a plan for after lunch."

Chapter Nine

I picked up the bill for our meal, telling Jayne that Pippa would pay me back.

As we stood outside, putting on our gloves and wrapping our scarfs around our necks, I told her what I wanted to do. She grinned and said, "Lead me to it."

While we'd waited for our food, I'd sent a quick text to Pippa's regular phone to say we were going for lunch and I was eager to hear about her day. My only purpose in doing that had been to let her know we were safely out of the flat. I'd tell her what I'd learned in person.

The address on Arianna Nowacki's business card was close enough we could walk it in a few minutes. I didn't call ahead, hoping to catch her by surprise. If she wasn't home, I'd have to phone, but I didn't like doing that unless it was necessary. Always better to catch people by surprise, I've found.

"Did you notice her booth at the conference?" I asked Jayne.

"I had a look at it. She was selling Holmes-themed jewelry. I saw necklaces and bracelets with sayings from the stories or the TV show, a key chain with a key for 221B, that sort of thing. I didn't think her stuff was anything special."

"I agree. We don't need to tell her that."

The address on Arianna Nowacki's card took us to an Indian restaurant. A small door was set into the wall beside the restaurant, next to which were buzzers for four flats.

I pressed the bell marked number three. We waited. I pressed it again.

"Hello?" said a tinny voice.

I nodded to Jayne.

"Hi," she said. "I'm sorry to bother you at home, but I thought I'd take a chance 'cause I have to go back to the States tomorrow."

"What is this about?" the voice asked. I recognized the Polish accent.

"I loved loved loved your jewelry at the Holmes conference. I went back to buy somethings today and you weren't there."

"Come in. Second floor." The buzzer sounded, the lock was released, and I opened the door.

The hallway was full of the deep rich scents of curry and spices. I breathed it in as we climbed the narrow dark staircase. We came to a small landing with two doors leading off. Jayne hesitated, but I continued on up.

"She said second floor," Jayne said.

"This is the first floor, the one above the ground floor," I said.

"Oh."

Up we went another flight. The staircase was narrow, the paint peeling, the light poor.

Arianna stood at an open door waiting for us. She was dressed in a large black T-shirt over leggings, and her bare feet showed toenails painted a bright red. Her hair was pulled into a rough ponytail and she wore no makeup. Her eyes and nose were tinged red.

"Hi," Jayne said, all American and bubbly. "Thanks so much for this. I hope you don't mind us barging in on you."

"Not a problem," Arianna said.

Jayne thrust out a hand. "I'm Jayne, and this is my friend Gemma."

"I know you," Arianna said to me. "You gave a speech last night, at the convention. You received an award."

"My uncle got the award," I said. "I just picked it up." Arianna waved us into her flat.

Her place was small, a cramped sitting room, one tiny bedroom, and a galley kitchen. Chaos might be the best word to describe Arianna's decorating style. Every chair and piece of furniture was covered with scarves, afghans, and throws. Potted plants, most of them lush and healthy, lined the floor beneath the grimy window. The coffee table was hidden under a pile of magazines, and more magazines, all of which had to do with fashion or gossip—or both—had tumbled onto the floor. A table shoved up against a wall appeared to be her work space. It was covered with containers overflowing with beads, crystals, and thin wire. Necklaces and earrings lay across the table, many of the pieces unfinished, amongst a jumble of magnifying glass, tweezers, and wire cutters.

I peeked into the tiny kitchen to see a mess of dirty dishes and pots and empty wine bottles. The bedroom door was open, and I caught a glimpse of tumbled pillows and bedclothes. Arianna didn't appear to think clothes needed to be hung up or put in the laundry hamper after wearing them.

"Pardon the mess," she said.

"Looks like my place," Jayne said with a laugh. "Why aren't you at the conference? Lots of people are like me. I looked at everything yesterday and went back to buy what I wanted today."

Arianna held a crumpled tissue in her right hand. She lifted it to her face. "A friend of mine died."

Jayne gasped. "How awful. You don't mean that man yesterday? The one who died at the banquet?"

Arianna nodded.

"Were you close?" Jayne said.

"We were engaged to be married." Arianna started to cry. She wasn't wearing the big diamond she'd been sporting yesterday.

"I am so sorry," Jayne said. "Perhaps we should go, Gemma. We don't want to bother Arianna at this difficult time."

Arianna wiped her eyes. "Oh, no. It is all right. You've come all this way. Now, what can I show you?"

While they talked, I'd studied Arianna's jewelry. It wasn't very good. Mostly colored beads strung on pieces of wire of varying lengths without originality or creativity. I'd barely glanced at her Sherlock-themed items in my first pass through the dealers' room on Friday, not seeing anything I might be interested in stocking in the shop.

"You like Sherlock Holmes?" she asked Jayne.

"I sure do! I wanted to get a couple of those pendants. The ones with sayings from the books. Do you have any here?"

Arianna moved a few boxes and rummaged through others. Eventually she found what she was searching for and held the box out. "Like these?" The tears were drying, leaving streaks on her cheeks.

"Oh, yes." Jayne picked up a chain with a metal disk hanging from it. YOU KNOW MY METHODS was carved into it. "This will be perfect for my mother's birthday. How much?"

"Thirty quid."

I swallowed a retort. I would have thought ten pounds excessive. No doubt that's what she sold it for on a street corner on Baker Street, but she'd upped her prices for the conference. Probably upped them more for people who'd come all the way across town looking for her.

"Your work is interesting." I pointed to a hideous silver bracelet with JOHN & SHERLOCK written on it in intertwined letters. "If you were at the banquet, you know I own a store in America."

Pure greed gleamed behind Arianna's dark eyes. "We can make deal. I give you good price."

"I'll have to think about it," I said. "Customs and duties and all that boring stuff. Do you sell in America?"

She had to admit she didn't. Not yet, anyway, but she'd like to expand her business.

"I might take that piece," I said. "Irene would love it, don't you think so, Jayne?"

"She'll adore it," Jayne said.

"How much?" I asked.

Indecision played across Arianna's face. She wanted whatever she could get for the bracelet, but she also wanted me to consider carrying her goods in the shop. Immediacy won out, and she said, "Fifty pounds."

I almost laughed.

"Forty then," she said.

"How about forty for both?" Jayne offered.

"Fine," Arianna said quickly.

While Jayne counted out the money, I walked around the room, pretending to study the rest of Arianna's things. "You do some good work."

"Thank you," she said.

"It's too bad you had to leave the conference early. People love this sort of thing. The people at the hotel this morning were saying the police think your fiancé was murdered. Is that true?"

"I don't know," she said.

"What did they tell you?"

"They told me nothing. I have not spoken to them."

"You should give them a call. You might know something important."

"I cannot help them. I don't like to get involved with the police."

I shrugged. "Your business, I guess. Were you and uh . . ."

"Randolph."

"Randolph. Were you together long?"

She shook her head as she stuffed Jayne's money into her bra. "Not long, no."

"You must be devastated," Jayne said. "Do you have any idea who'd want to kill him?"

"I am sad, yes, that he has died." She twisted the scrap of tissue between her fingers. "I told him only yesterday that I could not marry him." She buried her face in her hands and sobbed.

Jayne wrapped her arms around Arianna and murmured platitudes. Over the woman's shoulder she looked at me and raised an eyebrow. I made *keep her talking* gestures.

"That's awful. You must feel so guilty," Jayne said. "Even though you had nothing to do with his death, of course."

Arianna pulled herself free. "That is it. You understand. I feel guilt. His last hours on this earth were not happy ones."

I thought of Randy at the banquet. Laughing, drinking, chatting, having a great time.

I suspected Arianna was genuinely grieving. For now. But it was more of a self-pity party than any sadness for Randy. Jayne and I were giving her what she wanted, attention and sympathy, not to mention buying her cheap junk, and she was happy to take it.

"Why'd you break off with him?" Jayne asked. I wanted to know that too, but I might have been a bit more subtle about asking.

It didn't matter. Arianna was happy to tell us. "He was a cheat."

"No!" Jayne said. "Isn't that like a man? I was about to get engaged three years ago when I found out he was seeing a girl in the next town." That, I knew, wasn't true.

"I do not mean cheating with another woman," Arianna said. "He would not prefer any woman to me!" She puffed up her chest ever so slightly and patted the mess of hair. "No! He cheated with the money. I show you!" She went into the bedroom.

Jayne and I exchanged glances.

Arianna was soon back with the ring I'd seen her wearing in the hotel bar. She held it out to show us. Jayne squealed. "That's gorgeous."

"Is not gorgeous." Arianna marched up to the mirror over her worktable. She ran the stone in the ring across the surface of the glass.

Nothing happened.

"Is fake!" Her Polish accent got stronger as she got angrier. "Not real diamond."

"Oh," Jayne said. "The rat."

"We went to jewelry store. I picked out beautiful ring. It had to be made for my size. We went back for it next day." She spat on the floor, not minding that it was carpeted. "And I got *this*!"

"Gee," Jayne said. "Maybe he was cheated by the jeweler. You should tell the police."

"No police! I took it to be appraised. For insurance." I didn't believe that for a minute. She hadn't trusted Randy and she wanted to check his gift out. "He laughed and said jewelry was from friend of his. He'd get real ring later. He had big job and would soon get paid."

"What sort of big job?" I asked.

She shrugged. "Randy always about to get rich. I had enough."

That must have been the scene in the bar Jayne and I had been witness to. Notably, Arianna hadn't thrown the ring in Randy's face. She'd taken it with her, no doubt intending to sell it for fifty quid at a street market along with her other junk.

"And now," she said, "he'll never get rich."

"I'm sorry," Jayne said.

"You should talk to the police," I said. "You might know something you don't even know you know."

She shook her head.

"Up to you," I said. "But they'll find out that you knew each other."

Panic flashed across her face. "How?"

"Maybe they'll find something of yours in his flat."

The panic disappeared and she shrugged. "He moved two months ago. I've not been to new flat. He said it was not in nice part of town. Temporary until he could get something better."

"Is that so?" I said. "Do what you want. Thanks for your time."

"Give me your number," she said. "I will call you and we can talk about your store."

I hesitated. I didn't want her to think I'd be buying her goods to sell in the Emporium, but if she did remember something about Randy, I hoped she'd let me know. Although I didn't quite know how to ask that. I was supposedly here to look at jewelry.

"Gemma stocks lots of mystery books in her store," Jayne said. "She's really interested in crime. Maybe you could call us if you hear anything more about what happened to your fiancé. Ex-fiancé, I mean. Just 'cause we're curious."

"Uh. Good idea," I said. I rattled off my phone number. "It's a U.S. number, remember, so you don't want to call if it's not important."

Arianna pulled her own phone out of her pocket and quickly typed my number in.

We left the flat and walked down the narrow stairs. When we emerged onto the street, a light snow was falling and daylight was fading.

"It sure gets dark early here." Jayne pulled her gloves on. I hadn't taken mine off. It was highly unlikely the police would search Arianna's flat, but if they did, I didn't want my fingerprints to be found. Jayne's prints wouldn't be on file at Scotland Yard. Mine were.

And not from anything I'd done illegally. I once "helped the police with their enquiries" in a series of thefts on the street where I worked. Meaning I knew who'd done it, but they, suspicious bunch, thought I was responsible. Once we'd cleared that up, they should have deleted my prints. I suspected they hadn't.

It was, I realized, a lot easier to sneak about in the winter than in the summer. "London is much further north than Cape Cod," I said. "It's only four thirty."

We headed for the Tube station as wet snow began to fall faster.

"We now have," I said as we walked, "a good suspect."

"Do you think so?" Jayne said. "She seemed to be genuinely sorry he's dead."

"That means nothing. Plenty of killers have regretted what they've done as soon as it's done."

"Is that why she hasn't gone to the police, do you think? She seemed to me like the sort who'd love the attention. The grieving fiancée and all that."

"It's possible. Then again, she cuts a lot of corners with the little business she has going there. She was quick enough to suspect her engagement ring was fake. Which means she automatically thinks along those lines."

"When I get an engagement ring, if ever I do, I'd be too embarrassed to ask someone to check it out for me."

"Because that's not your instinctive reaction."

"Maybe she's in the country illegally?"

"Unlikely. Her English is nearly perfect and the Polish accent only gets strong when she gets emotional, meaning she's probably been in the UK for a long time."

"Did you find it interesting that she's never been to that flat we visited earlier, and Randy told her he wasn't living in a nice place?"

"I did. I suspect their relationship suffered from a lack of honesty in a lot of ways."

"What now?" Jayne asked.

"Let's go to Stanhope Gardens and report in. I want to check on my dad anyway, and the group should be back from Scotland Yard soon."

Chapter Ten

I texted Pippa and told her we were on our way back to Stanhope Gardens. We went to Tower Hill station to catch the Tube, but first I took a short detour so Jayne could have a look at the Tower of London from a distance. She gazed longingly at the massive fortress.

"We'll come back, I promise." I said. "Maybe we can get this business settled today and visit the tower tomorrow."

"It would be fun to skate around it." She pointed to the brightly lit ice-skating rink at the base of the historic fortifications.

"A whole new twenty-first-century use for a moat," I said.

* * *

My mother answered the door to my ring. "Your father's definitely on the mend," she said. "He's complaining about being bored."

"Any memories coming back?" I asked as Jayne and I stepped into the house.

"He says no. He's in his shop, if you want to see him."

"I'll pop out there. In the meantime, I bet Jayne would love a cup of tea."

Mum smiled at my friend. "As would I."

We hung up our outerwear, and I walked through the house in search of my father. The center hallway ends with the kitchen on one side and the conservatory on the other. There it opens onto a small terrace, used in the nice weather for dining outdoors. A low wall surrounds the terrace, and two steps lead down to the garden. Large trees, their branches bare now, and a six-foot-high brick wall surround the property. The large iron pots, which my mother fills with plants in the summer, were empty. A fine layer of wet snow lay over the bushes and the turned-over flower beds. Most of the yard was taken up by my father's woodworking shop. Lights shone from inside. I knocked lightly and went in.

Horace leapt to his feet and barked, and then he ran over to sniff the scents on my clothes to check on what I'd been up to today. I patted him on the head, and I looked up to see my father smiling at me. I gave him a hug. "Feeling better?" I asked.

"Much better. Still don't remember anything about last night. Dr. McMaster said it may never come back. Depends on whether or not my short-term memory had stored the events in my brain before I got hit."

I perched on a high stool and swung my legs in the air. I was ten years old again, sitting on the stool, enveloped in the familiar scents of freshly cut wood, mineral oil, and machine oil and breathing in sawdust, proudly telling my father my exam results.

Then I was twenty-seven again, having to tell him I was leaving England and joining Great-Uncle Arthur in America to help run the bookshop he'd bought on a crazy whim.

I picked a bowl off the table next to me. It was huge, almost two feet wide and a deep rich red in color. A matching set of salad servers rested inside. The shelves over my head were lined with bowls, candlesticks, cutting boards, toys, and sculptures of varying woods and sizes. "You've been busy."

"I've signed up for several craft fairs over the spring. I'm sure you've been busy today too. Tell me about it."

"Jayne and I went back to the conference for a short while, and then we went to the Tower of London." I spoke in total honesty, leaving out a handful of pertinent details.

"Highly unlikely you toured the tower. Want to tell me what you were doing there?"

"No. Pippa and I will coordinate. Better you don't know. Plausible deniability and all that."

He put the bowl in his hands down. "I don't want to be able to deny, plausibly or not, my daughters' activities on my behalf."

"Blissful ignorance, then," I said. "Do you have any contacts with people who work on art forgery?"

"One or two."

"Give them a call. Ask if there's any talk of fake Dutch masters, sixteenth or seventeenth century, floating about over the last couple of months."

"Randy was back in the game?"

"Looks like it. But we can't forget that he also had enemies of a more personal nature."

"It's so frustrating, Gemma, not being able to remember. For all I know I was a witness to whoever killed Randy, and I can't recall a single detail. Some old cop I am. If I were Sam Morrison, I wouldn't believe me either." He sighed heavily, and my heart rolled over. He looked so very old.

Horace was thinking the same as me. He nuzzled his nose into Dad's leg. Dad scratched behind his ears, and I smiled.

We never had pets when I was a child, mainly because of my parents' work schedule and Mum's allergies. I'd never wanted a pet, but then Violet came into my life and now I couldn't imagine life without her. I was glad Dad had Horace.

"The memory will come." I said. "And if not, I'm here. Did you hear from DI Morrison again today?"

"Unfortunately, yes. He was back early in the afternoon to badger me again. Anne called Dr. McMaster and had him speak to Sam to inform him that yelling at me wouldn't help my memory any."

"Did Morrison come with anyone?"

"A young woman. DS Patel. I didn't get her first name. She didn't say much, but she did look uncomfortable when things started getting tense."

"What happened then?"

"Anne made the phone call to the doctor, and the police left."

I hopped off the stool. "Mum and Jayne are making tea. Coming?"

"I want to get this piece finished." He turned back to his worktable.

Before following the sound of voices into the library, I called Ashleigh, my shop assistant. It was late in West London, and I hoped she'd still be up. I'd planned to check in every day, but with all that was happening, I hadn't had the chance today.

"Sorry about calling so late," I said when she answered. "But I've been on the go all day."

"Having too much fun, are you? *Westminster Abbey, the tower of Big Ben. Rosy-red cheeks of the little child-ren.*"

"I wouldn't have taken you for a sixties music fan."

"I have a wide variety of tastes."

That was true enough. "How'd the signing go yesterday?" A major best-selling author had agreed to do an event at the Emporium. His new book wasn't part of our usual mandate—not having anything remotely to do with Sherlock Holmes or his times—but it was a critically acclaimed "sweeping" and "important" historical novel about Cape Cod. I'd been delighted when the author agreed to come, but I'd already arranged this trip to London. Arthur had convinced me he and Ashleigh could handle the event on their own.

"It . . . uh . . . didn't happen," Ashleigh said.

"What do you mean, it didn't happen? Did he take ill?"

"Not exactly. Look, don't worry, Gemma. I know he said he'd never step foot in our store again, but that was only 'cause he was mad. He'll get over it. Someday. Probably. I offered to buy him a new pair of shoes, but he said those were handmade leather ones he'd had personally made by a family in Florence who've been crafting shoes for seven generations, and he wouldn't be caught dead in anything I—a mere store clerk—could possibly afford to buy to replace them."

My mouth flapped open, but no words came out. For one of the few times in my life, I was speechless.

"I don't think he even knows what some of those English words Arthur called him meant."

More mouth flapping in silence. Finally I said, "Arthur called a number-one *New York Times* best-selling author names?"

"Only after he threated to kill Moriarty for peeing on his shoes."

I groaned.

"Other than that," Ashleigh said, "everything's been great. No need to worry. Mrs. Fallingham said he was a jerk, so there." Mrs. Fallingham was one of our store's most loyal and influential book buyers.

"There is that, at least," I said. "If she likes the book, she'll recommend it to her friends."

"Oh, no," Ashleigh said, "she didn't buy one. You know how much she adores Moriarty. She said the author was so obnoxious, she'll tell everyone to boycott him."

I envisioned the storage room of the Emporium— stacked to the rafters with boxes of the "sweeping" and "important" book I'd ordered for the signing.

"See you Wednesday," Ashleigh said cheerfully. "Bye! Have a cuppa for me." She hung up.

I could only hope 222 Baker Street wouldn't burn to the ground before I got home.

I went into the library to find Jayne and Mum sipping tea and nibbling on chocolate biscuits. Which, now that I am living in America, I am beginning to call cookies.

"Everything okay at home?" Jayne said.

"Perfect. I should leave Arthur and Ashleigh in charge more often." I sat down and Mum poured me a cup.

"Glad to hear it," Jayne said. "I have to admit I was concerned. Maybe we can make that trip to Paris next year after all."

"You're going to Paris?" Mum said. "How delightful. Do be sure and visit in the spring. It's as dreary in January as London is."

The front door opened, and we could hear a babble of voices from the entranceway.

"In here!" Mum called.

In came Pippa followed by Ryan, Grant, and Donald.

"I'll make more tea," Mum said.

Jayne got to her feet. "Let me help."

I lifted my chin to accept a kiss from Ryan. "Have fun?" I asked.

"It was great!" His cheeks were ruddy with cold and his blue eyes shone with pleasure. "I can't believe Pippa was able to organize a private tour like that with no notice. And on a Sunday too."

"I'm beginning to think," Grant said, "Pippa can do a lot of incredible things." If Grant had been a woman, I would have said he looked radiant.

I glanced at my sister. She was also smiling. Good heavens, was that a glow I saw surrounding her? Did she look radiant?

"As well as the offices," Donald said, "we had a fascinating tour of the Black Museum." He meant the police museum that isn't open to the general public. "And an excellent lunch to boot." Fortunately Donald hadn't worn his ulster today, and his cardigan was buttoned all the way up, hiding the Sherlock quote on his T-shirt. I wouldn't have wanted anyone at the Yard to think he was making fun of them.

"And you, Gemma?" Pippa asked. "How was your day?"

"Jayne and I enjoyed a walk in the City and near the Tower of London. We also had a nice lunch."

"Isn't that lovely," Pippa said.

Mum and Jayne reappeared with a bigger teapot, more cups, and a larger arrangement of biscuits.

"Where's Dad?" Pippa asked.

"In the workshop," I said. "He remembers nothing new."

"Grant," Pippa said, "would you mind going out and telling him it's teatime?"

"I'd be happy to." Grant almost skipped away.

"Gemma, why don't you and I take a moment to chat?"

"Sure," I said.

Ryan started to stand. I gave him a playful push in the chest. "Sister talk. Not for you."

I followed Pippa into the hallway and shut the library door behind me.

"Is every man in America dreadfully handsome?" she asked me when we were alone.

I grinned. "Not all. When they get older, some of them turn into Donald."

"Oh, yes. Donald. I can say one thing for your Donald. You can't beat that wide-eyed enthusiasm. We can't talk here. Anyone of them might come in, and I don't trust Mother not to listen at the door. We'll go for a walk."

"What will we tell the others?"

"Nothing. We'll simply go. Otherwise Grant and Ryan will try to come."

"They'll think we've been kidnapped."

She gave me a look. "Really, Gemma. But if you insist, I'll text Grant once we're outside."

"You exchanged numbers, eh?"

"I didn't want us to get separated in the city."

"Really, Pippa."

We tiptoed down the hallway, collected our coats, and slipped outside. Pippa grabbed the key for the locked garden across the street out of the silver bowl by the door.

We crossed the street, let ourselves into the garden, and found a bench beneath a lamppost. Snow was falling, drier and heavier now, and we sat in the circle of light. No one else was in the garden.

"There are no CCTV cameras in here," Pippa said. "As it's private property. There's one at the entrance to

the street itself, but it's no secret you're visiting and that
your parents live here. If you need to come or go unob-
served, there's a crumbling section of brick in the back
wall that's easier to remove than it looks, and the people
who own the house on the far side winter in the South
of France. The CCTV camera on that street is inactive.
Now, tell me what you learned."

Pippa sat quietly while I did so. I finished talking
at last and let her think over what I'd told her. "So, he's
back in the forgery business," she said at last.

"That's what I concluded."

"With money behind him. I'm thinking someone
put him up in that flat, at their expense, to give him
time and a place to make the painting, and threw in a
few bonuses such as a credit card with a high limit to
keep him happy. That someone might have had second
thoughts about the deal. Or Randy had second
thoughts his partners didn't appreciate."

"Maybe they didn't like him taking time off to make
the Holmes sketches and come to the conference. But we
can't lose sight of other people who might be involved,
never mind the ubiquitous person or persons unknown."

"Such as the angry former fiancée," Pippa said.

An elderly woman walked slowly toward us, followed by a King Charles spaniel on a leash. The dog ran
over to sniff at us. "Good evening," the woman said.

"Good evening," my sister and I chorused.

We were quiet until they'd continued up the path
and disappeared into the snowy darkness. When I was
sure the woman was out of hearing, I asked, "What did
you find out about the dreadlocked woman and the
bullet-headed man?"

"His name is John Saint-Jean, and he was easy to
locate from the hotel's CCTV cameras. I won't give

you any information on him, because I want you to go in with an open mind. You can pay a call on him tomorrow." Pippa rattled off an address in Mayfair. "As for the woman, nothing yet. It's possible, by your description, her hairstyle was a wig."

"If she wore a wig, she might have been attempting to disguise herself."

"Or simply wanting to look more interesting as an artist."

"If you have access to the CCTV footage," I said, "you must know what it shows of Randy's movements as well as Dad's at the time in question."

"I don't have access," she said. "But I know people who do who will answer any questions I send their way. The only CCTV camera at that end of the hotel is mounted above the entrance to the ballroom area facing toward the lobby. The camera can see the faces of everyone approaching the reception and the room where the dinner was held, and the backs of them leaving. Not, unfortunately, what went on once people had passed into the reception area. As of yet, no one stands out as of interest."

"You know people . . ." I said. "If you know the right people, why don't you get Morrison taken off the case and someone who hasn't already decided Dad's guilty put on it?"

"Not everyone in Scotland Yard is a friend of mine," she said. "I've already done more than I should. There are people both at the Yard and in the press who would like to see my office embarrassed."

"Speaking of this office," I said. "What is it you do, exactly, Pippa?"

She brushed a light dusting of snow off her lap. "The police are going through the footage, image by painful image, trying to identify and locate each of the more than four hundred people who were in the area during the after-dinner speeches, when Randy got up from his table, but had left before the authorities arrived. The conference organizers have handed over the conference registration list, but quite a number of people bought banquet tickets for any number of guests, such as you and your friends did for us, and those names were not recorded. Even if names were given, no one ever checked that names and addresses provided were legitimate. It's going to take the police forever to find and talk to everyone who was there. I'll give them a little nudge and drop the name of this jewelry maker you found."

"Arianna Nowacki. Maybe we'll be lucky and she'll confess when they question her."

"That, I am not counting on. I have to go to work tomorrow. Things are happening that I can't put off, even for this case. What's your plan?"

"I want to pay a call on Gallery Lambert."

"That's the name on the business card you found in the Canary Wharf flat?"

"Yes. I'll pose as a wealthy American art collector."

"Are you going to take Jayne? I like her very much, by the way. You're lucky to have a friend. I mean, to have a friend like her."

Pippa, I realized, had let her tongue slip. Pippa had no friends. She had contacts and she had "people" and her "office." But she had no friends. And that made me very sad.

I pushed the emotion aside to ponder another time. "Not Jayne. I'd like to take Grant. He can play the rich American, one not entirely averse to dealing under the table, better than Jayne. Besides, you never know when you're going to run into someone who won't take Jayne and me—young women—seriously."

"I agree," she said.

"Which brings up the question as to what on earth I'm going to do with the rest of them."

"I have no more suggestions," Pippa said. "Unfortunately, I can't get them into Buck House for a private tour." Buck House is the nickname for Buckingham Palace. "Her Majesty is in residence this week."

I stared at her.

She reached into her coat pocket. "I bought you a present." She handed me a mobile phone.

"What's this for?"

"It's untraceable. Use it if you need to leave your number with someone you don't want knowing you have a North American phone number. Or if you have reason to believe the police might want to check into whom you've been speaking to."

I took the phone and put it in my own pocket.

"I did enjoy our outing today." Pippa stood up. "Do you know, I've never been to the Black Museum? It was fascinating. I need to start doing more recreational things."

"You can come and visit me in Cape Cod," I said without thinking.

She smiled. "I might do that one day. Let me make a few calls. I can probably arrange something to keep your entourage busy."

"Never mind. I have an idea."

* * *

"You still haven't had a chance to visit the Sherlock Holmes Museum or go on the walking tour, Donald," I said once Pippa and I were back in the library with fresh cups of tea on our laps.

When we returned, my mother had looked questioningly at us, obviously not believing my sister and I would spontaneously go for a walk, but everyone else had taken the text to Grant at face value.

"Mum, are you planning a fun day out with Jayne for tomorrow?" I asked.

"I'd love to, dear, but I have court tomorrow and I cannot put this one off. The Crown has delayed and delayed, and I simply can't put my client through that any longer."

"Not a problem," I said. "There's so much to do in London. Jayne's been hoping to get to Baker Street and go on the guided walk also."

"Me? I don't . . . oh, yeah right. I can't wait."

Donald rubbed his hands together in glee. "Excellent. Who else is in?"

"I have no interest," Ryan said. "This weekend has been enough Sherlock for me as it is."

"Count me in," Grant said. "It's on my list of things to do." Typical. The people I didn't want tagging along after me wanted to come, and the one person I did want, didn't. "I have a much better plan for you, Grant. Pippa told me about a wealthy collector who's selling off his collection of rare books. His house is open tomorrow for interested buyers. Only for his friends and colleagues, but Pippa can get us an invite."

Grant's face lit up. *Okay, so I lied.* But I had to get him on his own tomorrow. I'd tell him then what we were really up to.

Unfortunately, Donald's face also lit up. "Do they have anything by Conan Doyle? I'll come also. Hopefully we can do both that and the walk."

"Uh, no," I said. "He only collected works by . . . uh . . . female authors. Jane Austin, the Bronte sisters, and the like."

"I have no interest in either the Sherlock Holmes Museum or in rare books," Ryan said, "but I'll join you and Grant, Gemma."

"Uh . . ." I said.

"Sorry," Pippa said. "The owner won't allow extra people. It's a highly exclusive event. Why don't you go on the tour, Ryan? It's bound to be fun, and I believe as well as a walking tour, there's a Holmes-related pub crawl."

If there wasn't such a thing as a Sherlock Holmes pub crawl, I was beginning to think Pippa would have one up and running by tomorrow.

Ryan got to his feet. "Gemma, can I have a word?"

"Now," Pippa said, "what are we doing for dinner?"

"Why don't I order takeaway," Mum said. "Indian or Chinese?"

"Indian."

"Chinese."

"Indian," I said.

"Chinese."

"Either."

Ryan didn't offer an opinion; instead he gave me *that* look.

"Lebanese," said Donald. "I've always wanted to try Lebanese, and I saw a place on Gloucester Road."

"Then Lebanese it shall be," Mum said. "I'll call them now. I think it's time to open a bottle of wine, and Henry has a few bottles of beer around here somewhere."

"I'll help," Jayne said.

"Gemma?" Ryan said. "A word, please."

Reluctantly, I stood up and followed him out of the library. He opened a door at random, and we went into the dining room. He turned to face me. He was not smiling. "What are you and Pippa up to?"

"Nothing," I said trying my best to look innocent.

"Don't give me that innocent look, Gemma Doyle. I enjoyed our outing today and was glad Pippa arranged it, but I couldn't shake off the feeling you were trying to get rid of us. And this scene just now? The two of you are pretty good at manipulating people, but that got out of hand. Pippa just happens to know of a one-day exclusive viewing for books that just happen to be right up Grant's alley? What's up, Gemma?"

I never can lie to Ryan. I can bamboozle, misrepresent, deflect, even ignore. But I can't lie.

"Pippa and I are concerned that DI Morrison is concentrating his investigation on Dad to the exclusion of other suspects. Real suspects."

Ryan groaned. "So you've taken it on yourselves to investigate."

"Not investigate so much as poke around."

"Same thing, Gemma. I'd tell you not to do it, but you won't pay any attention to me, and your sister certainly won't. I assume you have some nefarious plan for Grant tomorrow, a plan that doesn't involve looking at rare books. I'll come with you instead. Let him go to the Holmes stuff."

"That won't work, Ryan. You pretty much have C-O-P tattooed on your forehead." Ryan was no actor. But, more to the point, I didn't want to put him in any position in which he might be legally compromised.

Not that that was going to happen with a casual visit to a nice art gallery.

I smiled at him. He did not smile back.

The door opened and Pippa came in. She handed Ryan a glass of beer without a word. "Trust Gemma," she said. She closed the door on her way out.

Ryan studied me over the rim of the glass. "Guess I'll have to."

Chapter Eleven

Ryan and I desperately needed some alone time. Some relationship-building time. Dinner together, just the two of us, or at least a quiet nightcap in the hotel bar. Instead, we ate takeaway Lebanese food off paper plates in my parents' formal dining room and walked back to the hotel with the group.

"I'm very tired." I took Jayne's arm as we walked into the lobby. "Time for an early night." If I had any alone time with Ryan, I knew it would turn into him asking me what my plan was and me confessing.

"Really?" Ryan said. "It's only five in the afternoon Boston time."

"We're not in Boston," I said. "And you must still be jet-lagged. I am. Night all." I dragged Jayne away.

"I'm game for another beer," Grant said. As I'd been digging the last of the tabbouleh out of the container, Pippa's phone—one of Pippa's phones—buzzed and she'd risen from the table to take the call without even checking the screen. She never came back, so I assumed she'd been called in to work to "take the minutes." If the call had something to do with Randy's death, she would have told me.

"Not me," Donald said. "We have a busy day tomorrow, so I need my rest."

"Might as well," Ryan said.

* * *

My sleeping pattern was still messed up with the time change, and rather than going to sleep when Jayne and I got to our room, I sat up for a long time. I checked out Gallery Lambert, preparing for our visit tomorrow, and read what news I could find about the death of Randolph Denhaugh. The murder having taken place at a Sherlock Holmes convention had caused some amusement and tasteless jokes in the press. The police statement said an arrest was imminent, and asked people to come forward with information. Nothing at all worthwhile. An "imminent arrest," I knew, was police-talk for "haven't got a clue."

I put the iPad away and opened my book, accompanied by the peaceful sound of Jayne's deep breathing.

When I woke, sunlight was streaming in our window and Jayne was up, showered, dressed, drinking coffee, and using her iPad.

"Morning," I mumbled. "Anything interesting in the world?"

"Same old, same old. I'm reading about all the exciting and interesting things there are to do in London, which I am not going to do because I'm going to the Sherlock Holmes Museum and touring Baker Street. Why are you taking Grant today and not me?"

I explained my reasoning to her. Grant would present better as a wealthy, yet somewhat clueless, art collector than she would.

"Okay," she said, "I guess that's fair enough."

"I need you to keep Ryan occupied. He's getting suspicious."

"When it comes to you, Ryan is in a permanent state of suspicion. As he should be."

"I don't need him deciding he needs to come to my rescue and tagging along after us. That would only complicate everything."

"Because it's not at all complicated now." She snapped her arm up into a stiff salute and touched her forehead. "I have my orders. I'll follow them to the letter. Sir."

I went for my shower. When I came out, Jayne said, "Your phone buzzed."

> PIPPA: DREADLOCKED WOMAN IDENTIFIED BY
> POLICE. SHE PAID FOR LUNCH WITH CREDIT
> CARD. A NAME AND ADDRESS FOLLOWED.
> ME: WHEN DID THEY GET THE ID?
> PIPPA: YESTERDAY AFT
> ME: ANYTHING COME OF IT?
> PIPPA: DON'T KNOW

Meaning the police would have paid a call on her yesterday and they hadn't arrested her. So she should be free today.

I'd drop in on her after Grant and I visited the art gallery.

> I TEXTED GRANT: LOBBY. 10:30. DRESS RICH.
> He replied immediately: WHAT DOES THAT MEAN?
> ME: YOU'LL THINK OF SOMETHING.

"Breakfast?" I asked Jayne.

"I've arranged to meet Donald in fifteen minutes in the hotel restaurant. Want to come with us?"

"No."

* * *

I spent a lot of time deciding what to wear. I wanted to look like the wife of a man who bought fine art, but I hadn't brought anything very posh with me. My coat was a black woolen thing bought at an end-of-season sale three years ago which was pilling badly around the elbows. If we were invited into the gallery's private office for tea, I'd have to take the coat off. The forecast for today was for slightly warmer temperatures than yesterday and no rain, so I eventually decided on slumming it in jeans and a navy-blue blazer. I'd need some high-end accessories though, if I wanted to look the part.

I answered the door to a knock. Ryan stood there, grinning slightly, hair damp from the shower, freshly shaven, looking absolutely delicious. He held out two takeout cups and a small paper bag from Paul's Boulangerie. "Room service, madam."

I laughed and stepped back to allow him in. He put the drinks and bag on the small coffee table, threw Jayne's backpack on the floor, and sat on the couch. I dropped beside him and curled my feet up under me. Ryan handed me a cup and I took the lid off and breathed in the scent of hot fresh tea. He ripped open the bag to reveal two flaky *pain au chocolat*, fragrant and warm from the oven.

"Perfect," I said.

We sipped our drinks and nibbled on the pastries. "Everything okay back at home?" he asked.

"I might not have a business to go back to." I told him about the cat/computer mishap and the angry best-selling author, and he laughed.

"Nothing much happening at my end. I called Louise this morning, and she told me the WLPD was managing perfectly fine without me."

"She's probably lying. If the place was falling into rack and ruin, she'd hardly tell you."

"True." He looked rested and relaxed. Apart from murder at the conference and wondering what I was up to, the time off work was doing him good.

"Did you and Grant stay in the bar for long last night?" I asked.

"No. As soon as we sat down, I realized I was bushed. I didn't even finish my beer."

"Did you manage to get any sleep?"

"I did. Either Donald's snores were quiet last night, or I was so tired I was able to ignore the cacophony. I think Grant's developing a thing for your sister. She's all he talked about. She seems nice enough, although she's scarcely said two words to me the entire time we've been in the same room, but I didn't find an extensive list of her virtues all that interesting."

"She's an interesting person," I said.

"But not the most interesting of the sisters." He put down his cup and licked chocolate off his fingers. "What time are you and Grant meeting?"

"Half ten."

"Ten thirty? It's quarter to ten now. I saw Jayne and Donald heading for the restaurant when I was going out for our coffee. They'll be a while yet." He plucked my cup out of my hand.

*   *   *

I was in the lobby precisely on time, and Grant was waiting. Ryan had come down with me.

"I'm not going home tomorrow as planned," I said to the men. "I'll need to extend my stay in the hotel."

"I'm not leaving without you," Ryan said.

"I'll stay as long as I can be of help," Grant said.

I felt something warm move in my chest. "Thanks, guys."

We went to the reproduction-antique desk that served as reception to make the arrangements. The woman seated behind it smiled at us and asked me to take a seat.

I did so, but I didn't sit there for long.

The hotel was fully booked all through to the weekend, she told me with a shake of her head so regretful you might have thought she was being kicked into the street rather than us.

"You're unlikely to find anything else suitable in the immediate area. A big convention is starting on Wednesday. Something to do with the architecture of computer systems. Whatever that is."

"Thanks," I said, and got to my feet.

"What are we doing to do now?" Ryan asked.

"Start calling hotels, I guess," Grant said.

"I have an idea," I said. "Let me take care of it."

"Happy to." Ryan kissed me goodbye, wished Grant and me a good day, and headed off in search of Jayne and Donald.

"I need to make a call before we go," I said to Grant.

I phoned Dad. "Good morning, my dearest," he said. I was pleased to hear the light tone of his voice.

"Hi, Dad. Just checking in. Any developments?"

"No. Nothing from Morrison or anyone else since yesterday."

"I suppose that's a good thing."

"It is."

"How are you feeling?"

"Fine. The headache is almost gone."

"What headache? You didn't tell me about any headache."

"Didn't I? Not a problem, is it now, as it's almost disappeared. Your mother is in court today, and she left me strict instructions to check in with her regularly. Which I plan to do. What are you up to?"

I sidestepped the question. "Speaking of problems, we have one. We can't stay at the Bentley after tonight, as they're full up for the rest of the week. I'm worried that staying in London much longer, plus the cost of changing flights, is more than we, Jayne and Donald in particular, can afford."

"You can all come here."

"Are you sure?"

"We have the room if some of you double up."

"Thanks, Dad. Call me if anything comes up."

"What are your plans for today again?"

"Bye." I put the phone away and said to Grant, "Tomorrow we're all moving to Stanhope Gardens."

"Nice of your father to have us."

"You'll have to share a room with Donald."

"I can do that. If I have to. In the meantime, I cannot wait to see these books. I was up half the night, trying to find any whispers of what this soon-to-be-sold collection might consist of. They're keeping a mighty tight lid on it; I couldn't find a thing."

"Books? What books?"

"The ones Pippa told us about last night? The ones we're going to see today?"

"About that. I may have stretched the truth a tiny bit."

"Meaning?"

"First, let's go shopping." I turned to the doorman holding the door open for us. "Can you get us a cab, please?"

The taxi dropped Grant and me off at Harrods. Grant always dressed well, if not actually rich (because he wasn't), and today he looked the part of a well-off art collector in a brown sheepskin bomber jacket with checked white-and-brown scarf over a good gray wool sweater and dark jeans rolled up at the cuffs. Study brown leather boots were on his feet.

"We're going shopping?" Grant said. "Not what I was expecting."

We stood at the entrance to the famous store. Hordes of well-heeled shoppers and casually dressed tourists swirled around us. I told Grant what our goal was for today. "We're going to look at art, not books."

"Why?"

"My uncle Randolph was a known art forger. I believe he was engaged in that line of work when he died. The gallery I'm interested in, according to their website, specializes in school-of art. Meaning, not quite old masters but works by those who studied under them, or paintings that can't be positively iden-tified as created by one of the masters themselves. The public stuff they sell is expensive, as you'd expect, but not outrageously so. We're not talking Sotheby's here. I have reason to believe this gallery handles forgeries. Sixteenth to eighteenth century specifically. We're going to have a look around, that's all. You're the wealthy American art lover; I'm your meek little wife."

"Yeah, right."

"I can pretend, Grant. You'll look at what they have to show you and not be overly impressed. You were thinking something a little more . . . exclusive. See how they respond."

"They're not going to respond by telling me they have a fake Vermeer propped up next to the furnace in the basement."

"No. Maybe I'm clutching at straws here. For all I know, Randy picked their business card up out of the gutter because he cares about keeping London clean and didn't get around to throwing it in the garbage. But I want to see what the place is like. If I sense anything not aboveboard, so to speak, I'll tell Pippa."

"And what will Pippa do then, Gemma?" Grant asked. His voice was low and his eyes serious. "What *does* she do?"

"Pippa knows people. People who can do things. That's really all I know."

"I'm happy to go along with you on this, if you want my help. But I still don't understand why we're in Harrods. Do they have any connection with this art gallery?"

"There's no point in going somewhere under a false pretext if one can't play the part. You look perfectly fine. I do not."

"You look fine to me."

What do men know? I took his arm and led him into the store.

We emerged half an hour later. I had a new pair of leather gloves (one hundred quid) on my hands, high-heeled leather ankle boots (five hundred quid) on my feet, and a Burberry bag (seven hundred quid) over my shoulder. I'd been afraid Grant was going to faint when he saw the price tags. Pippa and her "office" would be getting the bill. I'd briefly considered splashing out on diamond earrings, but Pippa might balk at paying for those. The plain gold hoops I regularly wore through my ears would have to do. I couldn't carry my own things around, so I hadn't worn a coat or brought my purse, and my cheap wool gloves and trainers were now in a trash can in the ladies' loo.

"Are we going to grab a taxi?" Grant asked.

"It's faster on the Tube at this time of day, but we can't just walk up to the front door of the gallery. We'll call a cab once we're a mile or so away. I don't think I can walk very far in these boots anyway. Now, remember, you're an American, but you spent a lot of time in England."

"Which is true."

"So it is. Thus it's natural for you to come to London in search of what you're after. You are also no art expert, although you think you are. You've recently inherited a lot of money on the death of your father. He had absolutely no taste for the finer things in life, but you plan to acquire them, no matter the cost. You'll be putty in their hands. In case they ask for your number so they can call you later, I have a second phone with me. One with a London number, untraceable."

"Dare I ask where you got that?"

"No. I only wish you were older."

"Why?"

"So I could be the young new wife." I batted my eyelashes at him.

He rolled his eyes and said, "Don't lay it on too thick."

*　*　*

Our cab pulled up in front of Gallery Lambert. Grant got out first and assisted me. I gave him a radiant smile. It wasn't easy. We'd walked to Knightsbridge Tube station, down to the platform for the Piccadilly line, transferred to the Jubilee line to emerge at

Waterloo, and then up to the street to hail a cab to take us to our destination. I couldn't have been walking in my new boots more than ten minutes, and my feet were screaming in pain. I don't normally wear such high heels, and I was worried I'd topple over. Perhaps I should have gone for lower heels instead, but that wouldn't have made the impression I wanted.

Nor would falling flat on my face.

Grant took my arm and we went inside.

Gallery Lambert was minimalist and screaming of money. Paintings in the style of the old masters hung on walls painted in shades of terra-cotta. The lighting was dim, with individual lamps discreetly illuminating each painting.

"Gosh," I said in my best American accent, "these are nice, honey."

A woman, who looked like she might have stepped out of a modern painting, all sharp angles and harsh edges, was seated behind a reception desk. She smiled at us without a trace of warmth. Her skin was the color of bleached cotton, her hair chopped at the line of her chin and dyed a pure solid black, her mouth a thin slash of red.

I couldn't help glancing at the painting behind her desk of a woman in a stiff black dress trimmed with pearls and a high ruffled collar. She wasn't smiling, but compared to the live woman in front of us, she was all softness and warmth.

"Good afternoon," the woman—the living one—said in a terribly posh drawl. No doubt she'd gone to a top-ranked girls' boarding school that qualified her for nothing more than staffing the desk at a fancy art gallery and impressing the customers. The accent, however, was not English but Canadian.

"Hi," Grant said. "I'm Kevin Thornton from New York, and I was told about this gallery by a collector friend of mine."

The woman got to her feet. She'd had, I thought, some plastic surgery done, and it might not have been entirely successful. Her mouth was too thin, her tiny nose out of proportion for the bone structure of her face. A genuine smile touched the edges of her painted mouth as she studied Grant.

Me, she ignored completely. All the better to allow me to snoop around.

"Might I know the name of your friend?" she asked.

"That would be telling," Grant said. "You wouldn't recognize his name, anyway. My friend prefers to buy through an agent."

She laughed lightly. "Welcome, Mr. Thornton. I'm Vivienne. Are you looking for anything in particular?"

"I've recently come into some funds, and I'm eager to start building myself a good collection. My wife and I are in London on a little buying trip."

I wiggled my one-hundred-pound leather gloves at her. She did not look impressed.

Grant wandered over to study a painting of a dog and a brace of pheasant. "I don't recognize this name," he said.

"One of the lesser Flemish artists," Vivienne replied. "If you tell me precisely what you're interested in for your collection, Mr. Thornton, perhaps I can make some recommendations."

"I like the Dutch. You know, Rembrandt. Vermeer. Frank Hall."

"Frank Hall? Oh, you mean Frans Hals."

"Yeah. Him."

"Items of that quality rarely, if ever, come onto the open market," she said.

"Yeah, I know that. It would be nice to have one though, wouldn't it? Some of the paintings you have here are good."

I noticed the absence of price tags. Presumably if you had to ask how much they cost, you couldn't afford them.

"Our gallery owner, Mr. Julian Lambert, is in his office. Perhaps he can make some suggestions."

"Sure." Grant walked off to look at the other paintings in the room while Vivienne picked up the phone on her desk.

Mr. Julian Lambert was a short, slightly built man in an Armani suit, gold cuff links, and Italian loafers. His thick gray hair was expertly cut, his hands manicured, and he smelled of cologne. His accent was English and middle-class. If he'd been at the Sherlock Holmes conference banquet, I hadn't noticed him.

Grant repeated what he was after and Julian showed him the pieces on display, while Vivienne returned her attention to the computer on her desk. She tapped at a sleek keyboard. I couldn't get a good look at the screen without leaning over her shoulder. Her perfume, too heavily applied, carried a breath of the tropics.

"My father, Kevin Senior, didn't have much of an eye for art," Grant said. "Too busy building his business empire."

"I don't believe I'm familiar with that name," Julian said.

Grant grinned at him. "And that was my father's intention his entire life. No need to attract attention, was his motto. As it was for many of his business contacts." Grant tapped the side of his nose.

"Oh," said Julian. "I understand."

I didn't.

"At Gallery Lambert, discretion is our business."

"Glad to hear it," Grant said. "Now, all this is nice enough, but let's see what you have in the back."

"I'm afraid I have nothing in the back, Mr. Thornton."

"Call me Kevin."

"Kevin." Lambert gestured around the room. "What you see is what we have on offer. At this time." He loaded the last phrase with significance. Grant caught it and lifted one eyebrow.

No one was paying the slightest bit of attention to little old me. I might as well have been the invisible woman here. I tottered past the reception desk and around a corner to the left. This room was smaller, but similar to the main room, displaying the same type of art. As I'd told Jayne, I have no art education. I wouldn't be able to tell a fake from an original old master unless it was reproduced in crayon. One painting caught my eye. It was of a young woman, dressed in the severe black of her age, with a high ruffled collar that must have driven her nuts, her dark hair tightly confined to a lacy cap. The quality of lace and the number of pearls sewn onto her dress showed she was from a wealthy family. Something about her eyes attracted me. A sense of amusement, laughter even, lay behind them. She didn't take life too seriously, and there was something shockingly sensuous about the way she stroked the small dog on her lap as she stared out of the canvas. In a flight of fancy, I wondered if she'd been in love with the painter.

This sort of formal portrait was likely to have been commissioned to mark her engagement or wedding. I hoped she'd found happiness in life.

"Your wife has excellent taste," Julian said.

I blinked. I'd forgotten myself. A serious mistake. I turned to him with a smile. "This is lovely. Do we know who she is?"

"Unnamed woman painted by an artist who never received the fame he should have." Even if I hadn't been wearing the new boots, I'd have been taller than Julian. He sniffed and stretched his neck in an attempt to make himself look more imposing. "Very little is known about him, as he died far too young. Not long after this portrait was painted, in fact. That was in 1643, I believe."

"Do you like it, honey?" Grant asked me.

"I adore it." I giggled. "I have a birthday coming up."

"How much?" Grant asked.

Lambert named a sum that had me giggling again so as to avoid choking. Grant nodded wisely. "Probably a good deal. I'm not sure I want to start my collection off with unknown artists, though."

"But I like it," I said in my best little-girl voice.

Grant smiled at me indulgently. "We've plenty of other places to see, honey. Besides, I thought you wanted to go shopping at Harrods for your birthday present."

I pouted prettily. I hoped it was prettily. I've never actually pouted before. "I guess."

Grant turned back to Julian. My birthday present and I were dismissed. I continued looking around. A door opened off the small room. Leading, most likely, to Lambert's office and the storage areas. "I need to use the bathroom," I said. "Do you mind?"

Irritation flashed across Julian's face, but he covered it up well. "Not at all. I'll get Vivienne to take you. Viv!"

"No need to bother her. I can find my way." I wrenched the door open and stepped directly into an office. Lambert obviously brought clients here, as it was luxuriously furnished with a glass-and-chrome desk, a chair with good lumbar support, and two comfortable guest chairs. A credenza that probably also served as a filing cabinet held a silver tray with four cut-lead glasses, a silver ice bucket with tongs, and a bottle of Laphroaig. The computer on the desk was a top-of-the-line Apple with a twenty-seven-inch screen. At the moment, the monitor showed a packaged screen saver with alternating photographs of great beaches. Another door led out of the office going further back into the building.

Before I could even think about hacking into the computer or trying to open the credenza, Viv came in. "You'll need a key for the loo." She dangled it in front of me. She was of average height, meaning shorter than me, taller than Jayne, and lean and fit. Now that she was out from behind her desk, I could see that her legs, visible under a short tight skirt and sheer stockings, were well muscled, indicating a runner.

"Oh, gee, thanks so much."

"Through here." She opened the door at the rear of the office and held it for me. I stepped into an ill-lit corridor. Viv took two steps past me and put the key into the lock of the door on the other side. She watched me and I went inside. It was a standard office loo. I'd find no secret account documents or illicit old masters in here. I lingered for a few minutes, hoping Viv would give up and leave me alone, but when I came out she was standing there.

"Thanks," I said.

"My pleasure. Shall we join the gentlemen?"

"Why not?" I said.

"Ready to go?" Grant said when we were back in the main gallery.

"I guess so," I said. "I do like that painting, sweetie."

Grant winked at Julian. "We might come back, honey. Julian here is going to speak to some of his contacts and ask if they have anything else we might like."

I squealed in delight.

Julian pulled out his phone. "Why don't you give me your number, and I'll call when I have news."

"Take care of that, will you, honey," Grant said.

"Okay." I pulled out the burner phone Pippa had given me. I'd memorized the number, but I pretended not to have. I read it out to Julian, and he punched it into his own phone.

"We might have to go elsewhere to see the painting I'm thinking of," he said.

"I'm good with that." Grant held out his hand and the two men shook.

"You'll be able to catch a cab at the Tate," Vivienne said. "It's not far."

"Thanks," Grant said.

"Bye!" I followed Grant to the street and we turned right, passing an antique-furniture shop. He took my arm and we strolled toward the river. I tugged his arm at the first intersection and pulled him to the right. Once we were around the corner, I immediately bent over and pulled off my boots. "I might never walk again," I said in my own voice.

He put his hands on the small of his back and leaned back to release some of the tension. "That was fun. Can we do it again?"

"I don't know that we learned all that much. We'll have to see if he calls us."

"Did you see anything when you were in the back? He sent Vivienne after you mighty fast."

"Which doesn't mean they were suspicious. She had to unlock the loo door. Their security is good. They've got substantial locks on the door leading to the back alley, and the door is alarmed. A CCTV camera is mounted inside facing toward it. No doubt there's a camera watching the alley as well."

"Fair enough if they have half-a-million-pound paintings inside."

"You should have bought that for me." I lifted my leg and rubbed at my toes. "I wasn't acting about that. I loved it."

"I broadly hinted that if he could find something for my collection, I'd buy the painting as a gift for the little woman. I expect he'll call before suppertime."

"Good job. Now, get us a taxi please. I cannot take another step in these boots. We have a couple of other stops to make; I want to talk to the woman who accused Randy of stealing her ideas. But we'll have to visit a shoe store first."

Chapter Twelve

We never did make it to the address of the dread-locked woman who, Pippa had discovered, went by the name of Elsie Saunders.

Grant headed for a busier street to hail a cab. Once it arrived, I hobbled into it and we took Waterloo Bridge across the river.

"I need a shoe store," I said to the cabby. "Any shoe store, but nothing too expensive. I just want a pair of trainers."

"New boots, pet?" he said. Considering that when I'd gotten into the cab I'd been limping and carrying the right boot in my hand, he didn't need to be Sherlock Holmes to figure that out. He winked at Grant in the rearview mirror. "Me wife likes to buy shoes she can't walk in, too. They'll do anything to please us, won't they, mate?"

"And we love them for it," Grant said. I refrained from slapping him because at that moment my phone—my own phone—rang. Pippa.

"What's up?" I asked.

She didn't bother with pleasantries. "Dad's been arrested."

"What? When?"

"Moments ago. Morrison came to the house and formally arrested him. He was allowed to call Mum, and she's sent one of her partners down to the nick to represent him. She called me."

"What station? We're in a cab now."

"There's no point in you going there, Gemma. They won't let you talk to him. I know Brian Cohen and he's a darn good solicitor."

"I can pace nervously up and down."

"What's happening?" Grant mouthed.

"That would not be helpful," Pippa said. "Now Dad has officially been charged, I can do even less to help him, so it's all up to you. Keep on with what you're doing. How's your day going?"

"We made initial contact at place one and are waiting developments. On the way to the second option now."

She hung up without saying goodbye.

"What's happened, Gemma?" Grant asked.

I nodded toward the cab driver. "No one has taken ill, but otherwise I received news of an unfortunate development." I looked down, to draw Grant's attention to my lap. I crossed one wrist over the other, as though in handcuffs. Grant's eyes darkened and he nodded.

The cab pulled up to a nondescript shoe shop in a row of nondescript shops. "I've changed my mind," I said. "No need for you to wait." I handed the cabby money and we got out. I carried the leather boots.

I quickly found what I needed in a pair of cheap, but properly fitting, trainers. "I don't need the box," I said to the clerk. "I'll wear them home, but I'd like a bag for these."

"Those are super nice boots," she said.

"Appearances can be deceiving," I said. Jayne was much smaller than me, but Pippa's feet were about the same size as mine and she was accustomed to wearing killer heels. I'd make her a gift of the boots. Before presenting her with the bill.

"What now?" Grant asked when we were once again standing on the sidewalk.

Before going inside the store, I'd told Grant what precious little I'd learned from Pippa.

"I need to reevaluate my plan in light of new developments," I said. "And I need a cup of tea and some lunch. I only had half a *pain au chocolat* for breakfast."

A sandwich shop was a couple of doors down from the shoe store. We were in sight of Trafalgar Square, and I glanced at Lord Nelson, pointing toward Spain from the top of his column. A pigeon flew overhead. The square itself and the steps of the National Gallery were packed with people. We were only a block and a half from what had once been my mystery bookshop. If I had time, I might drop in and see how the place was doing. My ex-husband, whom I sold the business to when I left the cheating rat, had run the shop almost into the ground and had been forced to sell it. He had not, I'd been maliciously pleased to hear, received anywhere near what he'd paid me for it.

We got sandwiches as well as tea for me and coffee for Grant. The people next to us had a map of London spread out on the table and everyone was pointing at different directions as they argued, loudly, in German. They paid no attention to us.

I phoned my mother and got voice mail. "It's Gemma. Pippa called to tell me what's happened. Let me know if there's anything I can do, and what time you'll be home. Obviously we have things to talk over. Love you. Bye." I next phoned Jayne to check in. "How are things going?"

"Good, Gemma. We went to the museum and took pictures in front of 221 Baker Street. Ryan couldn't have looked more bored if he'd tried, but Donald was thrilled with everything. We're now having a drink in the Allsop Arms, waiting for the walking tour to start. What about you?"

"Nothing of significance. Let me speak to Ryan, please."

The phone was passed and Ryan said, "What's up?"

"Don't tell the others, but my father's been arrested for the murder."

"Okay," he said so calmly I might have been giving him an account of my shoe-shopping expedition. "Did they find new evidence?"

"I don't know. Pippa called me, but she didn't know anything more. Mum has sent one of her law partners down, so that's good."

"What do you want me to do?"

"Continue to keep the others occupied."

"I want to help, Gemma."

"I know you do, but you can't. Grant's with me and we're following some leads. I called because I want you to realize that I have to do this. Now more than ever."

"I know," he said, "but I don't have to like it. Just be careful."

"I will."

"I love you."

"Me too," I said, conscious of Grant listening while he ate his prawn-and-mayonnaise sandwich on a baguette. I put the phone away and picked up my own sandwich. Cheese and ham. Grant's looked better.

"Where to now?" he asked.

"I want to pay a call on a man I met at the conference. He showed a prurient interest in my uncle's activities."

"Am I invited?"

"You are. I think male backup will be required. After that you can meet the others in a pub or something and Jayne and I'll visit a woman of interest. The just-between-us-girls approach will work better for that one."

"Are we getting anywhere, Gemma?"

I decided to be honest. "Absolutely not." I had a bad feeling I was wasting my time trying to pretend—to myself if no one else—that I was accomplishing something. I'd taken one bite of my sandwich. I rolled it up in its paper wrapping and got to my feet. "Let's go."

"I haven't finished."

"You can eat as we walk."

"No, I can't. That's not good for the digestion. Sit down and finish your lunch. We can wait another five minutes."

I dropped back into the hard plastic chair.

"There's a good girl," Grant said.

I glared at him. But I did unwrap the sandwich.

"Do you think Pippa will be coming around to your parents' house later?" he asked me.

* * *

The bullet-headed man, who'd been identified as John Saint-Jean, lived in Mayfair. Mayfair is the most expensive section of one of the most expensive cities in the world. I could only assume he worked as a chauffeur or butler (although he didn't look the part) or a gardener and lived on the premises.

As we fought our way through sightseeing crowds to the Tube station at Charing Cross, I told Grant why we were paying a call on Mr. Saint-Jean. "As he knows who I am, having deliberately sought me out at the conference to make threats, there's no point pretending to be something I am not. You're coming with me to look imposing."

"I can do that." Grant scrunched up his face, puffed up his chest, lifted his shoulders, and spread his arms, assuming the pose one is supposed to take when being confronted by a black bear.

I do not know why I know that tidbit of information.

"Pippa wouldn't tell me anything about this man, wanting me to make my own impressions. Why she thought that was necessary, I don't know."

"Think we'll find him at home? It is the middle of the day on Monday. He'll likely be at work."

"He might live at his place of employment. I'm more interested in his employer than in him anyway. He told me people had sent him. I want to know who those people are."

We got off the Tube at Marble Arch and walked the few blocks to Culross Street where, according to Pippa's contacts, John Saint-Jean was employed.

The house we wanted was four stories tall, painted a clean crisp white with black trim, surrounded by an iron fence intended to be nothing but decorative. It was at the end of the row, close to Hyde Park.

We stood on the sidewalk, and I studied the house. The drapes were drawn, the small balconies empty. "Remember," I said. "Stand behind me, say nothing, and look tough."

"Grrrr," Grant said.

I pressed the bell, and the door opened before the sound had died away.

The man who stood there was dressed in a perfectly fitting black suit, wrinkleless white shirt, thin black tie, shoes polished to a brilliant black shine. His gray hair was cut close to his head and his gray mustache neatly trimmed. "Good afternoon, Ms. Doyle," he said in a deep rolling voice with a faint touch of Scotland. "You have been expected." I'd never seen him before.

Grant and I stepped into the house. We might have been in Baskerville Hall—all dim lighting, dark wood, deep-red carpet, upholstered chairs, and gilt-framed paintings of hounds and horses and red-coated men at the hunt.

"Sir John is waiting in the library. May I offer you tea, or perhaps something stronger? Sir?"

"Nothing at the moment, thank you," I said. "Before we meet your employer, do you know a man by the name of John Saint-Jean? Does he work here?"

"I know him, yes. He does work here. In a manner of speaking. This way, please."

He bowed ever so slightly and led the way deep into the house. The hallway was lined with painted portraits, most from centuries past, but one was of a man in a World War II–era army uniform and another of a woman wearing, of all things, twenty-first-century medical scrubs with a stethoscope around her neck. The butler caught me looking. "Sir John's niece, Dr. Rose Saint-Jean."

Sir John?

He opened a door at the far end of the hallway. "Miss Gemma Doyle and companion," the butler announced sonorously. Grant and I stepped into the room, and the door shut silently behind us.

The Baskerville Hall theme continued in the library. Logs burned in a large open fireplace, and the thick red-and-gold drapes were pulled shut.

"Speaking of Vermeer . . ." Grant muttered as he stared at a painting of a woman pouring milk from a heavy jug.

"Not Vermeer, I'm sorry to say. As you may know, Mr. Thompson, Vermeer pained only thirty-four works in his lifetime that have been positively attributed to him, and they are all either in public galleries or private ones open to the public. With the exception of the painting stolen in Boston in 1990 and the one currently in the Queen's own collection." The bullet-headed man rose from a cracked and faded brown leather armchair. He wore baggy brown corduroy trousers, worn at the knees, a beige fisherman's sweater with a hole in one elbow, and purple-and-gray plaid bedroom slippers that showed a great deal of use. "I have some items that might be more to your interest." He waved a hand toward the bookshelves lining the walls. "Feel free to explore while Miss Doyle and I chat. Are you sure I can't get either of you a drink?"

"I've changed my mind," I said. "A whiskey would do. No ice, splash of water."

"I believe I have something you'll like. Mr. Thompson?"

"The same. Thanks."

I didn't see him press a button or make any other gesture, but the door behind us opened and the butler came in. "Three whiskies, please, David. You're not normally a whiskey drinker, Miss Doyle, although Mr. Thompson is. But I think you'll enjoy this. It's made in small quantities at my estate in Scotland."

I'm not often gobsmacked, but I was now. I gave my head a mental shake. "You again have the advantage of me, as I believe I said the first time we met. You're John Saint-Jean?"

"Sir John. A hereditary title. Please, have a seat."

I dropped into a chair, beautifully upholstered in red-and-gold damask. The butler handed me a glass, then gave one to Grant, who was reading the spines of the books lining the walls. I might have heard him gasp. The butler served Sir John last and left the room. The door shut soundlessly behind him.

"I consider myself a good judge of character," I said. "I'm not often wrong."

Sir John smiled at me. And it was a warm smile, full of gentleness and humor. This was definitely the man I'd seen in the kitchen hallway at the conference. The same, but totally different. This one had an educated, upper-class English accent, about as far from the rough cockney as it was possible to get in England.

"I dabbled in amateur dramatics at Eton," he said.

"Why the pretext?"

"Saves money on a bodyguard or hiring security personnel," he said with a chuckle. "Looking the way I do. My appearance was the despair of my mother's life." He cracked his knuckles. "That plus a few skills I picked up in the SAS." He pointed to the tattoo on his neck, an eagle's talons reaching up from inside his shirt. "An unfortunate memory of an excessively drunken weekend in Kuala Lumpur in my younger days in the army."

"SAS," Grant said. "Special Air Service. The equivalent of our Navy Seals."

"Same principle, at any rate," Sir John said. "I'm sure you're wondering why I know so much about you and Grant, Gemma. May I call you Gemma?"

I nodded. "I'm not wondering, no. I assume you looked us up on the Internet."

"My bio on my book business website says I'm fond of a good single malt," Grant said.

"So it does. Yours, Gemma, says nothing. Outside of your shop in West London, you have a surprisingly low public profile."

"I have no secrets," I said.

"I have to confess I merely took a guess you weren't a whiskey drinker. Young women today rarely are."

"I'll take a guess that you have a camera outside your house watching the street and you were waiting for us. Thus you instructed your butler to let us in immediately and to use my name." I sipped my drink. I had to agree with Sir John. I didn't like it much.

"Quite." He stood up and walked to the window. He lifted a corner of the drapes and I saw a garden, empty urns, bare trees, naked vines crawling up a brick wall. "Enough playful banter. Randolph Denhaugh cheated me out of a great deal of money and then he dropped out of sight. I went to the Holmes conference because I'd received word he'd be there. My intention was to confront him and threaten him with dire consequences if I didn't get it back. When I saw you, I decided the indirect approach might be better."

"You had to know he and I weren't exactly on familiar terms."

"An opening gambit only. For the same reason I spoke to your mother prior to the banquet. After that, by the way, I left the hotel premises when everyone went through to dinner. I didn't have a ticket. I came straight home, which both David and the CCTV camera the next street over can testify, and did not go out again. Meaning I didn't kill Randolph."

"Why am I here?" I asked. Sir John hadn't summoned me, but he'd sat back and waited, confident I'd show up sooner rather than later.

"Your uncle's death means it's unlikely I will ever get back what I was cheated out of."

"He sold you a piece of forged art?"

Sir John nodded. "He sold me an old master and replaced it with a forgery at the time of delivery. I paid ten million pounds for a painting I might as well use to keep the fire going. I bought it two years ago. I only discovered the forgery recently, and have been searching for Randolph Denhaugh ever since. I got word he'd popped up at a Sherlock Holmes convention, of all things. You ask why you are here. I know you're investigating Randolph's murder . . ."

"The police are investigating."

"Them too," he said. "I wanted to tell you my story so you wouldn't be distracted investigating me, as well as to ask you to let me know if you learn anything about my painting. I'll have David bring the copy in before you leave."

"I'm not a detective or a private investigator. I don't care about your painting."

"No, but you do care that your father not be charged with the murder of his wife's long-lost brother."

I kept my face impassive. According to Pippa, Dad had been charged. Apparently that was one detail Sir John didn't know. Yet. "I'm a bookstore owner," I said. "I live in a pleasant seaside town on the far side of the Atlantic Ocean. I have a cat who hates me and a dog who loves me." I put my glass on the table. "Thank you for your time, Sir John."

"At the time of his death, Denhaugh was doing a job for a man named Julian Lambert, who owns a gallery—"

"Near the Tate Modern. Grant and I paid him a visit this morning."

He grinned. "You *are* good. The police haven't made that connection yet. My bet is that someone in the rarified world of fine art killed Denhaugh. There is no honor among thieves."

"So I've heard. Let's go, Grant."

"I know Phillipa quite well, by the way," Sir John said. "I must say I had a shock when I saw her at the Holmes banquet. I never would have expected to see her at a thing such as that."

I refrained from glancing at Grant.

The door opened and the butler came in, bearing a painting in a heavy, ornate gilt frame. He held it up in front of him. It was a family portrait. Mother, father, two girls, one boy, a dog. Dutch, mid-seventeenth century, very much in the style of Rembrandt.

"I'm pleased you tracked me down. I wanted to meet you and let you know I had nothing to do with the death of your uncle," Sir John said. "However, if in the course of your investigation, you happen to come across a picture exactly like this, do let me know."

"I'm not investigating anything," I said, "just poking around."

"Nevertheless, things do have a habit of popping up unexpectedly, I'm sure you'll agree."

While Sir John and I talked, Grant had been continuously throwing wistful glances at the bookshelves.

"None of my books are for sale, Grant," Sir John said. "But if you give me a call later, I'll put you in contact with a few of my friends."

"Thanks," Grant said.

"Next time you're in London, drop by. I'd love to talk books with you. Give my regards to Arthur, Gemma. Good day."

We walked down the long corridor behind the silent David, still carrying the forged painting. He opened the door and gave us a slight bow.

When we were standing on the sidewalk once again, I let out a long breath. "Wow. That was something." I waved in the general direction of where I thought the house's security camera would be.

"I couldn't believe the books, Gemma. I've never seen a private collection like it. And I've seen some pretty good ones."

I turned away from the camera, in case Sir John or his butler could read lips, which wouldn't have surprised me in the least. John Saint-Jean was full of surprises.

"Did he mean your uncle Arthur when he asked you to give his regards to Arthur?" Grant asked.

"He must have. He seems to know an uncomfortable amount about me and my family. Good thing I have no secrets."

"Interesting about the forged painting," Grant said. "We can now scratch him off the suspect list."

"Scratch him off? Oh no, he's zoomed to the top."

"Why? Didn't you like him?"

"I liked him enormously, Grant. What a fascinating man. If I was staying in London, I'd want to get to know him better. But just because he says he didn't kill Randolph doesn't mean he didn't. His alibi is his butler and CCTV footage? The butler will say what he's told to, and video footage can be altered. Particularly by someone who has the sort of contacts I suspect Sir John does."

"You think he'd kill for a painting? He didn't exactly look to be short of funds."

"He paid a lot of money for an old master and he ended up with a forgery. People like Sir John don't care to be made fools of. It's not about the money, although I'm sure that's part of it. What's the time?"

"Coming up to four."

We walked down the street, heading back to Marble Arch Tube station. My phone rang, and I couldn't push the button fast enough when I saw the name of the caller. My mother.

"You spoke to Pippa?" she asked.

"Yes. What's happening?"

"I'm at home. Your father is being held until tomorrow at the earliest." Her voice broke.

"What do you want us to do?"

"Brian Cohen, whom I've engaged to represent Henry, will be here shortly. You and Pippa need to hear what he has to say."

"On my way," I said.

Good thing I had new trainers. I set off at a run.

"What's happening?" Grant called as he chased after me.

Chapter Thirteen

Pippa reached Stanhope Gardens before us. She answered the door and said, "I'll ask Mum to give you a key."

"Bought you something." I handed her the bag containing the boots.

She took it very suspiciously, as well she might. "What's this?"

"A present. From you to yourself." I took off my new leather gloves and put down my Burberry bag. "Where's Mum?"

"Sitting room."

I walked quickly into the front room, leaving Grant with Pippa as Pippa said, "I don't need new boots."

The sitting room is painted a soft peach with a sage-green sofa and matching chairs, and looks out onto the street. The paintings are watercolors of pretty meadows and long-haired girls in big hats. The green drapes were open, and Mum stood at the window, staring onto the darkening street. Horace was curled up on the carpet in a corner of the room.

My mother turned when I came in and Horace leapt to his feet. Her face was drawn and her eyes troubled, and new lines had appeared at the corners of her mouth. Horace gave me a welcoming sniff.

"Did you have to leave court prematurely?" I asked.

"Fortunately not. For some reason, my client decided this would be a good week to visit Scotland."

"He didn't show?"

"No. The judge was not happy, with him or with me. On the bright side, my calendar is clear for the rest of the week. I've instructed my client to seek representation elsewhere."

"What's happening with Dad?"

"Let's wait until Brian arrives, shall we? At the moment I know nothing more than you do. You can tell me about your day when we're all here."

I sat down as she said, "I like your young man."

"You mean Ryan?"

She nodded. "I like him very much. He's obviously head over heels for you, as he should be." She sat on the couch, tucking her skirt neatly beneath her. She was still dressed for court. "The way he looks at you when you aren't aware is totally charming."

Fire burned in my cheeks. "Poor Ryan. I promised him I'd not spend a lot of time at the conference and we'd have a romantic few days in London. I planned to show him all the places that are important to me as well as things I know he'd like. Instead, he's trailing around after Donald admiring Sherlock Holmes tourist traps."

"He'll forgive you," she said.

She was probably right. I hoped so. In West London he'd get mad at what he considered my interference in his cases, and in things that were, in his eyes, none of my business. Here, in London, it wasn't his case. And it was obviously very much my business.

"You should plan on coming back in the summer," Mum said. "Then you can do all the romantic things you want to do, and in much more pleasant weather. Arthur can mind the shop, can he not?"

Which reminded me that I hadn't called West London today. Just as well. I probably didn't want to know.

Pippa and Grant came in with the tea tray. How nice to be back in England, where every problem can be solved over a cup of tea and a chocolate biscuit.

Mum poured while Pippa went to the window. Deep in my pocket the burner phone buzzed and I checked the display. Gallery Lambert. Grant was watching Pippa, and I said, "You should take this." I handed him the phone.

"Hello," he said. "Oh, hi. Yeah, I can do that. Hold on while I write that down. Great. See you then. Looking forward to it."

He gave me back the phone. "That was Julian Lambert. He's taken the bait. We're meeting at an art gallery, not his, tomorrow at three."

"Good," I said.

"A cab's pulling up," Pippa said. "A man with an expensive overcoat and a briefcase is getting out. Almost certainly one of yours, Mum. I'll get the door."

She and Horace were back seconds later, leading a short, round man in his late fifties who peered at the world through thick spectacles. Mum said, "Brian, thank you so much for coming. My daughters, Phillipa and Gemma. A friend of Gemma's from America, Grant Thompson. You arrived in time for tea. Please sit down."

Brian Cohen perched in an armchair. The dog came over to investigate the newcomer and Brian gave him a hearty rub on the top of the head. He had quick, nervous mannerisms and his watery eyes blinked rapidly. His right hand shook slightly as he accepted a cup of tea from Pippa. She'd noticed it before pouring and had not filled the cup to the top. I had total confidence in him: if he hadn't been a highly competent solicitor, Mum would not have retained him.

"First of all," he said once we were seated, balancing our own cups and staring expectantly at him, "Henry told me to tell you not to worry."

"Easier said than done," Pippa said.

"Quite," he said. "But in this situation I'm inclined to agree. The case against Henry is weak, extremely weak, and I'm confident I can have him sprung"—a glance at Grant—"as you Americans say, in the morning."

"Obviously something happened this morning," Mum said. "What was it?"

"Henry insists he can remember nothing about the evening in question at the time Mr. Denhaugh was killed. Henry was found in the company of the dead man, with no memory of how he came to be there or of what happened. That looks bad, naturally, but isn't enough to have charges laid without further evidence. Henry's doctor has made a statement to the police outlining the injury to Henry's head, saying memory loss of incidents occurring in the minutes before such an injury are common. The memories have not had time to transfer to permanent storage in the brain before the trauma wipes them out."

Pippa picked the important words out of Brian's statement. "And that further evidence is?"

Before he could answer, Horace leapt to his feet, and a fraction of a second later the doorbell buzzed.

Pippa and Mum exchanged glances, and Pippa got up and peered out the window. "The remainder of Gemma's entourage has returned from a fun-filled day on Baker Street. I'll let them in."

I stood up. "I'll get more cups and make another pot."

I ran into Jayne in the hallway. "Help me with the tea, please."

"Happy to."

"Did you have a nice day?"

"It was pretty good. Donald's enthusiasm was so infectious, I think even Ryan enjoyed it. What about you? Did you learn anything?"

"My dad's been arrested."

She stopped in her tracks and stared at me. "No! That's awful. What happened?"

"His solicitor's here and about to tell us." I switched on the gas, filled the kettle, and put it onto the hob while Jayne took more of the Royal Doulton teacups out of the cupboard. "I didn't get a chance to call on the dreadlocked woman, as I'd planned," I said. "Can you come with me when I do that?"

"Sure. Are you okay, Gemma?"

I turned to face her. "No. I am not. I'm dreadfully worried and I fear all I'm accomplishing running all over London is trying to pretend to myself that I'm helping." I didn't cry, but I felt tears well up behind my eyes.

Jayne gathered me into her arms and held me tightly. "You're doing all you can do, Gemma, and absolutely no one I know could do it better."

I pulled myself away and gave her a smile. "Thanks." The kettle screamed, and I filled the teapot. "Let's go and hear what the solicitor has to say."

I carried the tray into the sitting room. Ryan took it from me. He looked into my eyes, and I gave him a smile. He nodded in return.

Introductions had obviously been made while Jayne and I were busy. Jayne took the place on the sofa next to Mum and Horace sat at her feet, staring intently at the chocolate biscuit on her plate. Brian picked up where he'd been cut off. "As you would expect, the police have been interviewing everyone they can locate who'd been at the conference. It's taking a long time, as conference attendees, hotel staff, and other guests amount to a great many people. They heard several reports of an acrimonious altercation on Friday between Randolph Denhaugh and another man."

"Meaning Henry," Ryan said.

"When asked, witnesses identified Mr. Doyle from a photographic lineup. Those witnesses include one of the security guards. She claims she heard Mr. Doyle make threats against Mr. Denhaugh. Henry was heard to warn Mr. Denhaugh to stay away from you, Anne."

"So," Ryan said. "What of it? Henry was angry, and Randy was being obnoxious. Threats made in front of a room full of people mean nothing."

"That's right." Donald munched on a biscuit. So interested was he in the conversation he hadn't tried to tell me all about his day at his pilgrimage site—Baker Street.

"Threats mean nothing, I'll agree," Brian said. "Unless the person threatened turns up dead shortly thereafter, with the person who threatened him standing over his body. Which is precisely what happened in this situation."

"I wouldn't take a case to court if that was all I had," Ryan said. "Is it different here?"

"No," Brian said. "DI Morrison can try, and he will, to have Henry held, but I will argue before a judge tomorrow that his evidence is not only perilously weak, it is backed by personal and professional animosity from the investigating detective toward my client."

"Do you know if they found any fingerprints on that lamp?" I asked. "The one that was on the floor next to Dad. The base was a particularly unattractive shade of orange. Is that what Dad was hit with?"

"That's what the police believe, yes. So many fingerprints were on it, it's going to be almost impossible to trace the people who most recently used it."

"Which is what I'd expect," I said. "It's a lamp sitting on a side table in a public area. Plenty of people would have touched the base when they turned it on or off, and the cleaner wouldn't scrub it down daily."

"What about the rope?" Ryan asked. "The one that killed Randy?"

"They've had no luck there," Brian said. "Fortunately, the events happened indoors, so Henry did not have gloves on him. I intend to point that out in the strongest of terms before the judge tomorrow. Although DI Morrison is reminding us that absence of evidence . . ."

"Isn't evidence of absence," Ryan said.

"Precisely. Morrison will also mention that Henry was not searched at the time. So he could have had gloves concealed on him."

Mum snorted.

"Rest assured," Brian said, "I will be reminding the judge of the unlikelihood of anyone carrying gloves to a formal dinner at which they have left their coat in the cloakroom, never mind them accidently leaving a length of rope in their pockets."

"That the killer brought the rope," Mum said, "means the act was premeditated."

"Almost certainly," Brian said. "I will also imply a fair amount about police failure to secure evidence at the scene. In case that is not sufficient, I've arranged to meet some of my police contacts this evening for a drink once we are done here, and I'm confident I'll have proof of Morrison's antipathy toward Henry to bring before the judge."

"In the meantime, Henry sits in jail," Jayne said.

"For one night only, hopefully," Brian said. "Now, I must ask you all if you know of anything I should be aware of as I proceed. For good or for ill."

I glanced at Pippa. She dipped her chin, ever so slightly, indicating that I should go ahead.

"I've been poking around," I said. "Randy was an art forger and spent some time in prison for it, so that's a matter of record. He claimed to be out of the business, but I strongly believe he was back in it. Unfortunately, I can't tell you why I know that and my evidence is . . . uh . . . illegally obtained."

"Gemma!" Ryan said.

"It's only slightly illegal," I hastened to add.

"Grant, what on earth did you let her do?" Ryan said.

Grant threw up his hands. "Wasn't me. We didn't do anything out of order today. Strange, yes, but not illegal."

"Whatever you know, Gemma, helps to draw a picture," Brian said. "Please continue."

I left out what I'd observed in the Canary Wharf studio and told Brian, and thus the whole group, about Grant's and my visit to the home of Sir John Saint-Jean.

"That is interesting," Brian said. "Criminal activity on the part of the deceased is always good for deflecting blame from an estranged relative."

"We don't want to deflect blame," Jayne said. "We want Henry to be declared innocent."

"We'll take what we can get, Jayne dear," my mother said.

Jayne put her arm around Mum, and as an indication of how upset she was, Mum left it there.

"We mustn't forget that Randolph had some personal enemies who were at the conference," I said. "An angry ex-girlfriend, another woman who accused him of cheating her. He wasn't a very nice man. Sorry, Mum."

"Nothing I didn't know already," she said.

"That is all worth knowing," the lawyer said.

"I've been talking to some of these personal enemies." I snuck a glance at Ryan. "Legally this time. No one has come straight out and confessed, but I have someone else I need to visit. I was planning on doing that today, but came back here to meet with you."

"Apart from the argument at the conference, which was reported to the police by bystanders," Brian asked, "did Henry and Randolph have any other contact this past weekend?"

"Not that I know of," Pippa said.

Donald, Ryan, and Jayne shook their heads.

"We were only there for Gemma's talk on Friday afternoon and at the banquet Saturday evening," Mum said.

"We ran into him Thursday evening in the bar of our hotel," I said. "The rest of you didn't notice him there, but he recognized us. Us, meaning he recognized Mum and Dad. Dad spoke briefly to him on our way out. It was obviously the first time they'd spoken in a great many years. Dad and I left together, and spent the rest of the evening in the company of this group."

Brian put his empty teacup on the side table. "I have to be off. Anne, I'll give you a call after I've spoken to my friends on the police force."

"I have an idea," I said. "Ryan, why don't you go with Brian to meet these police contacts?"

"Why?" Ryan said.

"Why?" Brian said.

"Why?" Pippa said.

"Because Ryan's a police officer and Brian's a defense lawyer. There's always some animosity between those two camps. Ryan can talk to them on a professional yet friendly basis. You know, visiting American cop, eager to meet his fellow officers. Hands across the water, and all that."

"Might be worthwhile," Ryan said.

"I'm not . . ." Brian said.

"Excellent idea," Pippa said. "People always talk more freely in casual company. Ryan can report directly back to us. In the meantime, Gemma and I will let you know if we learn anything you can use."

"Thank you, Brian." Mum got to her feet, and Brian also stood. He took her outstretched hands in hers and stared into her eyes. The look he gave her was so positively adoring I turned away. "Anytime, my dear," he said, "anytime." He left the room and Ryan followed. Pippa and I went with them to the door.

"Are you sure this is okay with you, Brian?" Ryan asked, as I handed him his coat. "I don't have to come if you don't want me."

"It's not a bad idea," Brian said. "If we arrive at the pub before my contacts, you can tell me about policing in America."

Ryan gave me a kiss, told me to stay out of trouble (as if that ever helped), and they left.

"Nicely done," Pippa said.

"I thought so," I said modestly. "My first instinct was nothing but an attempt to give Ryan something to do. He won't be happy for much longer traipsing around the tourist traps of London. But on second thought, it is a good idea."

Back in the front room, everyone was quiet. Outside, night had fallen and the streetlamps had come on. Mum pulled the heavy drapes shut.

"Jayne," I said, "Feel like an outing?"

"Where?"

"I have yet to talk to the woman we saw accusing Randy of stealing her ideas. Time to do that now. If she has a job, she should be getting home soon."

Donald leapt to his feet. "I'll come as well."

"Thanks," I said. "But she'll be more open with a couple of women."

"I want to help," he said. "Everyone else is doing their bit. You took Grant with you today, and Ryan is off to meet police officers."

"Not this time, Donald," I said. I appreciated my friends' concern very much, and the knowledge that they cared about my father because they loved me brought a lump to my throat. But I didn't need Donald, with his ulster, his Baker Street Irregulars pin, and his total inability to pretend he was anything other than what he was, tagging along behind me. I struggled to come up with a plausible excuse, when Mum came to my rescue.

"Why don't you tell me about your day, Donald? I'd love to hear about it. I've never been to the Sherlock Holmes Museum."

He turned to her. "You haven't? Oh, you must, it was fascinating. And the walking tour! I consider myself to be somewhat of a minor expert on Holmes, but even I learned new things today."

I jerked my head toward Jayne, and she followed me into the hall. Pippa followed us. Grant followed Pippa.

"Your job," I said to Grant as I pulled on my coat, "yours and Donald's, is to keep Mum occupied and not worrying."

"I can do that," he said.

"I have the burner phone, so if Julian Lambert calls again, I'll answer it, tell him you're busy, and offer to take any messages."

"I'll put things in motion," Pippa said, "to see what I can learn about the painting Sir John Saint-Jean claims Randolph cheated him out of. Although, I have to say, I consider Sir John to be the least viable of our suspects. Someone with his background and training wouldn't bludgeon a man to death in a public place."

"Don't discount it," I said. "Anyone can act out in a moment of sudden anger. What do you know about him, anyway? He said he knows you, and he had to do some nimble footwork on Saturday evening to avoid running into you at the banquet."

"Let's just say that if Sir John Saint-Jean did kill Randolph, or anyone else, it would be an inconvenience to the powers that be to see him stand trial."

"What does that mean?" Grant asked.

Pippa said nothing.

"She means," I said, "that he's intimately involved in matters of national security."

"How do you know that?" Jayne asked Pippa.

"Let's go," I said. "I'll outline our plan, not that I have one, on the way."

Jayne and I stepped outside. The light snow continued to fall, soft and beautiful in the glow of light from the streetlamps. A man walked past, a golden retriever trotting at his side, and a group of schoolboys in their neat uniforms chased each other up the road.

"Hold on," I said. "I forgot my scarf."

I hurried up the steps and threw open the door to see Grant and Pippa standing close together. Very close together. So close together that their arms were around each other and their lips touching. They flew apart, looking as guilty as school kids caught necking in the bushes.

"Sorry," I said. "Forgot something. Never mind. Don't need it." I slammed the door behind me and dashed down the steps.

"Everything okay?" Jayne asked.

"Perfectly okay. Fine."

"Where's your scarf?"

"What scarf?"

"The scarf you went back for?"

"Oh, that. I decided I don't need it. Come along. Don't dawdle."

*　　*　　*

Pippa had told me the dreadlocked woman was named Elsie Saunders and she lived in Whitechapel. Jayne and I caught the Tube and crossed the city. The trains were crowded with people heading home from work.

Whitechapel's most famous resident was a certain gentleman known to history as Jack the Ripper. Jack, like the police officers who chased him and the women who feared him, wouldn't recognize the place today. At the turn of the last century, it was a slum, in the full, filthy, nasty, poverty-and-disease-ridden Victorian meaning of that word. Today it's a neighborhood of good restaurants, lively nightlife, small family homes, bustling markets, and shining steel-and-glass towers.

Elsie's flat wasn't far from Ten Bells Pub, the place where Jack's final victim, Mary Kelly, enjoyed one last drink before heading out to the streets and meeting her fate. These days the pub's a popular place for tourists wanting to soak up the Whitechapel atmosphere or enjoy a drink at the end of a Jack the Ripper walking tour. We passed a group of people, bundled up against the cold, standing on a street corner shifting from foot to foot, listening to a man perched on a milk crate.

As we passed, a woman stepped up to him. He turned her around, held her close to him, and pressed his hands against her exposed throat.

Jayne gasped and stopped walking. The woman giggled, a watching man laughed, and a flash went off as someone snapped a picture. I tugged at Jayne's arm and we continued on our way. "Is that a tour, do you suppose?" she asked me.

"Yes. We're at the heart of Ripper territory here. I'll give you your own private tour." I talked as we walked. What I don't know about Jack the Ripper (and that's a lot), I made up.

The address we'd been given was next to a convenience store. The building was three stories tall, made of red brick dark with age. Narrow windows overlooked the bustling street below, and a solid row of parked cars lined the curb. The front door opened directly onto the sidewalk—no decorative iron railings or flowerpots here. I studied the front of the building, looking for someone watching me through the curtains. Lights were on inside, but no one moved in front of them. I stepped forward and knocked on the black door. It opened almost immediately.

The woman was in her midforties, substantially overweight, with long blonde hair reminiscent of a rat's nest showing about two inches of gray roots. She wore a formless red tunic over lumpy bare legs. "If you're selling," she said in an accent that proved she'd been born within the sound of Bow's Bells, "I'm not buying. Not interested in finding God neither."

"Sorry to bother you," I said in an accent that originated very far from Bow's Bells. More like West London, Massachusetts. "I'm looking for Elsie? Elsie Saunders?"

"She's at work."

"What time does she get home?"

"She knocks off at nine. Sometimes she goes for a pint after. Sometimes not." Her eyes flicked toward Jayne, standing slightly behind me, and then she began to close the door.

"We're not selling," I said, "but my friend and I are interested in buying."

The door stopped moving. "What's that?"

"Elsie's an artist. A friend of mine told me she did the sort of work I might appreciate. I'd like to talk to her tonight. We're going home tomorrow."

"Guess it won't hurt none," she said. "Els works at Glennbow Art Supplies." She gave me an address. "Tell 'er I sent you and I want a cut." The door shut in our faces before I could even say thank you.

"Art supplies," I said to Jayne. "That sounds interesting."

"Do you know where that place is?"

"Haven't a clue. But as we're on legitimate business this time, I don't mind looking it up." I called up the address I'd been given on my phone.

Fortunately, Glennbow Art Supplies wasn't more than a ten-minute walk away.

The streets of Whitechapel were quiet on a Monday night in January, but we didn't walk as fast as I might have liked because Jayne kept stopping to stare at everything around her.

"It's all so fascinating," she said. "The way the old is mixed up with the new. Look at that house; it's practically falling over and looks like an opium den Sherlock Holmes would visit in pursuit of a case, and it's right next to that ugly office tower."

"This part of the city was extensively bombed during the war," I said. "When they rebuilt, they weren't always sensitive to maintaining integrity of the streetscape."

The art supply store was in a row of shops not far from Spitalfields Market. The large front window was brightly lit, featuring a colorful display of half-finished abstract canvases propped on easels and cans of spray paint arranged in color-splashed pyramids.

The bells over the door tinkled as we came in. Elsie Saunders stood behind the sales counter, ringing up a purchase for a multi-tattooed, multi-pierced man. He put his credit card in his wallet, picked up his bag, said "Cheers" to Elsie and "Hello" to us, and left.

"Hi." Elsie turned to us. "Can I help you?" She didn't appear to recognize us. She looked the same as she had on the weekend: colorful flowing dress, tons of cheap jewelry, numerous piercings. When I looked closer, I could see that her hair, tied into masses of dreadlocks, which Pippa suggested might have been a wig, was the real thing. Meaning, she had not been in any sort of disguise at the conference.

"Hello," I said.

"This is a nice store," Jayne said.

"Thanks," Elsie said. "Visiting from America, are you?"

"Yes," I said. "We're here for the Sherlock Holmes convention." I didn't put on an American accent. If Elsie had heard me speak at the conference, she'd be suspicious of why I'd be pretending now.

"I think I saw you," Jayne said. "Were you there?" Before coming in, I'd suggested to Jayne we take the tag-team approach and both talk to Elsie. I'd also decided not to pretend we'd been sent to her house by a contact. That might fool her friend, but Elsie would likely not have anyone recommending her art to visiting Americans.

"I was there."

"Sherlock lover, are you?" Jayne said. "That's so great."

"I was hoping to have a space in the dealers' room," she said, "but by the time I went to pay for my table, they were full."

"A table? Are you an artist?" I asked.

"Yes, I am."

The door opened and two young men came in. Elsie nodded at them in greeting, and they made a bee-line for the cans of spray paint stacked against one wall.

"Do you do anything Sherlock related?" I asked.

Elsie talked to us but kept one eye on the shoppers. "I specialize in pen-and-ink drawings of scenes from the books."

Jayne's eyes opened wide. "Oh, I'd love to see them! Are they any good?" She laughed. "Sorry, silly question. Of course you think they're good."

The young men carried a basket piled high with cans of paint to the counter.

"Give me a minute here," Elsie said to us. She rang up the paint, put the cans in a bag, and accepted the money.

The young men left, and we were again alone in the store.

"I'd like to see your work," I said. "I own a shop specializing in Sherlockiana. Sounds like the sort of thing my customers might like. Do you have a studio we can visit? We don't have a lot of time, I'm afraid. We leave tomorrow."

"I keep a few pieces of my work here. In the back. The owner lets us use some of the space to show our own art. He pretends he's being generous, but it allows him to get away with paying less than everyone else on the street."

"Can I see them?" I asked.

"Sure. Let's say it's my tea break, okay?"

"Fine with me," I said.

Elsie locked the door, flipped the sign, and led the way through the store to a small room off the back hallway. She opened the door, switched on the lights, and walked in. The art in this room was eclectic, to say the least. I saw some beautiful watercolors of London at night, all hazy and romantic, that I'd have enjoyed hanging in my own house. There was also a giant piece reminiscent of graffiti found on the sides of train cars, and some oils by an artist who seemed to be releasing his or her anger issues onto the canvas.

"Quite the variety," I said.

"Ben, that's my boss, and some of the other employees keep their stuff here too." She took a thin stack of papers off a table and handed them to me. "Have a look."

I looked.

The idea was there, but the execution was sorely lacking. In these sketches, Holmes—I had to take a guess it was supposed to be the Great Detective—was unrecognizable. The Hound of the Baskervilles looked as threatening as Violet immediately after supper, and at first I mistook the horse pulling a hansom cab for a tall thin cow. None of the drawings had the modern touches that made Randy's so unique and disturbing.

There were only four pictures. "Is this all? I have to say I was looking for something a bit more . . . edgy. Like the ones I saw at the conference."

I threw out the comment, expecting her to get angry and defensive and, if I was lucky, verbally attack Randy for stealing her idea. Instead, her eyes slid to one side. "I might have some others. These are proto-types, getting the concept down on paper. My idea is to approach Holmes from a different angle. Sherlock Holmes has been done to death. Anyone can imitate Conan Doyle's writing or the Sidney Paget illustrations. Just about everyone has. My art is a fresh interpreta-tion." A ragged fingernail stabbed at the figure of the supposedly spectral hound. "See this. Not what you were expecting, is it?"

"Not at all."

"Anyone can make a dog look scary. I'm saying it's what's underneath the surface that we really need to be afraid of."

"You are so right," Jayne said.

"If I'm buying for my store, I'll need more than this," I said. "Can I see your finished pieces?"

"They're at my studio. I'm not working tomorrow—I'm only part-time here; come around then."

I put my disappointed face on. "That's too bad. We're off home tomorrow. Sorry to bother you. Let's go, Jayne."

"I finish work at nine," Elsie said. "I was going to meet a mate for a pint after, but we can go to my studio instead. How's that?"

I pretended to give it some thought. "I guess we can do that, if it's not far. Is it?"

"No." She gave me a familiar address. Her flat. If her roommate was there and recognized us, I'd have to come up with some reason for tracking Elsie down at home.

We went back to the shop front and Elsie unlocked the door.

"What do we do now?" Jayne asked when we were standing on the street.

"We have dinner and go to her place at nine."

"Dinner sounds good, but why are we bothering?"

"She knew I didn't like the pieces she showed me."

"They were terrible."

"So they were. I'm wondering what else she has. Not more of the same, I'm hoping. It's entirely possible she and Randy were in the art forgery business together. Now, what do you feel like eating?"

We found a nice comfy pub with warm lighting and a cheerfully burning fireplace and enjoyed a good dinner of real English fish and chips. I used my burner phone to call Pippa's burner, and was told they were all—meaning her, Mum, Grant, and Donald—at a local restaurant.

"When you looked up Elsie Saunders for me," I asked, "did you check if she had any sort of record?"

"No. I only had her name."

"Can you do that?"

"I can put someone on it. Unofficially."

"Please do. She's about to show me some art on the QT."

"What does that mean?" Pippa asked.

"On the quiet. Meaning not something she displays publicly. Jayne and I are meeting her at her flat at nine. I'll have my other phone on in case you need to trace it. Or something like that."

"Understood," my sister said.

I next called Ryan, but it went to voice mail. I hoped he was having a pleasant time exchanging war stories over a pint of good British stout.

*   *   *

At nine o'clock Jayne and I were standing at the corner of Elsie's street, bundled up against the damp cold. Ten minutes later I spotted Elsie dashing across the street, her long coat streaming behind her. We stepped out of the shadows as she approached.

"Hey, there you are," she said. "I wasn't sure you were going to show."

"Why wouldn't we?" I asked.

She shrugged and pulled her key out of her bag. She opened the door and led us into a dark, narrow corridor. The scent of boiled cabbage, fried fish, and stewed tea hung in the air along with unwashed socks and wet wool left to dry over a radiator. Elsie flicked the light switch, which didn't do much to help break the gloom. She kicked aside a pair of purple rubber boots. "Don't mind the mess. My flatmate's a first-class slob."

We went into the small, dark sitting room. The furniture was shabby, threadbare sheets used as drapes, half-filled cups of scummy tea everywhere, the carpet dotted with cigarette burns.

"Temporary accommodation," Elsie said. "I needed a place to stop when I came to London. I'll be out of here soon. Wait here. I'll be right back."

Jayne and I eyed the unidentifiable stains on the chairs. We decided to remain standing.

True to her word, Elsie returned almost immediately, carrying a stack of drawing papers. She cleared the table by the simple act of shoving all the newspapers and a week's worth of laundry onto the floor. Then she laid out the papers and stood back with a flourish.

I hadn't intended to react at all, but despite myself, I sucked in a breath.

"Oh." Jayne said. "Those are quite . . . good."

And they were. They were so good they might have been done by an expert artist. By someone like Randolph Denhaugh. They were the sketches I'd last seen in the dealers' room of the conference. I'd come here expecting to see forgeries. Instead I saw what had to be stolen art.

Elsie stood back and let us admire them. She didn't look happy or proud, as she would have if the pieces were truly hers. Her eyes had narrowed and she glanced rapidly between Jayne and me.

"These look a great deal like ones I saw on the weekend," I said. "Some man was selling them."

"Yeah, those. They were mine. He was working for me."

"I thought you couldn't get a booth?" Jayne said.

Elsie's eyes darted around the room, and she rubbed her palms on the seat of her jeans. "Yeah, that's right. He agreed to handle mine as well as his things. He did sketches too. Not as good as mine, though."

"How much?" I asked. I had no intention of buying anything, but I wanted to give myself time to think. After Randy's death, Elsie must have gone into the dealers' room at the conference and swept up what she could get her hands on from his booth. Surely the room was locked after hours? It would have been during the banquet and overnight, but unlocked first thing the following morning. She could have slipped inside as soon as the doors opened, before most of the other vendors arrived, and helped herself as though she were clearing out some of Randy's things after his death. When I'd seen his booth on Sunday, the tables had been covered in drop cloths. The police would have taken his things away without knowing what should be there or if anything was missing.

Elsie had been quick to take advantage of Randy's death.

Had she brought that occurrence on? Not only in revenge at him stealing what she considered to be her idea, but so she could take his pictures and sell them?

"One hundred pounds each," she said. "Five for three hundred."

"That's a lot," I said. "A hundred pounds is almost a hundred and fifty dollars. I won't have any profit margin."

"They're original art."

"They certainly are that. Thanks for your time." I turned to Jayne. "We can talk to the man who had the booth and see what his prices are like. I didn't get his card. Did you?"

Jayne hesitated, not knowing what I wanted her to say.

"You can't talk to him," Elsie said.

"Why not?"

"'Cause he died. Didn't you hear?"

"He died?" Jayne said. "Gosh, no. When did that happen?"

"After the banquet."

"We left early," I said.

"After you got your award," Elsie said.

So she did remember me after all.

"Cops were crawling all over the place when we arrived on Sunday morning," I said. "People were talking about a death. I didn't realize it was him. We didn't stay after that. I . . ." I shifted my feet and glanced toward the window. "Don't care to talk to the police any more than I have to."

Elsie's eyes glimmered. She'd caught and understood the implication. "Fair enough. But if you want pictures like these ones, you'll have to buy from me."

"I'll keep it in mind." I headed for the door.

"You didn't need to waste my time," Elsie yelled at me. "Pretending you were interested. I've got better things to do, you know."

"Have a nice day," I called.

I wrenched open the door and Jayne and I fell into the street. The door slammed shut behind us.

"Were those Randy's drawings?" Jayne said as we walked quickly away.

"Almost certainly. Aside from the fact that they're identical to the ones we saw in Randy's booth, the quality is far, far better than the pieces she originally showed us. Elsie went back to the conference hotel first thing on Sunday morning and helped herself."

"You mean she stole them?"

"I mean precisely that. The police must have spoken to her as part of their investigation, but as they weren't American shop owners in London on a shopping trip, she would have left out that minor detail."

"Didn't someone notice his stuff had been cleaned out?"

"She didn't take it all. Not judging by what she showed us, anyway. If no one has claimed, legally claimed, Randy's sketches, the police won't know how much he had. Even then, it would be hard to tell what's missing if he didn't keep a detailed inventory."

"What are we going to do now?" Jayne asked.

"This isn't something we can keep to ourselves. Elsie stole the property of a murder victim. I'll talk to Mum and Pippa first, but they'll want me to tell the police. Which is exactly what I have tried to avoid here. I hate getting wrapped up in police inquiries. They are always so slow to follow my thought process. It makes them suspicious. Why are you grinning like that?"

"No reason."

"I hope Brian manages to get DI Morrison removed from the case, and they put a competent officer on; I'd be willing to talk things over with him or her."

Chapter Fourteen

I called Mum to check in and she told me she was at home, Grant and Pippa had gone for a drink, and Donald had returned to the hotel. She hadn't heard from Brian.

I wished her a good night and asked again if it was okay if we all moved into the house in the morning. "It will be nice," she said, "to have people around until this gets sorted out."

Jayne and I took the Tube to Gloucester Road station and walked the short distance to Harrington Gardens. Halfway to the Bentley, a car drove slowly past. It pulled into a loading zone and a young woman got out. She stood by her car, facing us. I'd seen her at the hotel Saturday night with the police, but hadn't spoken to her.

I was not pleased to see DI Sam Morrison emerge from the passenger seat, as unkempt and rumpled as ever. He wore the same stained tie as on Saturday night. I wondered if he owned only the one.

"Trouble," Jayne muttered.

"Leave the talking to me." I kept my pace steady.

"Happy to," Jayne said.

"Ms. Doyle." Morrison greeted me when we reached their car.

"Good evening, Inspector," I said.

"I was on my way to see you."

"Is that so?" My eyes flicked to the woman.

"This is DS Patel," Morrison said.

She was a short, round, dark woman, and she did not look friendly.

"Hi," I said.

"Hello." Her voice was cool.

"It's late," I said. "Can we talk in the morning?"

By which time, I hoped Morrison would be off the case.

"No time like the present," he said. "When I spoke to you on Saturday evening, Ms. Doyle, you told me you and your party were going to America on Tuesday morning."

"Our plans have changed."

"Your hotel will do." Morrison turned to Patel. "Leave the car here."

The four of us walked to the Bentley together. I hoped we wouldn't run into Ryan in the lobby. If he'd been spending the evening getting the dirt on the good inspector, he wouldn't be in a mood to be polite.

We saw no one but the night manager when we came in. His eyes opened wide when he saw who we were with, and I knew he knew who Morrison was.

"The bar downstairs is still open," I said.

"Your room will do," Morrison replied.

I rummaged in my bag for my hotel key as the four of us squeezed into the tiny lift.

Fortunately, our room had chairs and a sofa, so we didn't have to provide seating accommodations on the beds, which had been turned down invitingly for the night.

"Tea?" I asked when we were all inside.

"No," Morrison said. He then begrudgingly added, "Thank you."

"I'm having one," I said. "Jayne?"

"Not for me, thanks," she said.

I fussed with the kettle and tea things. I didn't want tea, but I wanted a moment to collect my thoughts and decide how much to tell Morrison and Patel. I'd hoped there would be a new detective assigned to the case when I went to report what I'd learned at Elsie Saunders's flat.

"You are aware," Morrison said, "that your father has been arrested for the murder of Randolph Denhaugh?"

"I'm confident he will be released soon."

"Because he can pay for a top solicitor."

"Because he's innocent," Jayne said.

Morrison gave her a patronizing smile. I wanted to smack him. Instead I poured myself a cup of tea and sat down. Patel stood against the door, her arms crossed over her chest. Morrison had taken the desk chair and swirled it around to face into the room rather than out the window. I joined Jayne on the sofa.

He didn't have anything new to ask us, just went over the same questions as on Saturday evening about what we'd seen. I didn't say much, leaving Jayne to answer the routine questions. Morrison was rude and obnoxious and totally offensive, but he seemed to think he was coming across as tough but fair. After about a half an hour of trying to trip us up, he abruptly switched tactics, maybe thinking he'd catch me off guard, and asked me if my father was known to have a temper. He then tried to get me to confess that I'd left England to get away from my parents. He didn't ask a single question about what we'd been doing since Saturday.

DS Patel didn't say a word the entire time; she just shifted uncomfortably from one foot to another.

At last Morrison stood up. "Thank you for your time, Ms. Doyle, Ms. Wilson. Do you know when you'll be returning to America?"

"Not yet," Jayne said. "As we told you, we own our own businesses, and this is the slow time of year, so we don't have to get back immediately."

"Are you staying in this hotel?"

"We're moving to my parents' home in the morning." I decided I'd have to tell Morrison about Elsie and the stolen sketches. Brian Cohen was going before a judge in the morning to ask that Morrison be removed from the case, but there was no guarantee the judge would decide in my father's favor. This wasn't information I could keep to myself.

"Uh, Inspector, before you go, there's something you might want to know."

He eyed me. "What might that be?"

"Randolph Denhaugh was selling sketches at the conference; were you aware of that?"

He almost rolled his eyes. "I know that, thank you."

"I suspect some of them were stolen. Not by him. I mean after he died."

Jayne nodded vigorously.

"No need to worry about that, Ms. Doyle. His sketches are in police custody," Morrison said.

"Are you sure you have them all?" I asked.

His eyes narrowed. "I can assure you ladies that no one snatched his property out from under our noses."

Oh, dear. This was not going well. Rather than asking me to explain, Morrison was already telling me I was wrong.

"We saw them," Jayne said. "Tonight."

"Where?" he asked.

"My father wasn't the only person Randy argued with at the conference," I said. "Have you been told about a woman named Elsie Saunders?"

Morrison's face was blank. He flicked a look at Patel. She nodded ever so slightly.

"What about her?" Morrison said.

"I told you about her Saturday night, although at that time I didn't know her name. She accused Randy, at the conference, of stealing her ideas for his art. She was escorted out of the dealers' room by the security guards. I saw it happen myself."

"Did you now?" he said.

DI Morrison really was a patronizing twit.

"She was at the banquet," Jayne said.

"Sunday morning she came back early, as soon as the room was opened," I said, "and helped herself to a few of his sketches. She left enough behind that it wouldn't be immediately apparent some were missing."

"And you know this how?" he asked.

"By a total coincidence," I said. "We were in Whitechapel earlier tonight. Jayne's interested in the Jack the Ripper story."

"That's right," Jayne said. "I can't get enough of it."

"We went to see the scene of the crimes. So to speak."

"Typical," Morrison said. "You've been reading up on ghastly historical crimes and you now think you're a couple of hotshot detectives. I bet you even have your own pet theories as to the identity of the Ripper."

"Other than that it was not the Duke of Clarence, as postulated in the excellent 1978 movie *Murder by Decree*, I do not," I said. "After seeing the sights of Whitechapel, we spotted an art supply shop. I'm an amateur painter. I do watercolors of Cape Cod scenes."

"They're very popular with the tourists," Jayne added helpfully.

"I was interested to see if they had anything I might like that I can't get at home. Elsie Saunders was working there, and I recognized her from the conference."

"And she just happened to tell you she had stolen art to fence," Morrison said.

"More or less," I said. "As it's the sort of thing I sell in my shop."

"Ah, yes. The Sherlock Holmes Bookshop and Emporium." He snorted. "So you think you're some sort of Sherlock Holmes, if not Inspector Reid."

"Who's that?" Jayne asked.

"Edmund Reid was one of the detectives on the Ripper case," I said. "He was played by Matthew Mac-fadyen in the TV show *Ripper Street*. And no, Inspector Morrison, I do not think I'm Sherlock Holmes." My temper was starting to rise. I took a deep breath. Telling Morrison what I thought of him would probably not be a wise move. Jayne touched my knee, ever so lightly, helping to ground me, and then she took her hand away.

Patel noticed, if Morrison did not.

My phone rang, and I reached for my bag.

"Leave it," Morrison snapped. I let it ring.

"You're a couple of shop clerks in small-town America," he said, "who are a bit too much into this Sherlock Holmes thing, never mind Jack the Ripper. I see what you're doing, Ms. Doyle. Don't think I don't."

"I'm giving you information pertinent to your investigation," I said.

"I'll decide what's pertinent. If you're trying to deflect my attention from your father, you're doing a mighty poor job of it."

"Elsie Saunders was seen to argue publicly with a man shortly before he was murdered. That is the exact reasoning you used to have my father arrested."

"I don't have to explain my reasoning to you."

"No, you don't, but you can't let your personal animosity blind you to what else might be going on."

I'd gone too far. I could see it in the narrowing of Morrison's eyes, the vein pulsing in his forehead, the way he clenched and unclenched his fists. Even in the worried glance Patel threw his way.

"If you continue to dream up possible suspects to distract me in my investigation," he said. "I'll arrest you for interference."

"You can't do that!" Jayne said.

"Can't I?" he said.

Jayne sputtered. I lowered my head and touched Jayne's leg, telling her to be quiet. No wonder my dad didn't get on with thus guy. Morrison's style of "detecting"—identify the guilty party and then look for evidence—would have been anathema to my father. I debated whether or not to mention Arianna's name. It was possible Randy's estranged lover hadn't even come to police attention. She'd argued with Randy, but in the bar, not the conference area.

I said nothing. Anything I did say would give Morrison another reason to accuse me of interference at best and obstruction at worst. Jayne sat silently beside me.

"I'm glad we understand each other," Morrison said at last. He puffed up his chest. He really did need to do something about getting a fresh tie. "You need to think things over, Ms. Doyle. If you're lying because you think you're helping your father, it will only go worse for you both. I'll expect a call from you in the morning after you've had time to think things over."

I sat meekly on the couch, my knees together, my shoulders slumped, my hands in my lap. I nodded without looking up.

Patel opened the door, and Morrison marched through it. I lifted my head, and she and I looked at each other. She touched her forehand with her index finger, gave me a nod, and left, closing the door behind her. She hadn't said a single word.

I jumped to my feet.

"What an awful man," Jayne said.

"Shush." I stood at the door, listening. I heard the lift ting to announce its arrival. I then went into the bathroom and turned the faucets in the tub on full blast.

"Are you going to have a bath?" Jayne said.

"I wouldn't put it past him to listen at the door. It's unfortunate that his wife has ceased to love him, and he's taking it out on everyone else."

"What on earth do you know about his marriage?"

"That he's still in one is clear because he's wearing a wedding ring. He's been married for some time as the ring is scratched and worn and much too tight. If his wife loved him, she'd care about his appearance, and point out to him, even if he didn't notice, that he has a stain on his tie, the same one it had Saturday night."

"Maybe he's been working so hard he hasn't gone home to change since Saturday."

"If he was working that hard, I'd be seriously surprised. No, he's been home. He changed his shirt. It's the same brand of white shirt, bought off the rack at a cheap store, but today's was marginally less rumpled than the one he'd been wearing on Saturday evening.

Men who keep a change of shirt at the office always have a fresh tie as well. It's obvious that his wife doesn't love him, or at least doesn't care about his appearance, and I am not at all surprised at that."

Jayne shook her head.

I found my phone and checked voice mail. Ryan, saying he was back and if I hadn't gone to bed to give him a call. It was eleven thirty now, but I was anxious to hear what he had to report, so I called him.

He answered the first ring.

"Did you have a nice night?" I asked.

"I did. Productive, too."

"We can't talk on the phone," I said. "Come to our room. Morrison was here and he just left, so he might still be in the hotel. Use the back stairs."

*   *   *

As he'd said, Ryan had spent a productive evening. He and Brian had met at separate times with two police officers. Both cops told the same story. My dad, who'd been a detective chief superintendent when he retired, had clashed with Sam Morrison on several occasions. It was generally believed Dad had prevented Morrison from getting a promotion at least twice. Morrison had friends on the force, but not many. He was known to be sloppy and pigheaded (that came as no surprise to me) and was generally unpopular.

But he'd solved some high-profile cases, more through dumb luck than any investigative skill, and that had saved him from being dismissed.

"The guys we met said we'd have no trouble getting retired cops to testify on Henry's behalf, if it comes to that," Ryan said. "Brian says what we were told tonight is enough for him to bring before the judge tomorrow to have the initial charges dismissed pending further investigation."

While waiting for Ryan to sneak up the back stairs, I'd rummaged through the mini-bar and found two miniature bottles of whiskey. Ryan had accepted one, and Jayne and I shared the other. "Never knew you to be a whiskey drinker, Gemma," he said.

"Always eager to learn new habits," I lifted my glass. "Cheers."

I told Ryan about our visit to Elsie Saunders. I didn't usually tell him what I was up to, as he never took my interference in police matters well, but I wanted to show my good faith tonight. I also told him Morrison had been completely uninterested in my suggestion Elsie was someone they might want to investigate further.

"Jerk," he said.

"I'll talk to Brian in the morning," I said. "The police might not be interested in following up the theft of Randy's sketches, but the defense team certainly will."

"We can hope your dad never comes to court," Ryan said, "but if he does, the police failure to investigate a viable suspect can be grounds for the whole case to be thrown out."

He finished his drink. "We're still moving into your parents' house tomorrow?"

"Yes."

"Please, please, don't make me share with Donald. I swear, Gemma, the man's snoring would wake the dead. It certainly keeps me awake."

"Time to brush my teeth." Jayne leapt to her feet and fled into the bathroom.

Ryan gathered me into his arms and we kissed lightly.

"I'll see what I can do," I said.

"What's up for tomorrow other than moving?"

I hadn't forgotten about Gallery Lambert. Grant and I were due to meet Julian Lambert tomorrow (now today) to look at paintings that for some reason weren't being displayed publicly. "Grant and I have an appointment at three, and no you cannot come, and no I am not going to tell you about it. Other than that, we'll have to wait to hear what happens in court."

"I enjoyed my assignment tonight. I wish you'd let me do more to help, Gemma."

"Let's see what tomorrow brings. Why don't we have breakfast together?"

"I'd like that. Call me when you get up."

"Good night." He kissed me lightly, and then let himself out. I watched him walk to the staircase and then I shut the door.

"It's safe to come out," I yelled through the bathroom door as I headed for my pajamas.

* * *

I woke to a buzzing sound. The room was pitch-dark, and not a trace of light edged the corners of the drapes. Jayne's breathing was deep and steady.

My phone. A text. I sat up and grabbed the phone, thinking that any call at this time of night couldn't be good.

My heart settled fractionally when I saw the number of the store. Two AM here in London was 9 PM in Cape Cod, and Ashleigh might have forgotten the time difference.

"Hi, Gemma!" my shop assistant said cheerfully.

So cheerfully, I was immediately on guard. "What's happened? Why are you calling?"

Jayne groaned and sat up.

"I don't want you to worry, that's all," Ashleigh said.

"Worry about what?" I asked.

"What's happened?" Jayne mouthed.

"I wouldn't bother you," Ashleigh said, "except that it's on Twitter so I was afraid you might see it. It sounds worse than it was. Things always do, don't they?"

"What's on Twitter? What are you talking about?"

"The fire in the store. Don't worry, we didn't lose too much."

Chapter Fifteen

B y the time I got off the phone, Jayne had switched the lights on, brought us glasses of water, and was checking Twitter.

"It sounds worse than it is," I said.

"That's good, because it sounds pretty bad. The fire department arrived. They put out the blaze before it had a chance to spread to neighboring stores. The fire inspector is assessing the damage."

"Ashleigh said it didn't even spread to the bookshelves and she put it out herself with a bottle of water she fortunately had in her hand."

"What happened?"

"One of Uncle Arthur's lady friends . . ."

"That numbers in the hundreds," Jayne said.

"So it does. Anyway, sometimes thinking she's back in the fifties, this lady isn't always mindful of modern regulations around smoking in public spaces. She lit up her cigarette in the store. Ashleigh was on her break and Arthur was minding the shop. He went upstairs for a few moments. He didn't say why, but Ashleigh suspects he was going for a drop of whiskey for him and his lady friend."

Jayne groaned.

"She, the lady friend, dropped her cigarette on the floor. She didn't bother to put it out first, and it caught the edge of the rag rug under the puzzle table."

"The dry dusty old rug with the loose threads and tasseled edges?"

"That one. And there she left it, smoldering away, when Arthur returned and they moved to the reading nook to enjoy their tipple. Ashleigh returned, fortunately bearing a bottle of water she'd picked up at the convenience store on the corner, the moment the rug went *whoosh!*"

"Ashleigh saved the store, probably the tearoom as well, not to mention Arthur and his friend. She'll be wanting a raise."

"Here's an interesting thing. Ashleigh was only alerted to the impending disaster by Moriarty, who set up a big fuss and drew her attention."

"Good for Moriarty. But what's interesting about that? Animals have good senses."

I pondered that for a few moments. Moriarty had saved my livelihood. Did he do that because he, deep down inside where he kept it hidden away, cared for me? Or because he lived in the store and didn't want to see it burn down around him and have to find new accommodations?

Jayne put her iPad away, switched out the lights, and we went back to sleep.

* * *

Drat that phone. I really needed to learn to turn it off in the night.

The next time it woke me, daylight was creeping into the room, Jayne's bed was empty, and I could hear water running into the bathtub.

More heart leaping into mouth, more heart settling when I saw the number. This time it was one I didn't recognize. "Hello?"

"Gemma Doyle?" A Polish accent, strong today, indicating the owner was under some stress.

"This is she. Can I help you, Arianna?"

"I . . . I hope so. I need to talk to you. Can we meet?"

"What's this about? I have a busy day planned."

"I'd rather not say on the phone."

"I assume this is something to do with the death of Randy Denhaugh. If you know anything about that, you need to take it to the police, not call me."

"I know nothing! And that is my problem. Please."

"Garfunkel's, near Gloucester Road station. Half an hour." I might as well have breakfast while I heard what she wanted to say.

"Thank you." Arianna hung up.

I climbed out of bed and knocked on the bathroom door. "We have breakfast plans. Be ready in twenty minutes."

*   *   *

I dislike being kept waiting. Jayne and I arrived at the restaurant with three minutes to spare. We asked for tea (for me) and coffee (for Jayne) and told the waitress we'd wait for the rest of our party before ordering our food.

Then we waited. And we waited.

"She didn't say what she wanted?" Jayne asked.

"No."

My phone buzzed. "Maybe that's her now," I said. "Oopsie."

"What's the matter?"

I lifted a finger and answered the phone.

"Good morning," Ryan said. "Are you sleeping in? I've been waiting for your call, but I'm getting mighty hungry."

"I'm sorry, but something important came up, and Jayne and I had to go out."

"What came up?"

"Nothing important."

"One sentence ago, you said it was important."

I heard Donald's voice in the background saying, "Let's have breakfast in the hotel. One last treat."

"You go with Donald, and I'll call you when I'm finished here," I said. "We can check out of the hotel and take a cab to Stanhope Gardens."

"I might not be free," Ryan said. "Donald wants to go to Speedy's Café."

"Where's that?"

"A café where some scenes in the *Sherlock* show were filmed."

Even I caught the annoyance in his voice. "I'll fill you in later, but right now I have to run," I said. "Bye."

"That didn't sound good," Jayne said when I'd hung up.

"It wasn't. Ryan's truly annoyed with me this time. I suppose I should have invited him to come with us, but I'm thinking Arianna will be more forthcoming with you and me, whom she's already met. Ryan sometimes looks too . . ."

"Male?" Jayne said.

"Not the word I was searching for, but it fits." I checked the time on my phone. "Five more minutes and then we're outta here, and I can call Ryan back and apologize. She could at least contact me if she's running late."

Arianna made it in four and a half minutes.

She rushed in through the street doors, not looking good. Hair mussed, makeup sloppily applied, coat buttons pushed through the wrong buttonholes.

"Sorry," she said. "Tube was slow." She took off her coat, threw it onto the bench seat next to me, and dropped into the place next to Jayne.

She glanced around the restaurant, nervous and jumpy.

"What's happened?" I asked.

"Good morning," said the waitress. "Can I get you something to drink?"

"Coffee." Arianna nibbled on a broken fingernail. When the waitress had gone, she blurted, "I need your help."

"Why?"

"I need a job in America."

I'd risen from my bed early, rushed out without taking a shower, offended my boyfriend, to meet someone who wanted a job as a store clerk? "Aside from the fact that we're not in America at the moment, and I doubt you have a work visa, I don't need any more employees at my store."

"I'll work for nothing. I have retail experience."

"Arianna, I can't offer you a job, paid or unpaid, if you don't have a visa, which is a moot point, as I don't want to."

The waitress set down a cup of coffee. "Are you ready to order?"

The only thing that kept me from gathering my bag and leaving Arianna to pay our bill was the look in her eyes. She was clearly frightened. Whatever had scared her had happened since Jayne and I talked to her on Sunday.

"I'll have the classic breakfast," I said.

Jayne ordered the veggie breakfast, and Arianna said, "Nothing for me."

"Someone has threatened you," I said. "And it has to do with Randy Denhaugh."

She gripped her coffee cup and nodded. The door opened, and she just about jumped out of her skin. Coffee splashed onto the table.

"Spill," I said.

"I'm sorry," she said, dabbing at the spreading puddle of liquid with a pile of napkins.

"I mean, tell me what's going on."

She sighed and stopped dabbing. "A man came to my door last night."

"What man?"

"I do not know. I did not see his face. He rang the buzzer. All he said was he wants the painting. Today, he will send me an address to take it to."

"What painting?"

Her eyes slid to one side. "I do not know. I'm innocent. I know nothing. I have to get away. Now! Today! You will take me with you?"

"I'm not leaving London today, and I'm not taking you anywhere. Besides, it's perfectly obvious you know what painting this caller is talking about, meaning you have two options. Give it to him, or call the police and report that someone has threatened you."

"I cannot call police."

The waitress brought our plates and asked if we wanted anything else. I said, "No thank you," and cut into my grilled tomato. There's nothing like a proper English breakfast. "If you can't call the police, that puts you in something of a pickle, Arianna. You know of the painting, but you don't know its present whereabouts. Some scheme of Randy's, I suppose."

Without asking, she took a piece of toast off Jayne's plate and bit into it. Jayne lifted her eyebrows in my direction, but didn't reclaim the toast.

Arianna chewed. I waited. "Yes," she said at last. "You are right. Randolph always had a scheme. A very wealthy man, I do not know who, hired him to recover a lost painting."

"You mean a stolen painting."

She nodded.

"Was he working as some sort of art private investigator?" Jayne asked.

"Randolph knew people," Arianna said. "People in the art world."

"People in the art underworld, at any rate," I said. "Which is probably no less nasty than any other underworld. Do you know where the painting is?"

"No. I do not think Randolph found it. But he did spend the money he was paid."

"Ah, so now we come to the crux of the problem."

"If I do not turn over the painting, they want their money back," Arianna said. "I do not have it."

"How did they know your name and where you live?"

"Randolph met them at my flat. He gave me money to go shopping."

"Of course he did," I said. "You really have been played for a fool, Arianna."

Her lower lip quivered and tears filled her eyes.

"When did this meeting happen?"

"Two weeks ago."

"Tell me about the person who phoned you. Did you recognize anything about his voice? What sort of accent?"

She shrugged. "The voice was strange. Like speaking through cloth? I don't know for sure if it was a man or a woman. Their accent was . . . a mixture of many."

"I can't help you," I said, "with a job or anything else. My advice is to go to the police. If you don't want to do that, you should probably lay low for a while and get out of Dodge."

She blinked in confusion. "Where is Dodge?"

"An American expression, meaning leave town. I try to talk like an American sometimes, to fit in back in Massachusetts."

"Like that ever works," Jayne said.

"Do you want me to come with you to the police?" I said. "I will, if you have no one else."

She shook her head.

"Up to you." I wiped the last of the runny egg yolk with my toast and then took money out of my purse. "I have places to go. First I need to use the loo. Be right back."

When I returned, I didn't sit down. I picked up my coat and said, "Let's go, Jayne. Coffee's on me, Arianna, and I paid for you to have something for breakfast. You need to spend some time thinking things over, and this is as good a place as any. Goodbye."

Jayne and I walked out of the restaurant.

"Should we leave her?" Jayne said. "She's in danger."

"We can't help her and she won't go to the cops, so anything that happens is on her. But I don't think anyone will bother with her again."

"Why not?"

"Because she doesn't have this painting they're after or the money they spent to try and get it, if what she says is true. Whoever called her this morning was just covering their bases in case she did have it."

We stood on the street slightly to one side of the doors. I could see Arianna, still at our booth. She'd signaled to the waitress, who was bringing over a menu.

"Randy's death hasn't benefited her at all," Jayne said. "If anything, it's put her in danger."

"That doesn't mean she didn't kill him," I said. "She doesn't look to me like the sort of woman who thinks things through long-term."

Jayne started to walk away.

"Let's wait here a few minutes," I said.

"Why?"

"No reason." I pulled a map out of my purse. "Sherlockians have been speculating for a long time about the actual location of Caulfield Gardens, the fictional street on which the flat used to dump the body in the *Bruce-Partington Plans* was situated. I think it's . . ."

"Gemma, your father is under suspicion for murder and we've just spoken to a woman afraid for her life, and you want to find the location of a fictional story?"

A large black Mitsubishi Shogun pulled up to the curb. A man and a woman got out. He was in a black suit under a rumpled overcoat, and she wore a plain brown trench coat. The driver remained in the car.

The couple went into Garfunkels. I watched as they crossed the floor with rapid, purposeful steps. Arianna's avocado on toast had only just arrived.

"Now we can go," I said.

"What's happening?" Jayne said.

"I called Pippa when I went to the loo. A precaution in case I'm wrong and Randy's business partners really do mean Arianna harm. They'll take care of her for a few days."

Jayne started to turn around. I grabbed her arm. "Let's go. Time we were getting back."

I kept hold of her arm as we headed down Gloucester Road.

"Who are those people?" Jayne asked.

"I've no idea," I said in total honesty.

I'd done what I could. I couldn't make Arianna go to the cops. She hadn't committed any crime, and she wasn't admitting to knowing anything about Randy's death.

She hadn't met the people he'd dealt with, nor could she identify the person who'd contacted her last night.

I'd tell the police, if someone was assigned to replace DI Morrison, what Arianna had told me, but all that meant was that my uncle Randolph was involved in nefarious activities. That hardly came as a shocking revelation.

The person who phoned Arianna wanting a painting recovered wouldn't have killed Randy. Not without getting their money first.

I thought about Sir John Saint-Jean. Had he been willing to do business with the man who'd cheated him out of his painting, in order to get possession of the real thing?

Possibly. I have no idea how people think at that rarefied level of dealing and finance.

I couldn't see Sir John threatening Arianna, though. He didn't seem the type. Then again, I had got him wrong on our initial meeting.

I thought about that for a moment. Had the caller really threatened Arianna with bodily harm? Or had he or she politely asked her if she knew where the painting was, and Arianna overreacted?

* * *

Around ten thirty we arrived en masse, suitcases and all, at the house on Stanhope Gardens. My mother greeted us warmly, trying not to look as though she regretted extending the invitation. She was dressed casually, for her, in cream trousers and a turquoise silk blouse. I gave her a kiss on the cheek. "Are you going to work today?"

"I thought it better not to. I told them I won't be in for the remainder of the week. Brian will call me when he has word."

"What time's the hearing?" Grant asked.

Mum glanced at her watch. "It should be getting underway any minute." The bags under her eyes were deep and tinged purple, and I could tell she hadn't had much sleep, if any, last night.

She led the way up the wide staircase, and we followed, suitcases banging against the stairs and wheels rattling. The hallway was softly lit by wall sconces and the weak winter light from the window overlooking the garden. This isn't a small house; several closed doors led off the corridor.

Horace followed us. He seemed to be trying to hide behind suitcases and legs, keeping himself out of view of Mum. Dad had told me the dog wasn't allowed in the bedrooms. I didn't rat on him.

"Jayne," Mum said, "I've given you the smallest room, but it has a window onto the garden and can be quite delightful in the morning. The last room on the left."

"Thank you," Jayne said.

"Donald and Grant, I hope you don't mind sharing," Mum said. "We had more bedrooms at one time, but we knocked out a wall and moved my study down to this floor a few years ago. I was grateful not to have to manage the stairs any longer. Henry's office is still on the upper level, although he rarely uses it these days, favoring time in his workshop."

"Happy to share," Donald said cheerfully.

Grant forced out a tight smile.

"Second on the right," she said.

Ryan and I got the big room at the front of the house, overlooking the street.

"Nice," Ryan said, bouncing on the king-sized bed, once we'd closed the door behind us. "And I don't mean just the room. Thank heavens I don't have to share with Donald any longer."

"I'm an improvement over Donald? Glad to hear it."

"Anyone would be an improvement over Donald."

I took a few things out of my suitcase and hung them in the closet.

"Forget unpacking." Ryan patted the bed and his eyes sparkled. "Come over and let's try this out."

I grinned at him, pleased he seemed not to be mad at me anymore for standing him up at breakfast. "No time. I don't know how long the hearing will take, but in case it's not good news, I want to be with Mum when Brian calls. Grant and I have an appointment later this afternoon."

"Normally, I'd complain about you going off with Grant without me, but seeing as how he got the wrong end of the stick in roommates, I won't mind too much."

I kissed him and dodged his attempts to pull me down beside him. "Let's go downstairs and act sociable."

We found the others gathered in the kitchen. Mum fussed about, in a very un-Mum-like manner, pretending not to be constantly checking the clock on the wall or her iPhone on the counter. Jayne helped with the tea things and chattered cheerfully about our expedition to Whitechapel yesterday, leaving out all the bits about Elsie Saunders pilfering Randy's art. Donald tried to interest Grant in an expedition to Speedy's Café.

Ryan and I pulled stools up to the breakfast bar. Jayne handed him a cup of tea.

"Oh, good," Ryan said. "More tea."

Mum's phone rang. She threw me a frightened glance as she reached for it. Her hand shook, ever so slightly. "Anne Doyle," she said.

I held my breath, but only for a moment. All the tension fled from my mother's face and she let out a

long, grateful sigh. She broke into an enormous smile.
"Thank you so much for calling, Brian. Yes, I'll be
here." She hung up. "Henry has been released."

We all cheered. Horace barked.

"The charges were not dismissed," Mum said, "but
the judge agreed the police acted prematurely in
detaining him. DI Morrison was in court, although he
was not called upon to speak. He left, Brian said, in a
rage."

"That's so great!" Jayne gave her a spontaneous
hug. My mother is not the hugging type, but this time
she returned the gesture with enthusiasm. When they
separated, tears filled her eyes.

"I'm so glad," I said.

Ryan lifted his teacup. "I'll drink to that."

"Is Henry coming home?" Grant asked.

Mum nodded. "They're on their way now."

"Perhaps we should get out of your hair for a
while," Grant said.

"Good idea," Donald said. "We can go to Speedy's.
There's a walking tour of places featured in the TV
program that might be of interest."

Ryan groaned.

"That's not necessary," Mum said. "You're all welcome to stay. Henry will be happy to see you."

I dumped my unfinished tea into the sink. "You
and Dad have things to talk over and he'll be tired.
He doesn't need to play host to us. Grant, remind me
what time our appointment is."

"Three."

"We have time for an outing, then. How about
lunch at St. Martin-in-the-Fields, Jayne? You'll love it.
A total tourist trap, but great fun. Ryan, you and Donald can go to . . ."

"Lunch sounds good," Ryan said firmly. "I like tourist traps."

"No, you don't," I said.

"Yes, I do," he said.

"Maybe Pippa would like to join us," Grant said. "She told me her office is in the center of town."

"Pippa wouldn't be caught dead in St. Martin's," I said. "Pippa wishes the government would move all the offices to some remote offshore island where tourists can't find them."

"Doesn't hurt to ask," Grant said. "I'll give her a call now."

I turned in time to see my mother smiling at him. Was Mum hearing wedding bells?

"I'll get my bag," Jayne said. "Ten minutes?"

"Sure," I said.

"I'll be ready," Ryan said.

"My guidebook recommends St Martin's," Donald said. "I'm happy to join you."

"Could I possibly borrow a scarf and gloves?" I asked my mother once everyone had dispersed.

"What's wrong with yours?"

"Nothing."

"I assume it has something to do with helping Henry, so very well. I'll get you something."

"Thanks. The Burberry scarf, please, and those blue leather gloves, the ones with the mink trim."

"The gloves were a gift. I've only worn them once."

"All the better."

* * *

We were standing in a bunch in the doorway, adjusting coats and scarfs, collecting bags and phones, and making plans, when a black cab drove up. Dad and Brian got out.

Mum flew down the steps and wrapped her arms around my father. He held her tightly for a long time. The neighbors would be shocked.

"As long as a taxi's conveniently arrived," Donald said. "We might as well take it." He ran down the steps and spoke to the driver.

Brian joined us in the entrance hall. He looked, I thought, highly pleased with himself.

"That was quick work," I said.

"Thanks to what Detective Ashburton and I learned last night, I was able to have a quiet word in police ears before going into court."

"Glad I could be of help," Ryan said.

"And you were," Brian said, "Police, I've found, always talk more easily to one of their kind."

Mum and Dad came up the stairs together, arms wrapped around each other. He looked tired but otherwise not too much worse for wear after a night spent in the nick.

I gave him a hug. "Do you remember anything more about what happened?"

He shook his head. "Still a blank."

"Upstairs with you," Mum said, "this instant. Have a shower and I'll bring up tea and toast."

The English cure for everything.

"We're going out to lunch," I said. "Unless you want me to stay?"

He gave my mother a fond look, but he spoke to me. "I'll be fine, Gemma. You and your friends have a nice day."

"We won't be long."

"I couldn't get Pippa on her phone," Grant said. "You should call and let her know what's happening."

"I suspect Pippa knew I'd be released before I did," Dad said.

"What does that mean?" Grant asked me.

"She's psychic," I said. Then, at his look, I added, "Only joking."

We piled into the waiting cab. I took the seat by the window on the left next to Jayne, with Donald and Grant facing us from the jump seats and Ryan up front beside the cabby. The driver pulled into the road and drove away. As we approached the intersection with Cromwell Road, I felt a tingling down the back of my neck.

DI Sam Morrison was standing by the iron fence surrounding the private garden. He was alone and he stared intently at the taxi as it went by. He caught my eye, and the look on his face sent a chill through me.

The cab found a break in traffic and sped away.

I sent my mother a quick text: MORRISON IS WATCHING THE HOUSE.

* * *

The restaurant in the crypt of the church of St. Martin-in-the-Fields, across the street from Trafalgar Square and the National Gallery, is a tourist favorite, and deservedly so.

The moment we entered the underground space, Jayne squealed as she caught sight of the soaring red brick arches and the rows of ancient tombstones laid into the floor. "Order me anything," she said, "anything at all!" She ran around the room, reading the fading inscriptions on the stones.

The place was crowded, but we managed to snag a big table as a group of German tourists, all guidebooks, sturdy shoes, and camera equipment, vacated it. Donald and I guarded the table while Grant and Ryan went for our food and Jayne rushed about, looking at everything.

"Jolly good to see your father this morning," Donald said. The longer we stayed in England, the more he was picking up traces of an accent. He'd be speaking the Queen's English better than I did soon.

"It was that."

"Have you given any thought to when we can go home?"

"Aren't you enjoying London?"

"I'm loving every minute," he said. "Except for your father's problem, of course. But home is still home and I'm not accustomed to being away."

"You don't have to stay any longer, Donald. I appreciate your support, I hope you know that, but I understand."

"I'll stay," he said firmly. "As long as I'm needed."

Once again, I felt tears forming behind my eyes. Donald wasn't needed in the least; if anything, it was complicating things trying to keep him busy and out from underfoot, but his concern for me and my family was genuine. Donald pulled his *Lonely Planet* guide to London out of his satchel, adjusted his glasses, turned to the section on St. Martin's, and settled back to read.

I was glad Dad had been released from jail, but I was well aware the case wasn't over yet. My father was still under suspicion for the murder of his brother-in-law, and Sam Morrison was watching my parents' house. Brian had argued in front of a judge that Morrison had a grudge against my father and he'd been removed from the case. His presence in Stanhope Gardens this morning could mean nothing good.

Like Donald, I wanted to go home. But I wouldn't, not until my father was completely cleared of all suspicion. And that, I knew, might take a very long time.

Ryan and Grant arrived with laden trays and placed drinks and sandwiches on the table and we all dug in. Donald read parts of his guidebook out loud to Jayne, and Grant checked a text under the table that left him grinning like a lovesick fool. Only Ryan's face was dark and serious. Like me, he knew this wasn't over. Not by a long shot. He reached for my hand under the table and ran his index finger across my palm.

"You need to go home." I spoke in a low, private voice. "You're using up all your vacation time."

"I called the chief and explained. He's given me another week."

"Might not be enough," I said.

"I'm not leaving without you, Gemma. And I have the feeling you're not leaving until this is over."

"You're right about that. I'm not. I couldn't."

"I called Louise this morning to check in. She didn't come right out and say I wasn't needed, but she did imply that the crime rate in West London has gone down considerably since you left town."

I harrumphed. "That is most certainly not my fault."

"How's Arthur managing at the store?" he asked.

I thought of fires and flooded computers and angry *New York Times* best-selling authors. "Everything's fine, but he'll be getting restless soon." Great-Uncle Arthur was one of the world's great travelers. Even approaching ninety, he never could stay in one place for long.

I glanced at Jayne, munching her sandwich and listening to Donald natter. Jayne needed to get back to the bakery. Before we left, she'd put in long hours getting things done ahead of time and putting a week's worth of pastries into the freezer. Her staff was competent, but they weren't professional bakers of her quality.

Donald might have said he'd stay, but I knew he didn't have much in the way of extra money and my parents' hospitality would eventually run out.

As for Grant, he also had a business to run, but clearly he wasn't ready to go home yet. Not until he and Pippa came to an understanding.

I feared Grant would have his heart broken.

Then again, maybe I was being too hard on my sister. She seemed to be enjoying his company.

The very thought had no sooner crossed my mind than I saw her coming toward us. I blinked, in case I was imagining things.

No, it was Pippa all right, tapping her way across centuries of graves in her red patent-leather shoes with four-inch heels. Wonder of wonders, she was out of the office in the middle of the day and actually smiling.

Grant leapt to his feet, his face a picture of pure joy. "Pippa! So glad you could make it!"

"I snuck out of the office; wasn't that naughty of me?" She giggled. I checked to make sure this was really Pippa and not some foreign spy pretending to be her.

"I'll find another chair," Donald said, politely getting to his feet.

"No, thank you," Pippa said. "I can't stay for long, but when Grant said you were lunching here at St. Martin's, I wanted to take the opportunity to show him my favorite room at the gallery." She smiled at Grant. He smiled back.

"Great idea," he said. "Gemma, why don't we meet at ten to three on the steps outside the church where we came in? We can walk from here and be on time for our appointment."

"Fine," I said.

"I've been wanting to visit the National Gallery," Donald said, gathering his book and coat and putting on his gloves. "I'll come with you. It's always better, I've found, to visit these places in the company of someone who knows their way around, particularly when I don't have time to see everything."

Ryan chuckled. Grant sputtered. Pippa said, "Let's be off, then." She looked at me. "You'll keep me appraised?"

"Of course."

"Appraised of what?" Ryan said.

"Developments," I said.

"That means nothing," he said.

"Trust me," I said.

"He will," Pippa said.

"Two against one," Ryan said, "I haven't got a chance."

"Coming, Jayne?" Donald asked.

Jayne glanced at me.

"Pippa's taste in art is not mine," I said. "I'm thinking of spending the time at the Portrait Gallery. I always love saying hello to Henry the Eighth and Elizabeth the First."

"I'll come with you, then," Jayne said. "History is more to my liking than art"—a glance at Ryan—"if that's okay?"

"Happy to have you," he said, meaning it.

Pippa, Grant, and Donald left. I settled back to finish my lunch, and then we also gathered our things. We'd barely risen from our seats before a pack of Japanese tourists in matching red-and-yellow jackets descended on our table.

When we emerged onto the street, the sun was shining in an unusually (for London in January) bright blue sky.

Ryan held my hand as we crossed the busy sidewalk heading for the curb. Traffic was heavy in both directions. Behind us, I heard Jayne say, "Hold on a sec. My sunglasses are in here somewhere." Ryan dropped my hand and stepped back. I stood at the edge of the road, waiting for the light to change. I looked across the street and felt a sudden, unexpected tug of emotion. Trafalgar Square, full of pigeons and tourists, hawkers and performance artists. Admiral Nelson standing proud on top of his column; the four plinths, one in each corner of the square. The wide bustling steps of the National Gallery, the building packed full of the greatest art in the world.

My city.

My city smelled strongly of fumes from delivery lorries, ancient drains, too many people crowded too close together, the occasional passing dog, cooking odors.

And something else. Something soft, almost flowery, unexpected, unidentifiable.

A hand on my back. A shove. I stumbled and fell forward.

A white panel van heading straight toward me.

Chapter Sixteen

"Gemma. Gemma! Are you all right?"

I groaned, blinked, and opened my eyes. Ryan's intense blue ones, full of fear, were looking straight into mine. "Gemma?"

"I'm here. I'm . . . I'm fine. I think. Help me up." I lay on the sidewalk, my legs sticking into the roadway. I yelped and pulled my feet in.

A look of pure relief wiped the fear from Ryan's eyes, and he gripped my arm. A soft hand took the other, and between them Ryan and Jayne leveraged me to my feet. I tried to take a step, but my legs gave way and I wobbled. Pain shot through my right knee and I cried out. My friends gripped me harder.

We were surrounded by chattering voices and concerned faces. Traffic had come to a complete halt. The face of the driver of the panel van had gone almost pure white and his dark eyes were round. Behind him, a man leaned out of a sleek black SUV and yelled something rude at us.

"We're okay here!" Ryan waved at the van's driver. The man nodded in acknowledgment and put his vehicle into gear. Traffic began to move again.

A policewoman, young, pretty, and efficient, trotted up. "What's going on here?"

"My friend fainted," Jayne said, "and fell into the road. She had a close call."

The policewoman pointed behind us. "There's a bench over there. She needs to sit down."

"I'm okay," I said.

"Are you sure, madam?" she asked. "Do you need me to call an ambulance?"

I tried to smile. "No, thank you. A moment's rest is all I need."

She turned to the crowd of onlookers milling about, hoping for something to happen. "Nothing to see here. Move along."

Show over, they began to disperse.

"What happened?" Jayne said to me.

"Like you said, I fainted."

Ryan looked highly dubious. As well he might. I gave him an encouraging smile. "All's well that ends well."

"You had a fright. You need to sit down," Jayne said. "Come on."

Ryan continued to hold my arm as we followed her. I lowered myself to the bench. My two friends crouched in front of me, peering into my face, searching for signs of illness or distress.

"I'm okay. Really."

"You're lucky we were so close behind you," Jayne said. "Ryan saw you stumble and jumped in front of that van to grab your arm and pull you out of the way. It missed you both by inches."

"An exaggeration," Ryan said modestly.

"No, really," Jayne said. "You fell, and then Ryan was there, stopping cars. Sorta like Superman."

"Whose real name, I now know, is Clark Kent," I said.

"What's that got to do with anything?" Ryan said.

Jayne and I exchanged a look. I laughed. "Private joke."

"I can't claim all the credit," Ryan said. "Jayne moved as fast as I did and helped pull you out of the way."

"You can call me Superwoman," Jayne said, not at all modestly.

"Which I will from now on." I closed my eyes and leaned back on the bench.

"Do you remember . . . ?" Ryan said.

"Shush," Jayne said. "She needs a moment to rest."

I wasn't resting. Not in the least. I thought back over the seconds before I fell. Before I was pushed.

That I'd been pushed, I had no doubt. I'd felt a person standing too close, even in the crush of people waiting to cross. A hand, firm, purposeful, on my back. A solid shove. I'd seen nothing. I'd been looking across the street, over the blur of traffic, thinking of London. I'd not seen anyone familiar as we left the church and walked to the street. I'd smelled something, though, in the fraction of a second before I'd been pushed. Something out of place in busy, wintry London.

Citrus.

I opened my eyes and jumped to my feet. "Shall we go?"

"Go where?" Ryan said.

"To the Portrait Gallery, of course. We're still wanting to see Henry and Elizabeth, aren't we?"

"Yes, but . . ." Jayne said.

"No buts." I took her arm and gave it a squeeze so hard she squealed. "This time I'll wait for the light to change before crossing. I didn't faint, by the way." I decided not to mention what I knew had happened to Jayne and Ryan. Not yet anyway. "Someone bumped into me, I suspect. It's so crowded around here; they were probably bumped by someone else and that started a chain reaction. I'll remember not to stand so close to the curb from now on."

* * *

While we toured the gallery, admiring the kings and queens, politicians and scoundrels, and other distinguished personages of Britain past and present, I pondered how to get rid of Ryan. He was a suspicious sort, and was clearly having trouble believing I'd fallen accidently. Grant and I, in the disguise of newly wealthy art collector and silly wife, had an appointment to view possibly purloined art at three o'clock. I didn't need an American police officer trailing along behind, glaring at anyone who approached me. I briefly considered explaining to Julian Lambert and his contacts that Ryan was my bodyguard, but the fact that I needed a bodyguard might cause the art dealers to not be totally forthcoming with Grant.

At two thirty, I excused myself to visit the loo. I called my mother. "Just checking in," I said. "How's Dad?"

"He lay down for a short while, but said he couldn't sleep and is now up. He's in the workshop with the dog, the door firmly closed. I suspect he's calling his police friends for updates on the case."

"Would I be correct in assuming they are not permitted to speak to him about that?"

"You would be. Which doesn't mean they won't."

"Any further sign of Sam Morrison?"

"No. He didn't come to the door, and when I peered out after you called, I didn't see him. Are you sure . . . ?"

"Of course I'm sure. I'd recognize that ugly mug anywhere."

"Henry took Horace for a walk a short while ago. He didn't mention seeing anyone."

"He might have, but not wanted to worry you."

"Precisely."

"I don't think you two should be alone."

"Why ever not?"

"Who knows what Morrison's thinking? He was embarrassed in court, and he probably got a strong talking to from his bosses. He might even have been placed on suspension. You need a bodyguard."

"I don't think—"

"Fortunately, I happen to know the right person. Ryan can be tough when he wants to be, plus he and Dad can talk over the case. Dad needs someone to toss ideas against, and he shouldn't be discussing things openly with his former colleagues."

"You mean, you want to get rid of Ryan for a few hours."

"If you put it like that. I'll let you talk to him. You can tell him you're concerned about Morrison, but you don't want to say anything to worry Dad."

I found Jayne and Ryan admiring the portrait of Charlotte Bronte by George Richmond. "I called Mum to check in, and she asked to talk to you." I handed Ryan the phone. He took it, and Jayne and I walked down the row of paintings. "I've always liked this one," I said, stopping at a painting of a richly dressed lady. "The fabric in that dress looks so real I want to touch it."

"I can't imagine dragging that outfit around after me all day," Jayne said. "Do you suppose they got awfully hot?"

"Good thing this is a cold climate. Be hard to keep that hem clean in streets of mud."

Ryan caught up to us and handed me back my phone. "Your mom says Morrison's been spotted hanging around."

"I thought I saw him as we were leaving," I said. "I wasn't sure if it was him though."

Ryan gave me *that* look. The one that says he knows I'm up to something. "She asked if I'd mind coming back to the house."

"Didn't Morrison get taken off the case?" Jayne said.

"Yes," I said. "So if he's watching the house, Mum has reason to worry."

"Anne also thinks Henry would like some company," Ryan said. "Someone to talk the case over with."

"And you can do that because you're a cop too," Jayne said, so helpfully I might have prompted her myself. "That's nice."

"Although, seeing as how Gemma's mother is a defense attorney, she isn't exactly ignorant of the law or of police methods," Ryan said.

"Not the same," Jayne said.

"Off you go," I said. "We'll be fine on our own."

"I'm still not happy about your *falling* incident," Ryan said.

"I'm meeting Grant in fifteen minutes," I assured him.

"Knowing that you and Grant are up to something you won't tell me about is supposed to make me feel better?"

"Yes," I said.

Ryan didn't look entirely convinced. I gave him a smile. "I'll be fine. Trust me."

"I trust you to get into trouble, but I also trust you to get yourself out of it. And that sister of yours certainly knows far more than she's letting on. Okay, I'll go, but only because your mother asked."

We headed for the exit.

"Did you enjoy that?" I asked Jayne.

"So much. It was great seeing the faces of people I've only read about in books. I'd love to come back and finish."

"Maybe we can do that another time. They do a nice afternoon tea in the restaurant." We walked out into the sunshine.

"You're just as well to take the Tube," I said. "A taxi is not any faster in this traffic. Jayne, you go with Ryan. Mum will need help preparing dinner for us all. I'll see you both back at the house."

"I . . ." Jayne said.

I waved cheerfully and trotted off. This time I stood far back from the curb while waiting for the traffic to stop.

* * *

Grant was waiting for me on the steps of St. Martin-in-the-Fields as arranged. I was pleased to see he'd come alone.

"Pippa had to go back to work," he explained, "and I managed to persuade Donald to visit the British Library. Pippa said they might have some of the writings of Sir Arthur Conan Doyle on display this week. I think she lied."

"Naughty, naughty," I said. "Why are you looking at me like that?"

"Are you going to go dressed like that?"

"Like what?"

"For one thing, that coat looks like you lay down in the street in it. You went to so much trouble yesterday, not to mention expense, to dress up."

"This will have to do. I couldn't come out in an entirely new wardrobe and sexy, yet unwalkable-in, shoes and not expect Ryan to ask questions. It's slightly warmer today, so I can manage without my coat and I have a few handy accessories that'll make the look." I took off my coat and dug in my bag to pull out the scarf and leather gloves I'd borrowed from Mum. Underneath my coat I'd worn jeans and a cashmere cardigan that didn't look entirely off-the-rack and matched the color of my mother's gloves. I spotted a woman shuffling along, eyes on the tips of her toes, mumbling to herself. Her coat was ragged, the hems of her trousers filthy, and her left trainer had a hole it. As well as being a popular tourist attraction, St. Martin's does what it can to care for the homeless of central London.

"Be right back," I said to Grant.

I approached the woman. "Would you like this?" I held out my coat.

She probably wasn't much older than me, in her early thirties, but her eyes were far too old for her years and her skin had an unhealthy yellow sheen. She studied me through red and rheumy eyes full of suspicion. "What's that then?"

"Just a coat. I don't need it anymore. My husband doesn't know it yet, but he's going to buy me a new one."

She studied me for a long time, trying to read my face. I smiled and held out the garment, and at last she snatched it and hurried away before I could change my mind.

I went back to Grant.

"What on earth did you do that for?" he said.

"I've been told that once upon a time you could find luggage storage lockers around town, but no longer. I can't take that old coat with me, not if I'm trying to make an impression as your trophy wife, and if I leave it somewhere it'll be gone when we get back. Might as well give it to a needy person. It's warm enough today that I'm not entirely out of place in just a sweater, scarf, and gloves."

Grant pulled out his phone. "We're going to the Black Star Gallery. I've programmed the address into the GPS. Let's go."

We walked down the street together. I kept us well away from the curb.

"What's the plan?" Grant said.

"I won't know until we see what's on offer. We might not have one."

Just as well I hadn't lain awake last night trying to come up with a plan: no one was there to meet us. The gallery we'd been directed to had some nice paintings for sale, eighteenth and early nineteenth century mostly, from artists I'd never heard of, at prices that were steep but not excessive. The staff, an older woman in horn-rimmed glasses and a black wool dress she appeared to have been poured into, and a younger man, constantly rubbing his hands together, were polite enough when we arrived. The politeness faded considerably when Grant explained we were here to meet with Julian Lambert, as arranged.

The man shrugged, and the woman said, "Doesn't he own a place on the other side of the river, near the Tate?"

"That's right," Grant said. "He asked us to meet him here. He said you have a painting I might be interested in."

"You must be mistaken," she replied with a sniff. "I know Julian Lambert by reputation, and he would be highly unlikely to do any favor, no matter how small, for anyone."

Grant looked at me. I shrugged. "Sorry to bother you," he said.

"If you're in the market for fine art," she said, "we have some excellent pieces from the estate of a stately home, which have recently come on the market."

"Maybe another time," Grant said. "Thanks."

We stood on the street corner. "That was odd," Grant said.

"Very." I glanced up and down the street. I could see nothing or no one out of place or familiar to me. "When did Julian's assistant call you and recommend we meet here?"

"It was Monday, a couple of hours after we left his gallery."

"Which means something happened between us meeting him and that phone call, something that changed his mind about showing us the art he initially planned to recommend."

"Any idea what that could be?"

"No. Unless somehow he discovered we are not what we presented ourselves as."

"How would he do that?"

"Followed us, perhaps. Or had someone else follow us. I didn't spot anyone, but he might have a much larger operation than I expected."

"Operation?"

"As in criminal contacts. To organize an undetectable tail that quickly would take some considerable degree of coordination."

"What do we do now?"

"We have a cup of tea, of course." I'd spotted a pub across the street and headed for it. The street was narrow but not much less busy than St. Martin's Place. I took care not to get too close to the edge of the pavement and checked carefully in both directions, as my mother had taught me, before crossing at the light.

"Gemma," Grant said, as I stepped cautiously into the road. "Did something happen after Pippa, Donald, and I left you earlier?"

"What do you mean?"

"You seem more hesitant than usual. Fearful almost."

"Traffic in London can be a nightmare," I said. "I'd forgotten how bad it gets."

I pushed open the door of the pub to be enveloped in the scent of an overheated radiator, greasy food, and spilled beer. "I'll have tea," I said to Grant.

The place was almost empty, and I found us a table close to the fireplace. Without a coat, I was feeling chilly.

I sat down and closed my eyes.

Julian Lambert had been prepared to show Grant and me some pieces of art—expensive art—he thought would appeal to a new, and naïve, collector. He'd phoned Grant a few hours after he'd met us to set up the meeting. But there'd been no meeting, and he didn't intend there to be one.

Something had to have happened after we left his gallery. Maybe he'd checked up on Grant and decided he was iffy. But a thorough check would have taken time, more time than he had given it, particularly considering it had been night in the United States. Then again, whatever happened might not have had anything to do with us. Maybe he'd simply received a better offer for whatever he had in mind for Grant to purchase.

Still, he could have called and made excuses. It was rude to send Grant on a wild-goose chase, and not an act inclined to make Grant view doing business with Julian in the future in a favorable light.

I hadn't forgotten someone had tried to kill me not long ago. To kill me had to have been their intent. If Ryan hadn't been close and acted so quickly, I would have fallen directly into the path of the van. I shivered.

No one outside my immediate circle knew I was having lunch at St. Martin's and going to the Portrait Gallery after. We'd arranged the lunch only ten minutes before leaving the house, and the gallery visit on the spur of the moment. Grant had phoned Pippa and told her where we were, but I had to believe Pippa's phone was unhackable. Grant's was not, but if someone was listening in on him, I'd have to believe they were listening to us all. Not impossible to do, but not easy either.

Sam Morrison had not followed us, I was positive of that. I would have seen him lurking about on street corners. He had seen the cab we left in and could have asked one of his friends to locate it. The cab driver let us off on one of the busiest street corners in the world and drove away without giving us a backward glance. Even if Morrison had tried to follow us, I couldn't see any reason for him to want to kill me. He'd clearly dismissed me as not someone worth bothering about.

A thought struck me. Did he want revenge on my father?

It was possible, if Morrison was that angry at being humiliated in court, and that vengeful.

But in that case, I couldn't see how he could have arranged to have me followed and attacked so quickly.

The shove into my back had been hard, purposeful, and directed. It had not been some random person pushing his or her way through the crowd. Might I have been the victim of a random act of violence, or mistaken for someone else? Such a busy intersection was the perfect place for a sudden, spontaneous act of murder. As was most of central London, including the intersection outside this very pub. But until I knew exactly what was going on, I wouldn't allow myself to believe it had been accidental.

I let out a long breath.

Perhaps it had been an act of random chance. Not of the victim, as I'd speculated, but of the location.

Even if someone who meant me harm didn't know I was going to be crossing St. Martin's Place, it was known I'd be in the general area around this time. Because Grant and I had been lured to the Black Star Gallery.

Had that person simply seen me standing in the street among so many others and taken the opportunity that presented itself? I tried to create a mental image of the scene as we'd come out of the church. The traffic, the crowds, the noise, the pigeons in Trafalgar Square. The scent of exhaust fumes, damp clothes, restaurant ovens. Jayne called for us to wait a moment; Ryan dropped my hand to fall back, but I carried on. Someone near me had been smoking a cigarette, but I hadn't seen their face. The scent had passed on by as the smoker went on their way.

The strong fresh odor of citrus. Close to me. Very close. Might someone have been eating an orange as they pushed me into the street? That seemed unlikely.

"Gemma?" Grant said in a soft voice.

I opened my eyes. He had a half-finished pint of beer in front of him. My tea was cold. "What's the time?"

"Quarter after four. I didn't like to disturb you."

"Time we were going then. The others will be getting worried."

"Did you think of something?" he asked.

"No," I said.

But I had.

Chapter Seventeen

I was pretty sure I knew who'd tried to kill me, and why, but I needed time to think over what to do next.

I also needed, before doing anything further, to find out if there had been any fresh developments.

There had been one, and it was significant.

A new detective had been assigned to the case. My mother phoned as Grant and I were leaving the pub. The police, she said, had come to the house to interview Dad and her as well as Ryan and Jayne. They wanted to talk to Grant and me also.

"We're on our way," I said. "Half an hour maybe."

"One other thing," she said. "Henry got word that DI Morrison has been placed on leave, pending a review of his behavior around the arrest of Henry Doyle, which was subsequently determined to be so premature and unfounded it was thrown out of court with strong words from his lordship the judge about wasting valuable court time."

"Morrison is not going to be well disposed to the Doyle family."

"We can only assume that is the case," my mother said.

Grant and I took the Tube to Gloucester Road station and walked quickly to Stanhope Gardens in the deepening dusk. If Grant was aware that I was paying particular attention—even more than usual—to my immediate surroundings, he said nothing.

DS Patel met us at the door. She might have looked marginally less stressed than when I'd seen her last, but she was as silent as ever. Ryan had followed her, and he gave me a hug. "Everything okay?"

"Okay," I said. "Absolutely nothing happened. And you can check with Grant if you don't believe me."

"Somewhat like the curious incident of the dog in the nighttime," Grant said. "That we met with no one and no one was interested in meeting with us, was the curious incident."

Ryan raised one eyebrow. At last Patel spoke. "I wish you people would stop pretending this is an episode of *Sherlock*."

"Fear not, I don't believe that for a moment," I said.

"DI Robinson is in the library," she said. "She's waiting for you, Ms. Doyle."

"Lead on," I said.

DI Robinson was in her midforties, married for a long time, judging by the tightness of the band of the gold ring on her left hand, and she had at least one very young child, judging by the porridge stain on the back of her right shoulder. I assumed the late-in-life child had been a surprise and Robinson was having trouble squeezing the baby into her busy work schedule. Her husband resented the amount of time she dedicated to her job, and thus he hadn't bothered to point out the food residue before she left the house.

Either her colleagues didn't like her much, or they were too afraid of her to point it out. I decided, by the tone of voice Patel had used to refer to her, that it wasn't the former, and by the lack of aggression in the inspector's eyes, that it wasn't because anyone lived in fear of her. They simply accepted that she was having a difficult time balancing all her responsibilities and let it go.

She was sitting in my father's chair, and although I didn't like to see anyone else there, I said nothing. She stood when I came in, Patel introduced us, we shook hands, and I sat down, aware Robinson was studying me as intently as I had done her. I waited for her to speak.

"Tell me about Saturday evening, at the conference banquet," she said in a Birmingham accent. I did so.

Our interview took a long time. I told her everything I remembered. Unprompted, I then told her about Elsie Saunders and how I suspected she'd pinched some of Randy's sketches. Robinson's face showed no reaction, but when I mentioned Arianna Nowacki and the argument with Randy in the bar, her eyes flicked suddenly to Patel, who was unfortunately standing directly behind me so I couldn't see her, and I knew this information came as news to the detectives.

"You might also want to speak to Sir John Saint-Jean," I said. "He had a history, so I've been given to understand, with my late uncle Randolph. He spoke to my mother before we went in to dinner."

"Is that the bald man, tough looking, in your mother's words, who wanted her to give a message to her brother?"

"Yes," I said. "It would seem my uncle was involved in business to do with forged and stolen art. Plus, on a personal level, a lot of people didn't like him all that much. I trust you're focusing your inquires in those directions."

"I'll keep all that in mind."

"Good."

"I'm curious as to what you're doing here, Ms. Doyle."

"Me? I'm visiting my parents."

"Other than that. Your friend Ryan Ashburton is a detective in Massachusetts. At the Met we don't take kindly to vacationing police officers investigating crimes in our jurisdiction."

"Ryan hasn't . . ."

"No, he hasn't," she said. "He hasn't been doing anything but visiting the popular sights of the city and talking to your father in general terms about police work. But you, with no qualifications whatsoever, seem to be running all over London investigating."

"Perhaps I'm just nosy," I said. "Be that as it may, I have been trying to help my father, yes. Considering that DI Morrison was prepared to railroad him, someone had to conduct a proper investigation."

"And you thought that someone should be you? The owner of a Sherlock Holmes bookshop?"

I'd sat here debating how much to tell Robinson about Julian Lambert and his gallery, the misdirected meeting, and the shove against my back.

But now Robinson was putting me in mind of my nemesis Detective Louise Estrada, back home in West London, who never believed a word I said. If I deduced that the sky was blue, Estrada would accuse me of trying to cover up the fact that the sky was green.

Dealing with suspicious police officers can be highly tedious.

Although, in fairness, I had absolutely no proof anyone had pushed me. Things do happen in overcrowded streets.

"Thank you for your time," Robinson said, dismissing me.

I didn't stand up. "Are you aware DI Morrison was seen this morning watching this house? And that that happened after the court hearing?"

"Mrs. Doyle mentioned you told her something to that effect."

"I told her because I saw him. Can I trust you'll be mentioning it to your supervisors?"

She said nothing.

I got to my feet. "I'll be staying in London for the time being, if you need anything."

"Unlikely I will," she said.

"I hope you can get home in time to put the baby to bed tonight," I said. "Your erratic schedule must make it difficult."

"What the . . . ?" She shot a look at Patel. I was half turning and saw Patel give her boss a shrug and me a suspicious look.

* * *

I found everyone huddled in the kitchen. Despite Jayne's presence to assist, there was no sign of dinner preparations.

"What do you know about DI Robinson?" I asked Dad.

"Nothing," he said. "Never heard of her. I called a mate, and he told me she transferred in from Birmingham, but then she went on maternity leave and only just returned to work."

"So she has no ax to grind," Grant said. "That's good."

"But a reputation to make," Mum said. "Even more so if some of her colleagues resent her for taking time off to care for a new baby."

"Tea, anyone?" Jayne asked.

Ryan groaned.

"Oh, Gemma," Mum said, "The police dropped a package off for you earlier. It's Arthur's statue. They don't need it any longer. I put it in your room."

I'd been rather hoping the police would keep it. I didn't fancy lugging it all the way home in my suitcase. It might even put me over the weight limit on the plane.

"Let's have dinner out," Dad said. "How about Steak and Co. on Gloucester Road? I feel like a good steak."

We chorused our agreement.

"Why don't you see if Pippa's free tonight?" Grant said.

"She might be," Dad said. "I saw on the news that that standoff in the South China Sea ended peacefully."

"Why would that affect her dinner plans?" Grant said.

"Her boss might have had to go in to a meeting," I said. "And want her to take the minutes."

"He works her too hard," Grant replied. "Don't they have recording devices in the British government these days?"

"Pippa must have been mistaken," Donald said to Grant as they headed for their room. "The nice people at the British Library told me they don't have a Sir Arthur display at the moment, but they hope to have the opportunity to put on something next year. They took down my contact information so I can be informed if it happens. I'd like to come back to London to see it."

My mother had signaled to me that she wanted to speak privately, so I hung back after everyone went to get ready for dinner, including Dad. Horace stayed behind, clearly wondering what was happening about dinner.

"The police will be releasing Randolph's body the day after tomorrow," Mum said. "I've been on the phone discussing the arrangements."

"Why is it up to you?"

She sighed heavily. The strain of the last few days showed in the fine skin around her mouth and the shade of purple under her eyes. "There is, it would appear, no one else. He was married at one time, but that ended a number of years ago. The police gave me the number of his ex-wife, and I called her. She lives in Italy, and doesn't want to be bothered. She was downright rude about it. He had no children, at least none that I can locate."

"That's sad," I said.

"It is, isn't it?"

I thought of Arianna, supposedly his fiancée prior to Friday. Unlikely she'd want to be saddled with making funeral arrangements.

"He brought it on himself," I said.

"Yes, but that doesn't make it any less sad."

* * *

Before changing to go out for dinner, I knocked on Jayne's door. Horace had followed me up the stairs, after first checking that Mum wasn't watching.

"Come on in!" she called, and the dog and I did so.

This room was pretty and feminine in shades of peach and cream. The bed was small, with ruffled pillows and a thick down comforter, and the curtains were pulled back to give a view over the lights of the garden to the dark shapes of the rooftops of the houses behind. Horace sniffed Jayne's suitcase and the shoes she'd laid out next to the closet.

"You need to go home," I said.

"No, I don't," she said. "Not without you."

"I might be a while." I sat on the bed. The dog settled his muzzle in my lap and I stroked it.

"A while as in permanently?"

"Definitely not. Just while my parents need me. Dad's not out from under the cloud of suspicion yet."

"This case might never be wrapped up."

"I'm aware of that. Uncle Arthur and Ashleigh can manage the store."

"No, they can't."

"All the more reason for you to go home. Someone has to keep our businesses afloat. Isn't that right, Horace?"

The dog snuffled in agreement.

"But that's not why I'm here," I said. "You and I are going on an outing tomorrow, if you're willing."

"Of course, I'm willing. Where?"

"We're going to look at art. Our intentions in doing so are not honorable."

"Are you going to tell me what that means? Okay, foolish question, you never do."

I went back to my room. Ryan was propped up on the bed, reading his phone. "Any news from West London?" I asked.

"Nope," he said, far too quickly, closing the phone with an audible click.

"Nope meaning yes. What's happened now?"

"Nothing you need to know about."

Meaning something I desperately needed to know about. "Now I am worried. Tell me what's happened, or I'll assume the entire town has been washed away in a flash flood, bearing Uncle Arthur and Moriarty on a raft made of Sherlock pastiche novels."

"That paints an interesting picture. I guess you'll find out anyway. I went onto Twitter to check the police updates."

"And?"

"Nothing of importance there. Things do seem to have been quiet in town this week. But a reference to . . . uh . . . your store caught my eye."

I dropped onto the bed beside him. "Let me see."

He pressed his thumb on the button to open up the screen. I leaned over his shoulder to read. A reference had been made to the Sherlock Holmes Bookshop and Emporium, all right. Several references. And none of them good.

The tweets were warning people to stay away. I saw words such as RUDE STAFF and VICIOUS ANIMAL.

I groaned and took out my phone. I called the store.

"Hi, Gemma," Ashleigh said. "Hope you're still having fun. Have you been on the London Eye yet? I was watching a BBC program last night, and everything looks so interesting."

"An absolute riot," I said. "Unfortunately, they get Twitter in England."

"Oh. I guess you saw."

"What happened?"

"It's not as bad as it seems, Gemma. No one pays any attention to those sorts of things. Everyone uses Twitter to complain. We all know that."

"What happened?"

"This bus tour group came in. I don't know why anyone would come on a bus tour to Cape Cod in the winter anyway. They should know better. Probably because it's cheap."

"Ashleigh, get to the point."

"I am. The group consisted of older ladies and gentlemen. One of the women said she loved Benedict Cumberbatch, and one of the men said something not polite about English men."

"And Uncle Arthur happened to be there at the time."

"Yeah. So he made a comment about uncouth colonial upstarts, and the old man reminded him that we'd kicked you people out back in 1776."

"Oh, for heaven's sake."

"It escalated from there. Some of the women took Arthur's side, but another guy started mocking the whole Sherlock Holmes thing, and Arthur said the reason he didn't like it was because he was too stupid to understand it. The woman who liked Benedict laughed and the man got mad at her. Arthur ordered them out of the store. They left after exchanging more insults. The woman who liked Benedict bought a wall calendar."

I was not consoled by news of the sale of one calendar. "Twitter says something about a vicious animal?"

"Yeah. That. Moriarty took a swipe at the arm of the guy who didn't like Sherlock. He didn't draw blood, though. Not that I saw."

"Ashleigh! We're lucky he didn't complain to the town."

"He threatened to, but one of the women said he was a sissy if he went crying to the police about a cat scratch. Don't worry about it, Gemma. I think their bus trip wasn't going very well even before they got to the Emporium."

* * *

We enjoyed a pleasant dinner and avoided any talk of what was keeping us in London. My dad seemed in fine form, laughing with Jayne, talking books with Grant and police with Ryan. Mum smiled and sipped at her glass of wine, but when she glanced at Dad, I could see the shadow of worry behind her eyes. Donald regaled us with the plot of the *Bruce-Partington Plans*, much of which happened not far from where we currently were.

Pippa had not joined us, and Grant tried, and failed, to hide his disappointment.

As we lingered over coffee and dessert, I said, ever so casually, "I want to pay a call tomorrow morning on Arianna."

"Who's Arianna?" Dad said.

"Randy's fiancée. Ex-fiancée. She needs to know about the funeral arrangements." I didn't mention that at my request Pippa had had Arianna placed under unofficial protection, which meant she could be just about anywhere in the country.

"Can't you phone her?" Ryan said.

"That's not something you discuss over the phone."

"Sure it is, if it's someone you arranged to meet only because you thought they might have murdered the deceased."

"I'll go with you," Jayne said.

"Thanks."

"Might as well tag along," Ryan said.

"Not a good idea," I said. "She's likely to be . . . emotionally fragile."

"In which case the presence of a strong young man would come in handy," Donald said, not at all helpfully. "Women like that sort of masculine support, or so I've been told."

I pretended to consider the idea; then I said, with a reluctant shrug, "Probably better if Ryan stays with Dad in case DI Robinson comes back with more questions. Or if Morrison comes to the house. No one saw him hanging around this afternoon, or as we were coming out for dinner?"

"You're the only one who's seen him, dear," Mum said.

"You are such a lousy liar, Gemma," Ryan said, scraping up the last of his Bakewell tart.

I took offense at that. I've always believed I'm an excellent liar.

Chapter Eighteen

I didn't bother to dress up for today's expedition. That I'd been discovered was obvious, so I might as well go as myself.

Mum laid out a breakfast of sliced melon and croissants with jam and butter for us to enjoy in the conservatory, to take advantage of the morning sun, she said. Rain was expected later and would last the rest of the week.

Grant had gone out before the rest of us were even up. "A breakfast date with Pippa before she goes into the office," Mum told me as she sliced the fruit.

"That boy doesn't know what he's getting himself into," Dad chuckled as he put the butter dish onto a tray.

Mom reached up and tousled his hair. "Exactly what happened to me when I met a totally unsuitable young police recruit. I've regretted it ever since." The glow in her eyes put the lie to her words. Dad snatched up a piece of watermelon.

No one in my family is a morning person, so we sat in comfortable silence over our breakfast. Dad read the *Guardian*, Mum the *Times*. Jayne studied a food magazine she'd been handed on the street yesterday, and Donald flipped through his guidebook, in which he'd made so many notes it was easier to see things he wasn't interested in than those he was. Ryan read the news online. I pretended to be doing the same while I decided how best to proceed with my day.

After breakfast, Dad announced he was taking the dog for a walk and asked Ryan to join him. As he did so, he jerked his head in the direction of my mum, indicating he had something private to say to Ryan.

Mum didn't so much as look up from her paper, but she said, "Good idea. If Sam Morrison is hanging about outside, I'd prefer you didn't confront him alone, Henry."

Dad muttered something about "eyes in the back of her head" under his breath. Ryan couldn't say no, although I could tell he wanted to. He'd have preferred to keep an eye on me.

I smiled at them and told them to enjoy their walk. Horace bounded on ahead and stood at the door, tail wagging and tongue lolling, while Dad took the leash off the hook.

With a sudden pang, I missed Violet, my cocker spaniel, so very much.

Mum had taken the dishes to the kitchen, and Jayne ran upstairs to get her purse.

"We'll wait for you outside, Ryan," Dad called, opening the door and being dragged out by Horace.

Ryan and I were left alone in the hallway. "Whatever you're up to, Gemma," he said in a low voice, "please be careful."

"I will." I touched his cheek. Sometimes I thought I didn't deserve this man. He was so incredibly patient with me. He knew I had to do things my way, and he knew that if he asked me to change, I'd say I would. But he also knew that even though I might want to, I couldn't.

I'd not told him I suspected the person who'd shoved me into the traffic yesterday had done it deliberately. Even Ryan would try to stop me from going out on my own if he thought someone intended to do me harm.

"I love you," I said.

He gave me a crooked grin. "And I love you too, Gemma Doyle, but I can't help wondering what brought that up."

"It's not like I don't ever think of it, and I suddenly remembered, *Oh, yes, I love Ryan Ashburton. I'd totally forgotten.*"

"Wouldn't put it past you." He kissed me on the forehead.

"If you see DI Morrison, don't let him and Dad confront each other."

"Probably easier said than done, so let's hope he's gone on to bother other innocent people. I have my phone on me, and I expect to hear from you regularly."

"Will do," I said as Jayne clattered down the stairs and called, "Ready!"

Ryan left, closing the door behind him.

"Did you phone ahead to tell her we're coming?" Jayne asked.

"Phone ahead? No, I want to catch her unawares."

"Is that wise, Gemma? She might not be at home."

"Home? We're not going to anyone's home. I don't even know where she lives."

"Didn't you say we're going to Arianna's to tell her about the funeral for your uncle?"

"Oh. Her. I gave Mum her number. She can call."

"But you said . . ."

"Never mind what I said, Jayne. Arianna had nothing to do with the attack on me yesterday, seeing as to how she was in close protection at the time. I have to assume that whoever the attacker is, they are the person responsible for, or at least involved in, the death of Randy."

"What attack on you? You don't mean when you fell into the road? I thought someone bumped you by accident. That's what you told Ryan."

"What Ryan doesn't know is better for me. I'm pretty sure I was pushed, Jayne. Yes, it could have been a random nutter, someone who doesn't like tall women with curly hair, but I can't afford to assume so. As I haven't offended anyone in London, at least not in the past five years, I can only conclude that someone wants to stop me asking questions about the murder of Randolph Denhaugh."

"Did you tell Inspector Robertson?"

"What would have been the point? She's hardly going to assign a close protection unit to watch over me. Not that I'd want that in any event. That would definitely put a stop to me asking questions. Let's go."

At that moment Donald clattered down the stairs. "Another lovely day in London."

"So it is," I said. "We'll see you later."

"As you're going into town," he said, "I'll come with you." He took his umbrella out of the polished brass stand by the door. At some point yesterday, he'd bought himself a proper English brolly, large and black with a solid wooden handle. He twirled it in the air. All he was missing was the bowler hat. "They say you can never count on the weather remaining fair in England." He opened the door. "Ladies. After you."

He tagged along after us to the Tube station. "What are your plans for the day?" I asked.

"I've no plans," he said. "Other than accompanying you two on your outing."

"Did Ryan put you up to this?"

He blinked rapidly. "Ryan? Why ever would you think that?"

"Which means yes," I said. "Oh all right. Come on." We swiped our Oyster cards to get into the Tube station.

* * *

Gallery Lambert was opening as we arrived. That wasn't by accident, as I remembered their hours of business as posted on the door on my previous visit.

"Whatever happens," I said to my friends, "do not talk. Leave it up to me."

"As I have absolutely no idea what's going on, Gemma, I have nothing to say," Jayne said. "I need to call the bakery. Fiona texted that they're having a problem with one of the suppliers and I need to straighten it out. You go ahead; I'll be in when I'm finished."

"Okay," I said. I held the door open for Donald to go first.

The woman behind the desk looked up at the sound of the bells over the door. She glanced at Donald, and she instantly discarded him, unimpressive in rumpled beige raincoat and thick glasses. Her gaze slid behind him, and the moment she saw me, the artful look of total boredom fled in a flash to be replaced with something approaching shock.

She quickly wiped that expression away and forced out a smile. I've seen more genuine smiles on sharks at the aquarium. She stood slowly, a rippling river of expensive black cloth. "Good morning," she said in her polite Canadian accent. "Mrs. Thornton, isn't it? How nice to see you."

"So nice to see you too, Vivienne. I love your perfume."

She blinked. "My perfume?"

"Such a delightful scent of citrus. It puts me in mind of sitting under an orange tree after an afternoon rainfall in the tropics."

"Uh. Yes."

"Although you might apply a bit too much sometimes, if you don't mind my saying so."

She glanced at Donald. "Will Mr. Thornton be joining us today?"

"Mr. Thornton is temporarily indisposed," I said.

Behind me the door opened and Jayne came in. "Hi," she said.

Vivienne ignored her. "I'll ask Julian to join us."

"No need. I know the way to his office. Donald, Jayne, why don't you two stay here and admire the art. But hands off, this stuff is expensive. Right, Viv?"

"Uh, right."

She snatched up the desk phone as I marched past. Her smartphone and earbuds lay on her desk.

The office door flew open the moment I put my hand on it. Julian leapt back in shock, not expecting to see me so close.

"Hi," I said, in imitation of Jayne. Friendly and American. "Got a minute?" I didn't wait for his answer, but pushed my way past him into the office. "Nice digs you got here, Julian."

"What do you want?" He didn't bother pretending he thought I was a prospective buyer.

"Ten thousand dollars for starters."

The edges of his mouth turned up in a smile. "Unlikely. You can drop the fake accent."

"Fake?" I said in my own voice. "I thought it was rather good."

"It was. Until you dropped it the next street over when you stopped to take off the borrowed shoes."

"Not borrowed, but newly bought. That had been a mistake." I kept my tone light, but inside I was kicking myself furiously. *Half a disguise is none at all*, as Mary Russell said to Sherlock Holmes in *The Game* by Laurie R. King. I'd been in such a rush to get the painful boots off, I'd not waited until I could be sure of being unseen and unheard before returning to my own persona.

"I own the antique furniture shop next door, and we share an internal door." Julian was shorter than I, but he did his best to peer down his long patrician nose at me. "It's the shop at the end of the row with the small window overlooking the side street."

"Convenient."

"It can be." He sat down. "Now that I know you and your husband, if that is who that American gentleman was, do not intend to buy art from me, we have no further business to discuss."

"But we do." I didn't take a seat. "Not the buying and selling of art, but other matters. You sent your assistant, Viv there, to attempt to, as the Americans say, bump me off."

"You're imagining things."

"She wears a distinctive perfume. I noticed it a fraction of a second before I was shoved into St Martin's Place in front of an approaching panel van. You arranged for me to be at the Black Star Gallery at three o'clock, and my working theory is that Viv intended to attack me as we arrived or left the gallery, where, as you know, we were not expected. She must have come early, intending to scope out the surroundings, and spotted me outside St. Martin-in-the-Fields. Fortune favors the brave, and she took her chance. Fortune also occasionally favors the lucky, and my friends were close enough to save me. I was on high alert after that, so she couldn't try again. Am I getting close?"

"No."

"No matter. Since you know I'm an Englishwoman, I want ten thousand pounds, not dollars, not to take my complaint to the police."

He smiled at me as he might an indulged child, stretched his neck, and lifted his chin so he had a good view of the ceiling. "If some disturbed street person, who happens to wear a knock-off perfume similar to that of my assistant, attempted to harm you, that's unfortunate. The police will not be at all interested."

I kept my face impassive, but inside my heart lifted. I'd been right, without even knowing why. Now I did. I'd seen that stretched neck and that tilt of the chin before: on a gentleman dressed in full Victorian evening wear at the reception prior to the Sherlock Holmes conference banquet. At the time, I'd thought it was part of the costume. Turns out it had just been Julian, being the arrogant fool he was, with a mannerism as distinctive as a fingerprint. "Probably not. So I'll need fifty thousand. Pounds again, not dollars, not to tell the cops you murdered Randolph Denhaugh because he tried to back out of your deal to forge an old master."

Not as cool as he thought he was, our Julian Lambert. His right eye began to twitch. His neck tightened even more.

I didn't expect him to break down and tearfully confess everything to me. All I wanted was some admission of guilt, some indication I was right, something I could take to the police so they could start investigating him and his relationship with Randy. Nothing he said to me would be admissible in court, but I needed something, anything, to take to the cops other than my suspicions. Once the police started looking, they'd turn up something, and that would lead to something else, and the whole edifice of art theft and fraud and murder would begin to crumble.

No matter how much of a couple of crooks Julian and Vivienne were, they'd never have tried to kill me because Grant and I made an amateur attempt to pass ourselves off as wealthy, and slightly unscrupulous, collectors. All they had to do was shut the door in our faces next time we dropped by. They could have even threatened us with the police. I assume offering to purchase art with money you don't have is a crime.

That they'd decided they needed to get rid of me, permanently, could only be because they knew I was investigating Randy's murder. I'd wondered how they knew that, and also how they knew I was the one they should go after, not Grant.

And now I knew: I'd told them.

If Julian had overheard Grant and me talking after we left the gallery, he'd have realized I was the one calling the shots, so to speak. Not my pretend-husband. I couldn't remember the entire conversation between Grant and me, but I'd planned to continue poking around and call on Elsie next. I might well have mentioned Randy's name, thus letting Julian know why we were here, pretending to be people we were not. If Julian had been at the banquet, and I was now positive he had been, he might have seen me there. Seen me, yet not immediately recognized me when we first came into his gallery. I'd dressed differently, acted differently, spoken differently. Julian hadn't paid much attention to me, assuming Grant was the one who controlled the purse strings.

"I haven't the slightest idea who you're talking about," he said.

"Sure you do. You and Randy Denhaugh worked together: him forging the paintings, you finding the buyers. You put him up in a nice flat in Canary Wharf . . ."

His eye twitched and his neck tightened still further.

". . . to give him time and a place to forge a Dutch old master. I don't exactly know what went wrong this time, but something did. I suspect he changed his mind about the deal." What had Randy told me he was doing at the convention? *Earning a living.* The words had been spoken in tones of pride. He had, I believed, intended to go straight. That week, anyway.

Obviously, any criminal partners he had would have objected to that.

"I saw you at the Sherlock Holmes convention banquet on Saturday evening," I said. "Nice disguise. You hadn't bought a ticket for the dinner, meaning there's no record you were there, so the police didn't come around to question you."

All the blood drained from his face.

Convenient for him that all a man needed to do was slap on a pair of fake muttonchop whiskers and a bushy beard and pull a top hat low over his eyes, and he wouldn't look at all out of place in nineteenth-century costume.

"You hid in one of the small rooms while Randy was at dinner, and then you texted him or left a voice mail asking him to meet you outside the banquet hall, no doubt using a burner phone. But you had to take his phone after you killed him. You'd given him your name when asking to meet." On that, I was merely speculating. But, if I was even partially right, a panicked man would conclude I knew everything.

"Fifty thousand, and I'll walk away." All I wanted was for Julian to agree and make some sort of arrangement to pay me the money. I could take that to DI Robinson and let her handle the rest.

"I don't think so," came a tinny voice from a small box on the gleaming glass-topped chrome desk.

And I realized I'd made a dreadful mistake.

Julian wasn't the mastermind here.

Vivienne was.

She sat at the front desk, looking haughty and beautiful, and let Julian pretend to be the boss. Meanwhile, they kept an open intercom so she could listen in on what went on in his office. I'd thought the earbuds were feeding her music so she could appear to be even more detached from the boring people who dropped into her gallery. Instead she was listening to everything that was said in his office.

"Come out here, please," she said. "Now. Your friends are admiring our goods, but I don't think they're going to buy. They don't seem to like our prices."

Julian grinned at me. "After you."

I went back through the door into the main gallery. Vivienne was sitting on her desk, her well-muscled stockinged legs crossed, facing Donald and Jayne, who were standing very close together. Jayne's eyes were wide and frightened, and Donald looked simply confused.

Vivien held a small pistol in her perfectly manicured hands, and her right shoe, ballet flats today, dangled casually from her toes.

"That's not necessary, Viv," Julian said. "She was bluffing. She doesn't know anything."

"She knows a heck of a lot," Vivienne said. "I assume you're Henry Doyle's daughter."

"Yes."

"Which means she has the resources to find out a heck of a lot more," Vivienne said. "She can't be allowed to do that."

For a moment I wondered what resources she thought I had. Then I understood: she thought I was Pippa.

"It was never my intention that anyone else be involved," Vivienne said. "Julian should have had the sense to lock the door behind him when he killed Randy. Instead a man walked in. Not just any man, but a retired chief superintendent." She looked at her partner out of the corner of her catlike eyes. "But you're not that smart, are you, Julian?"

He said nothing.

"Julian then compounded his error by hitting the newcomer and running away without checking to be sure he was dead. I couldn't believe my luck when I heard that Henry Doyle couldn't remember what had happened."

"Wouldn't have mattered," Julian mumbled. "No one could identify me in that ridiculous getup."

"The little details always matter," Vivienne said. "Haven't I taught you that, at least?"

I didn't like the way she referred to the potential murder of my father as a little detail.

I also didn't like the smug expression on her face, or the way she held that gun, loose and relaxed, on my friends. She would have been at the reception—unlikely she let Julian do much on his own initiative—but I hadn't seen her there. The room had been very crowded and she was short enough to disappear in the mass of people.

"You can't kill us," I said. "This is your place of business. Everyone in the area can identify you."

"A minor inconvenience. The death of Randy, and thus his inability to finish the commission, means we're out some money, but it had to be done. Julian and I can make ends meet if we have to, can't we, darling? We've tickets for Brazil next week, after we receive the next portion of the down payment. Thanks to your interference, we'll have to advance our plans by a few days."

"Why?" Jayne asked. "If he was making a painting for you, why did you kill him?"

Vivienne gave her a smile so cold I shivered. "I have a contact in the Met who was kind enough to let me know Randy had been chatting to the art fraud division." She shook her head. "Foolish man. I knew him well enough to be confident he wouldn't have told the cops everything they wanted to know up front. He liked to drag things out, play for time to get the best deal he could. And then off he went to that conference to try to sell his ridiculous little sketches."

"I don't understand what's going on here," Donald said. "But I suggest you put that gun away, young lady, before someone gets hurt."

"You do, do you?" she said.

"Yes, I do. Gemma, tell her . . ."

Vivienne's eyes flicked toward me. "Who's Gemma?"

Donald lifted his big black umbrella and slashed it down across Vivienne's extended arm. She yelped and dropped the gun. Donald swung the umbrella again, keeping her at bay, while Jayne ran forward and gave the gun a good solid kick. It skittered across the floor and slid under the desk. Julian yelled, and I jumped at him, intending to knock him to the ground. He swung around and aimed a punch at my face. I saw the blow coming and ducked in the nick of time. His closed fist glanced off my cheek, but it threw me off balance and left me momentarily stunned. Julian moved to hit me again, but Donald yelled, "Gemma!" and ran at the other man, swinging the umbrella. Julian grabbed it and the two men struggled for control. Jayne leapt on Vivienne. If she hadn't been so fond of striking a pose, sitting on the edge of her desk, flashing her legs like a forties-era noir femme fatale, Vivienne wouldn't have made such an easy target. Jayne knocked her backward, but she recovered quickly and rolled to one side. They struggled, but Vivienne was a hardened criminal and Jayne was a West London baker. Vivienne soon got the upper hand and shoved Jayne off her. My friend fell heavily, hitting her head on the floor. Vivienne jumped off the desk and glanced around her, searching frantically for the gun. Her shoe had fallen off when Jayne jumped her. She shoved her foot into it.

Donald had a firm grip on the solid handle of the umbrella, and Julian only had hold of the sharp tip. I kicked out and got Julian hard in the right knee. His grip on the umbrella relaxed enough that Donald regained control and wrenched the umbrella out of Julian's hands. Julian collapsed into a corner, and

Donald stood over him, welding the umbrella as though it was the sword of the elaborately attired eighteenth-century nobleman watching over them from inside his gilt frame.

Vivienne bolted for the street door.

The fog in my head, caused by Julian's blow, cleared. "I've got her!" I yelled. "Donald, stay with him! Jayne, call 911! I mean 999."

I ran outside in time to see Vivienne turning the corner into the side street, the very one in which I'd taken shelter to foolishly divest myself of part of my disguise. I put on a burst of speed and rounded the corner, barely missing a young couple strolling toward me, holding hands and staring dreamily into each other's eyes.

"Sorry," I said. I needn't have bothered. I doubt they even noticed me.

Up ahead, moving fast, Vivienne was heading for the wide plaza surrounding the Tate Modern. The place was crowded with tourists and art lovers. Vivienne shoved her way through the throngs and I followed.

She looked like the type who ran for exercise, whereas I could usually find an excuse, even in winter, to skip the gym. I sprinted after her, aware of running footsteps behind me. I glanced over my shoulder to see Jayne gaining on me. Jayne went to the gym regularly.

"I told you to call for help," I said.

"I did. They're on their way. Where's she think she's going?"

"I doubt she knows. She's running in panic."

Vivienne was heading for the pedestrians-only Millennium Bridge that crosses the Thames River in front of the Tate Modern and Shakespeare's

Globe Theatre. She pushed her way past the walkers and joggers and tourists posing for pictures with expansive views of the city in the background. She knocked a small boy flying and didn't even pause to say sorry.

Jayne and I were hampered because we were not quite so rude. We dodged bikes and wove around the foot traffic, not simply plowing through as Vivienne had.

"Excuse me. Excuse me," I said. "Coming through. Sorry. No need to be so rude, sir."

"What's going on?" someone yelled.

"Nice day for a jog," I replied.

The mother of the small boy Vivienne had knocked out of her way was helping him to his feet. He didn't seem hurt, but his father—a massive brute of a man with shoulders like an American football player—stood firmly in the center of the bridge. "'Oy!" he yelled. "What do you people think you're doing?"

"Make nice," I said to Jayne, as I dodged his imposing bulk.

"I am so sorry," Jayne said, gasping for breath. "That woman snatched my friend's purse and we're trying to get it back."

"Wait here, Marg!" he called. I heard his footsteps fall into step with Jayne's. "Can't 'ave that. Bad for tourism."

Vivienne reached the bottom of the bridge. She ran on. I was getting a bad stitch in my side and the distance between us was lengthening. If she could disappear into the traffic and slip down a side street or into a shop, I'd lose her. I summoned something deep inside me and put on one last burst of energy.

The traffic on Queen Victoria Street was heavy, a steady stream of cars, buses, taxis, and lorries. It was midmorning and we'd emerged from the bridge into the center of the city's financial district.

Vivienne reached the street and momentarily hesitated. She glanced around her, seeing sidewalks packed full with streams of office workers heading for meetings or in search of sustenance. Making up her mind, she ran into the road, after first checking the traffic to her left. All was momentarily clear, so she dashed into the break.

A car hit her, coming from her right.

Vivienne the Canadian had forgotten that in England we drive on the left-hand side of the road.

Chapter Nineteen

I had a strong sense of déjà vu as vehicles screeched to a halt and pedestrians came running from all directions. Vivienne had bounced off the bumper of a two-person Fiat and lay in the road in a crumpled heap. I dropped to my knees beside her. She groaned and looked up at me. I could see no immediate sign of damage; she appeared to be only stunned. Vivienne moved as though to try to stand up. I put my hand on her chest and pressed her back down. She fell with a moan as sirens sounded in the distance.

"Gemma, it's me. Get up. We've got her."

I looked around at the sound of my name, and to my considerable surprise saw Ryan Ashburton holding his hand out to me. I took it and he lifted me to my feet.

"What the heck?" I said. "What are you doing here?"

Two uniformed police officers crouched next to Vivienne. A yellow-and-green ambulance attempted to push its way through the line of stopped cars.

"That woman is to be placed under arrest." Pippa flashed her wallet at a third police officer. He moved toward me.

"Hey!" I said.

Pippa paused for the briefest moment and then said, a touch reluctantly I thought, "Not that one. The one on the ground. Accompany her to the hospital and see that someone remains with her at all times."

"Yes, ma'am," the officer said to her. "Sorry," he said to me.

Grant Thompson stood on the sidelines, watching Pippa with his mouth hanging open. Ryan didn't let go of my arm, but guided me (more like force-marched me) out of the road.

Jayne ran up, followed by the big man.

"That's 'ow we deal with handbag snatchers in England," he said proudly. "The streets of London are once again safe for you Americans. Cheers." He trotted back to join his family.

"Nice work, Jayne," Pippa said.

"Thanks," Jayne said.

"What?" I said.

"Let's get out of the way and let these people do their jobs," Pippa said. "DI Robinson has been called. She'll want to talk to you, Gemma. We'll wait in the boat."

"What boat?"

My sister spun on her heels and walked back the way we'd come, past the buildings lining the walkway to the riverfront. A Metropolitan Police launch, used to patrol the River Thames, was pulled up to the muddy banks next to the Millennium Bridge. People leaned over the bridge railings to watch the activity. Quite a number were taking pictures.

Pippa jumped lightly on board. A handsome officer leapt forward to offer a helping hand to Jayne. Ryan shoved me up, and then he and Grant climbed in. It made for a very crowded craft.

I found a seat on the gunwales. "Okay, is someone going to tell me what's going on? I can't possibly believe you happened to be out for a pleasant cruise and saw that I could use some assistance. Donald! I forgot Donald! He's at the gallery watching over Julian Lambert."

"That's been attended to," Pippa said. "Mr. Lambert is under arrest."

I turned to Jayne, who squirmed uncomfortably under my accusing glare.

"Might as well tell her," Ryan said.

"You told me to call 999 when you ran out of the gallery," Jayne said. "I had a better idea, and I called Pippa."

"Why do you have Pippa's number, and why would you call her rather than the police like any normal person would in such a situation?"

"I didn't need the number," Jayne admitted. "She gave me a burner phone with it programmed in."

"You've been spying on me," I said to my sister.

"Someone has to. And before you get too mad at Jayne, she did take some convincing that I had your best interests at heart."

I thought of the way Pippa had almost let that cop arrest me and said nothing.

"You didn't make a call to the bakery, did you?" I said to Jayne.

"No. I lied about that so I could take the time to tell Pippa where we were."

I mentally kicked myself once again. We'd arrived at the gallery at ten o'clock. Five AM in West London. Far too early for Jayne to be making arrangements with suppliers. I'd been so focused on my mission, I hadn't even noticed. As Vivienne had said, only a few minutes ago, it's the little details that matter.

"And thus," Pippa said, "I was able to organize the launch and have it ready when we needed it. The fastest way to get around London is on the river."

"And you?" I said to Ryan.

"I didn't believe for a minute," he said, "that you were going to talk to some woman about funeral arrangements. Pippa and I had earlier come to an understanding."

"An understanding?"

"That you needed to be watched," Pippa said.

"I wouldn't put it quite like that," Ryan said. "She and I were together, waiting for Jayne's call to tell us where you were."

"And I just happened to tag along," Grant said.

Suddenly, out of nowhere, I was angry. I got to my feet and faced my sister. "You knew everything but you let me put myself, not to mention Donald and Jayne, in danger. Vivienne had a gun. If things had gone slightly differently, she might have killed us all."

"But I didn't know everything," Pippa said calmly. "I didn't, in fact, know anything. Gallery Lambert and Julian Lambert were nowhere on my radar or that of the official investigation into Randy's murder. I still don't know who that woman is we arrested. The thing is, Gemma, I trusted you to find out."

"Oh," I said.

"I told you my office couldn't be involved. My hands were tied." She glanced around. At the police launch, the listening officers, the people watching from the bridge, police cars, ambulances, onlookers on the road, people snapping pictures. "In that, I seem not to have been entirely successful. I fear questions will be asked behind closed doors." Her phone buzzed, and she sighed as she checked the display. "I should get this."

"What sort of doors?" Grant said.

We all turned at a shout. DI Robinson and DS Patel were on the riverbank, thick black mud ruining their shoes. "Is someone going to tell me what's going on here?" Robinson yelled.

A smaller boat, also marked POLICE, pulled up on the other side of us.

Pippa put her phone away. "My ride is here. I'll leave you to it, shall I? Perhaps I'll see everyone later at the house. I'm sure you'll be able to keep my name out of this, Gemma."

"That should be easy," I said, "seeing as to how I didn't need your help."

She smiled and let the officers assist her into the other boat.

Chapter Twenty

Before we were escorted off the police launch, I'd had time for a quick conversation with Ryan. "What about Dad? I'll confess I might have suggested you act as his bodyguard to keep you busy, but I genuinely believe he might be in danger from Sam Morrison, out for revenge."

"Not a problem any longer. Henry got a call this morning, not long after you left, from one of his friends at Scotland Yard. Morrison has decided to take early retirement, effective immediately, with a nice benefit package. He and his wife are leaving this evening to enjoy two weeks in Spain. Apparently his marriage has been on the skids lately because of pressure at work, and he's hoping the news of his retirement, plus the vacation, will mollify her."

That came as an enormous relief. One less complication to worry about.

"I suspect," Ryan said, "your sister mentioned to his superiors that he'd been seen watching your parents' house. They couldn't have that."

DI Robinson hadn't been all that happy with me. I'd solved the case for them, at risk to my own life, and all she could say was she should arrest me for interfering in her investigation.

I spent a long time at the police station, being questioned by DI Robinson and DS Patel, and otherwise cooling my heels. They left me in a nice interview room with a young constable assigned to fetch me copious cups of tea, while they pursued "developments." Many of these developments were conducted in whispers with an assortment of officers in the hallway. I tried to listen in, but they make thick walls and doors in police stations these days.

Finally, I was woken from a light nap in an uncomfortable chair, and told someone would drive me home.

It was very late and the station was quiet. Only one person occupied the hard plastic chairs in the lobby. Ryan Ashburton jumped to his feet when he saw me. A sports magazine fell to the floor. "Good to go?" he said.

"Yes," I said. "Thanks for coming down. Have you been here long?"

"Long as you have." His jaw was covered in dark stubble and his eyes were red with fatigue. He gathered me into his arms and I fell into them gratefully. I closed my eyes and listened for a moment to the steady, reliable, comforting beat of his heart.

The young officer cleared his throat. "Car's waiting outside, sir."

"Lead on," I said.

"I'm to give you this." The officer handed me my phone, which Robinson had temporarily confiscated. I was glad to see it. I'd worried that "temporarily" meant "forever."

We didn't say much as the car drove through the dark, empty streets of central London. I checked my phone. "Only one message," I said to Ryan. "In all that time."

"We all knew where you were," Ryan said. "Who's the message from?"

"Ashleigh at the store." I checked the time. Four AM, eleven PM in West London. "It's too late to call her back. I dread to think what might have happened now."

"Why? I thought you said everything was fine."

"Depends on your definition of fine. The building still stands. Uncle Arthur and Ashleigh are still alive. Last I checked, at any rate."

The house at Stanhope Gardens was shrouded in darkness. A single light burned over the front door.

Not even Horace met us when we came in.

"Tea?" I said.

"If I never have another cup of tea in my life, it will be too soon," Ryan said. "Are you ready for bed?"

"No."

"I'll have a beer then."

We tiptoed through the house to the kitchen. On the way, I let Horace out of the library, where he spent the night. I put the kettle on while Ryan rummaged in the fridge for a beer and some cheese to have with crackers.

When the tea and plate of snacks was ready, we carried a tray into the conservatory, followed by Horace.

I switched on the light, and a deep groan came from the day bed.

"Sorry." I hit the switch again, but it was too late. Pippa, all tousled hair and pillow lines on the pale skin of her face, blinked at us from under a comforter.

"And so she returns," my sister said. "Triumphant."

I didn't feel triumphant. "What are you doing here?"

"In the house? Waiting for you, of course, so we can discuss developments."

"Don't you know everything the police know?"

She snorted and threw off the blanket. Ryan quickly turned away. My sister was dressed in nothing but her bra and knickers. "My boss reprimanded me, strongly, for allowing my office to be involved in a personal matter."

"You have a boss?"

"Of course I have a boss. We all have a boss. Although, I suppose, the head of our country does not. Come to think of it, I suppose you don't either, owning your own business. As for what I'm doing in the conservatory, all the beds in this house have been taken." She rummaged among the pile of clothes on the floor and pulled on her skirt and blouse, both badly wrinkled. "You can look now," she said to Ryan, and he did so, blushing furiously.

We kept our voices low, but my dad was the first to come down, wrapping his terry cloth bathrobe around him. One by one, yawing and stretching, the others joined us.

My mother headed straight for the kitchen to put the kettle on.

"How'd it go?" Jayne looked so adorable in her blue kitten-patterned shorty pajamas, I was glad Jack Templeton wasn't here to see her. "Are they going to give you a medal or something?"

"If anyone deserves a medal," I said, "it's you. Have you ever thought of taking up life as a spy?"

"Now there's an idea," she said.

"Perish the thought," Pippa said. Grant, who'd taken the time to get dressed, sat on the arm of her chair. He smiled at her and she smiled back.

Pippa, I thought, seemed to be doing a lot of smiling lately.

"What happened while I was temporarily detained?" I asked. "Did you learn anything more?"

"Let's wait until everyone's here," Dad said.

At that moment, Mum brought the tea tray in. Donald followed her, carrying a plate of biscuits. I laughed, and Pippa threw me a worried look. "We look like we're in a Noel Coward play," I said.

Mum wore a lavender satin negligee and matching fuzzy slippers, and Donald was in a pair of gray-checked men's pajamas with a buttoned shirt, which looked to have been ironed before he wore them. Who, I wondered, irons their pajamas?

"Henry's memory has come back," Mum said.

"Great!" I said. "What do you remember, Dad?"

"So little, it scarcely matters." He accepted a cup of tea.

"Biscuit, Henry?" Donald said.

"Thanks. I remember leaving the ballroom for a break during the speeches. The bar had closed and the bartenders had left. I took a seat and Randy came up to me. He must have seen me leave the room. He said he wanted to talk, and suggested we go someplace private as the banquet was about to end."

"Do you know what he wanted to talk about?" I asked.

"He didn't say. It wouldn't hurt to hear him out, I thought, away from Anne. I had to go to the men's room first, so I told him that. I needed some time to think about whether I wanted to get into another conversation with Randy. When I finally made up my mind and walked into the room where we'd arranged to meet, I saw a man, dressed in Victorian dinner clothes, and Randy, lying on the floor. I didn't suspect foul play at first. I thought he'd had a heart attack and the man had come in to help. I might have shouted something. The man turned, and grabbed at a lamp on a side table. It was only then I realized that Randy had a rope wrapped around his neck, and the man had not been helping. I reacted too late. Getting old, I fear. My reflexes aren't what they used to be. He must have hit me with the lamp. Next I knew, I was on the floor, beside Randy; I tried to stand, and then you and Pippa were there. Even now that I remember seeing my attacker, I can't identify him. Dark clothes, a hat, lots of whiskers and a beard." He shrugged. "Could have been anyone."

"I feel so bad about Randolph," Mum said. "I hadn't seen him in all those years; we meet again, and he's killed before we can even try to rebuild our relationship."

"If it helps," I said. "I think he was serious about going straight. At the time anyway."

"Oh, yes," Pippa said. "He was."

"What do you know?"

"No more than we all know. Yesterday evening, while you were having tea with DI Robinson, Dad had a visit from his former boss."

"As I was under suspicion for a while," my father said, "naturally enough Greg stayed away. Soon as he got word that Julian and Vivienne had been arrested for Randy's murder, he paid me a visit and told me what was happening. The police went back to the Canary Wharf flat. This time they sent a squad from the art fraud division. They found something interesting almost immediately. Didn't even need all their lab equipment and expensive consultants."

"What did they find?" I asked.

"The painting Randy was presumably working on . . ."

"The one on the easel."

"Right. It wasn't far along. The first layer of one of the background colors, the initial paint for the drapery, was being filled in. He used twenty-first-century paint."

"Do you think he slipped up?" Donald asked.

"I can't believe that," Dad said. "Not someone with his experience. It had to be deliberate. If the painting had been finished, the overlay of period-appropriate paint would fool a knowledgeable collector or dealer on first inspection, but not a detailed study."

"What do you suppose he was up to?" Ryan asked. "Trying to trap whoever had commissioned him, or out to cheat them?"

"His deception wouldn't have remained hidden for long," Pippa said. "It would be discovered soon, perhaps even before he got the final payment for the work. I have to conclude he intended to help the authorities prosecute the art fraud ring."

"I agree," Dad said. "Randy, being Randy, was being cagey. He'd been out of the business for a while, dabbling in his own art."

"Including sketches of Sherlock Holmes?" Jayne said.

"Yes. Two months ago, he moved into a nice flat in Canary Wharf, one owned, incidentally, by a shell company, with everything he needed to create a forgery of a seventeenth-century Dutch masterpiece. The original of the painting is currently hanging in a private collection. The family who owns that painting is in the process of selling off much of their assets in order to raise money for substantial legal bills related to other matters. Randy would have understood that the plan was to replace the real picture with his forgery in time for the auction, and no one would be the wiser.

Except for the people who'd arranged the deal, Julian and Vivienne, and the original owner of the painting, who would get to keep it and pay off his bills as well."

"I've often wondered what sort of person wants to own art they can look at only in the secrecy of some locked room," Grant said.

"Owning such a thing is a power trip in and of itself." Pippa helped herself to a second chocolate biscuit. I don't think I'd ever seen Pippa eat a biscuit before, never mind two.

"Was your office aware of this art theft ring?" I asked.

She raised one perfectly formed eyebrow. "Petty theft? I hardly think it would be worth our time."

"Randy went to the art forgery division of Scotland Yard," Dad said. "Do you remember asking me to find out what I could about that, Gemma?"

"I do now. I forgot to ask if you learned anything."

"I asked a few questions, but got nowhere, so didn't bring it up with you. Tonight, Greg came by and told me. Randy offered to tell the police where and when he was going to deliver the finished product. The incorrect layer of paint was intended as a backup clue in case something went wrong. He was, as I said, as cagey as ever."

"Too cagey for his own good," Mum said.

"Yup," Dad said. "The police didn't know what painting they were after, or who else was involved."

"Julian and Vivienne were the ones behind the plan," I said. "They had a customer who needed money fast and at the same time wanted to keep his masterpiece. They arranged for Randy to make an imitation, and set him up in a place where he could paint in comfort. Then they'd sell his to the owner of the original, who'd then sell the fake as the genuine item."

"I can't imagine several months of Randolph's work, never mind his living expenses, came cheap," Mum said. "And then the fees of the dealer and the auction house on top of it. Is this painting worth that much?"

"The auctioneers were planning on opening the bidding at fifty million pounds," Dad said.

"Goodness," Mum said.

"Julian and Vivienne must have guessed he was up to something," Jayne said.

"Randy took time away from the project to make his own art and sell it at the conference," Pippa said. "That in itself would have worried them."

"Under the name Veronica Raymond," Dad said, "the woman Gemma met as Vivienne from the art gallery has come to the attention of police in Toronto and New York. She disappeared from North America two years ago. She had some minor plastic surgery done, enough to keep her unrecognizable from CCTV footage. No one knew where she was until you, Gemma, had her on the run."

"If the police knew Randy was involved in art fraud and theft," I said, "why didn't they go after his associates in that world for his killing? Why on earth concentrate on you?"

"Sam Morrison was handed the investigation when the 999 call came in. He suffers from a serious case of single-mindedness."

"It was also, I suspect," Ryan said, "a situation of silos. The art fraud division didn't speak to homicide and vice versa."

"Sadly," Dad said, "that still happens."

"Happens everywhere," Ryan said.

"Art fraud did take a look at it," Dad said. "But they didn't know who Randy's business partners were. As I said, he was cagey."

"What do you suppose they were doing at the reception?" Mum asked. "Surely it was not a coincidence that they were Holmes fans?"

"Julian and Viv didn't have tickets for the banquet," I said. "When they found out Randy was talking to the police—"

"You can be sure the Met is working hard on finding that leak," Dad said.

"They would have known they had to act quickly," I said. "Vivienne said something about Randy and what she called his ridiculous little sketches, which leads me to think Randy enjoyed making them wait for him to finish the painting. He told them about the conference. They knew where he'd be Saturday night, so they decided to get rid of him then and there. It wasn't a bad plan. Julian wore a disguise so complete, about which no one would ask any questions, he wouldn't be identified by CCTV cameras or witnesses. If Dad hadn't walked in when he did . . ."

"Can all this be proven," Ryan asked, "in a court of law?"

"Greg told me Julian and Vivienne can't incriminate each other fast enough," Dad said. "Vivienne was the mastermind, so to speak, and art fraud will be spending a lot of time searching her business accounts and records of every painting that's passed through her hands."

"But Julian killed a man," I said. "A lot more serious charge than theft, even at the multi-million-pound level."

"He claims," Dad said, "he only wanted to talk to Randy, but things got out of control. Besides, Vivienne made him do it. She claims they came to the reception to talk to Randy, to tell him they were concerned that he was falling behind schedule, and Julian killed him totally on his own initiative. Regardless of whose idea it was, Julian came to a party with a length of rope in his pocket, and that will ensure he's charged with intent." He stretched and Horace leapt to his feet. "Let the lawyers sort it out. As I'm up so early, might as well take the dog for a walk."

I yawned, and my mother said, "To bed with you, young lady. I haven't forgotten you haven't slept."

"I dozed at the police station," I said.

"And we can only assume that's really comfortable." Jayne stood up and began collecting used teacups.

"Just what I need," I said. "Two mothers."

"What I need," Ryan said, "is a cup of coffee. But first, I'll come with you, Henry."

"You haven't slept either," I said.

"No, but I'm wanting to hear the details of how the police will proceed with this investigation."

"Breakfast will be ready when you get back," Mum said.

"I'll help Gemma, get myself dressed, and then give you a hand," Jayne said.

"I can take myself to bed," I said.

"No, you can't," Jayne said.

* * *

I started awake as a weight settled on the bed beside me. Soft lips caressed my cheek.

"Ummm." I rolled over. Ryan's lovely blue eyes stared deeply into mine. I reached for him.

He leapt off the bed. "I was sent to get you. We have company."

"What time is it?"

"Five after nine."

I rolled back over. "Tell DI Robinson I'm deathly ill and more questions will push me over the edge."

"It's not Robinson, and our visitor is insisting you'll want to be there." He pulled the covers off me. "Be downstairs in five minutes."

Grumbling, I got up and staggered into the bathroom.

Once again like the cast of a Noel Coward play, the family gathered in the library. Everyone was dressed, and they had that wide-awake, sparkly look that meant they'd had adequate cups of tea or coffee and a hearty English breakfast. Even Ryan looked like a man ready to dive eagerly into another day. He was a detective, and used to getting out of bed at all hours and going days without sleep.

Whereas I was a bookstore owner, accustomed to a good night's sleep every night, followed by enjoying several cups of tea before so much as thinking about coming alive. I rubbed at my head, trying to flatten some of the curls.

The family and houseguests had been joined in the library by the visitor. Sir John Saint-Jean stood as I entered. "Congratulations," he said. "I hear you singlehandedly brought down an entire network of art thieves."

"If you want to put it like that," I said modestly.

"I do," he said.

"I don't," Pippa said. She'd changed out of the clothes she'd thrown onto the conservatory floor and also looked rested and refreshed. "I'd only just arrived in the office this morning when I got a call from Sir John. He said he had something to tell us and wanted you and me to be here." She turned to our visitor. "We're here. What's so important?"

The doorbell rang.

"You might want to answer that," he said.

Pippa and I exchanged a look. I hadn't seen Sir John make a single move, but he'd summoned someone to the door at exactly the right moment.

Dad, followed as always by Horace, left the library. They were back a moment later with David, Sir John's butler. David carried a large parcel, about three feet square and two inches thick, wrapped in heavy brown paper tied with string.

It could only be a painting.

"If you don't mind, Mrs. Doyle," Sir John said. "I'll rearrange a few things." He moved photos and knick-knacks off the mantel above the fireplace, and when he'd cleared a space said, "Put it here please, David."

David propped the parcel on the mantel and stepped back.

Sir John ripped the paper away with an excessively dramatic flourish.

Mum gasped and her hands flew to her mouth.

"Well, I never," Dad said.

"Wow!" I said.

"Where did you find it?" Pippa asked.

"Is that what I think it is?" Grant said.

"What is it?" Jayne and Donald asked.

I'd never seen this particular painting before, but I'd seen many by the artist. His style was unmistakable. Sir John Constable, one of England's most renowned landscape painters. This was a small work. Small but perfect.

My mother dropped into a chair. She began to cry. My father's mouth hung open. For perhaps the first time in their lives, they did not offer tea to a morning visitor.

"Is this my grandparents' Constable?" Pippa asked. "The one stolen by Randolph more than thirty years ago?"

"It is," Dad said.

"I'm pleased to be able to return it to you." Sir John's eyes sparkled.

"It's been gone for a long time," Pippa said. "How did you find it?"

"As I told Gemma, I've been trying to find the painting your uncle cheated me out of." He explained to the others what he'd told Grant and me. "In the course of that search, combined with some small tasks I've been able to perform for Her Majesty's government over the years, I've made valuable contacts in the international world of art theft."

"And you just happened to trip upon my family's Constable?" Pippa said.

"Not exactly. I got a letter in the post the Monday after the Sherlock Holmes conference banquet."

"I'll bite," Pippa said. "What sort of letter?"

"From Randolph Denhaugh. He said he knew I was wanting to talk to him, but he'd rather not talk to me. He apologized for any . . . unpleasantness . . . between us. He wanted, so the letter said, to make amends, but unfortunately my painting had disappeared into the abyss that is the shadier parts of the art world and he didn't know where it ended up. He'd seen me lurking about—his words, not mine—at the Holmes conference on Friday. He wanted to make amends to his family and thought I'd be the best person to find the work he'd stolen from his parents all those years ago."

No one said anything for a long time as we simply stared at the beautiful work of art.

"Why didn't he tell us where to find it?" Pippa said.

Sir John cracked his knuckles. "I've made some contacts over the years you might not want to be seen associating with, Ms. Doyle. The present, now previous, owners of this painting professed to be shocked, shocked, to hear it had been stolen."

"You didn't believe them?" Ryan asked.

"Not for a moment. If they, who do not reside in Britain by the way, had been innocent, I would have merely reported the location of the painting to the proper authorities, and let you sort it out in court. Instead, I convinced them to place it in my care."

"You threatened them," Pippa said.

Sir John raised one eyebrow and David coughed discreetly.

"Why didn't you tell me this when we met at your house?" I said.

"Because I didn't have the painting. I was conducting negotiations and not yet fully confident of a successful outcome. I landed at Heathrow not much more than an hour ago, and came directly here."

"This is simply astounding," my mother said. "I don't know how I can thank you enough. I only wish my parents had lived to see it one more time." Dad had gone to stand by her, and he laid his hand on her shoulder.

"I simply followed your brother's directions, Mrs. Doyle. You have him to thank."

Mum wept some more.

"Will you stay for tea, Sir John?" Pippa asked.

"Thank you, but no. I had a long flight."

Pippa and I walked Sir John and David to the door. "You've made my mother very happy," I said.

"I'll be in my office later this afternoon," Pippa said. "Please pay me a visit. I'm looking forward to a chat about where you were yesterday."

"I didn't go to the Hermit Kingdom," he said.

"No. But your sources had been there."

He turned to me. "I'm thinking of vacationing in America this summer. I'd love to visit your shop and pay a call on Arthur."

"You'd be very welcome."

"Good day," Sir John said. David touched the brim of his hat.

"The Hermit Kingdom?" I said to Pippa when the visitors had gone. "You mean our painting has been in North Korea all these years?"

"If not in that country, then in the private rooms of an embassy somewhere."

"And Sir John's been . . ."

She tapped the side of her nose. "Need to know, Gemma. You do not need to know. I have to go to back to work, but I'd like one more peek at it before I leave." She linked her arm through mine. "Shall we join the others?"

Chapter
Twenty-One

We were able to rebook our flights to Boston for Friday evening.

"I cannot wait to get home." Jayne punched SEND on the airline's website to finalize the bookings. "This vacation stuff is exhausting. Sure you don't want to come into the city with us?"

"No thanks." I shut the cover on the iPad.

Jayne, Donald, and Grant planned to visit the Mithraeum, the temple to the Roman god Mithras, which recently opened in the basement of an office building in central London. After that, they were going to the Museum of London and on a tour of Roman London. Donald, it turned out, was almost as much an enthusiast of ancient Rome as he was of Sherlock Holmes.

I hadn't heard from Ashleigh again, and I was dreading what I would hear when it was daytime in West London and I could return her call. Hopefully, Uncle Arthur's cigarette-wielding friend hadn't returned to finish the job, and no more *New York Times* best-selling authors had blacklisted us. I'd cautiously checked Twitter and the website of the *West London Star* and had been relieved to find no news of the Emporium or Mrs. Hudson's Tea Room. I wasn't going on the group outing. I'd seen the Roman stuff many times before, and although the Mithraeum sounded interesting, I needed some serious downtime.

By downtime, I meant Ryan-time. Once we'd waved the others out the door, Dad and Horace had escaped to his workshop, and Mum was in the library staring at the Constable, Ryan and I headed out.

We walked slowly through the streets of Kensington, holding hands, peering into shop windows, talking about our friends and our lives. We found a little French bistro on Cromwell Road and took a table at a back corner.

"I'll have to come to London for Julian and Vivienne's trials," I said. "I've no idea when that will be. I hope not in the summer when we're so busy."

"I'll try to get some time off," he said, "and come with you."

I reached out and touched his hand where it lay on the table. "That would be nice, but I have the feeling you don't want another vacation in London."

"I do if I'm with you," he said. "When we come again, and assuming we can get some time alone, what would you like to show me in London?"

"Not the Sherlock Holmes Museum?"

He pretended to shudder. Or maybe it wasn't a pretense. "Anything but that. What's your favorite place?"

"There's so much I love, but if I had to pick a favorite, it would probably be the sculpture hall in the Victoria and Albert."

"That's just down the road from here."

"Yes, it is."

He threw money on the table. "Let's go. I want you to show it to me. I want you to tell me why you love it."

"I'd like that. I'd also like to tell you that I love you."

He held out a hand and lifted me to my feet.

* * *

"See that piece hanging from the ceiling?" I said as we entered the center rotunda.

"It's amazing." Ryan threw his head back to get a good look. And it was amazing, blue and green glass formed into enormous balls and twisting tendrils.

"Do you remember the pieces stolen from Rebecca Stanton's house the day Jayne and I catered the fundraising tea for the theater festival?" I asked.

"How can I ever forget?"

"Same artist," I said. "Dale Chihuly."

Ryan looked around, at the soaring arches, the marble pillars, the ancient gilt statues on the second-floor veranda. "It doesn't seem to fit in here," he said. "It's so modern."

"I think it does. Art's not static, nor should it be frozen in time. They had to reinforce the ceiling for this piece."

Ryan and I spent hours in the V&A. I was delighted that he seemed to be enjoying it as much as I always did. At one point, I left him having a coffee in the café and slipped outside to stand on the steps and phone the Emporium. To my enormous relief, Ashleigh said she'd called me yesterday just to check in, and that everything was going great in my absence. They didn't miss me one bit.

I didn't know how I felt about that, but I said, "Glad to hear it."

"Arthur has some grand scheme in mind," she said.

"Not glad to hear that," I said. "What is it?"

"He won't say. Except that it's going to be the talk of West London this summer."

"I'll be in the shop first thing Saturday," I said. "I'll put a stop to it. Whatever it is."

"Maybe you should give him a chance, Gemma. I think he feels bad about what happened with Mrs. O'Reilly."

"Who's Mrs. O'Reilly?"

"Cigarette lady."

"Oh, yes. Her."

"He's sorry about offending those customers from the bus tour. I think he's sorry, anyway. What he actually says is that if they didn't want him to insult them, they shouldn't have insulted him first."

"That's not the way customer service works," I said.

"This big idea is a way of making up to you. You should be nice about it, Gemma."

"I'll try," I said.

*　*　*

After the museum, Ryan and I went for a drink in a pub before walking back to Stanhope Gardens. I hadn't heard anything about dinner plans, so I assumed we'd be going out again.

Instead, on the way back from their expedition, Jayne had stopped at a supermarket. She and Mum were in the kitchen, chatting while they chopped and mixed and simmered and sautéed, sipped wine and laughed together.

The others, including Pippa, had gathered in the library. My father poured me a glass of wine and handed Ryan a beer. Pippa and Grant each had a whiskey.

"Would you like to see what I bought today, Gemma?" Donald asked. His big brown briefcase was tucked under his chair.

"Sure."

He opened it, brought out a stack of papers, and handed them to me.

I flicked quickly through them. "These are Randy's drawings. Where did you get them?"

"From his partner," Donald said.

"His what?"

"Jayne told us Elsie Saunders had some of Randy's sketches," Grant explained. "Donald insisted on going around to her place and buying them."

"You do know she stole them, Donald? After the man was dead?"

He grinned at me. "Ms. Saunders and I came to an arrangement, facilitated by Jayne. I made the check out to a charity that works with the homeless in Whitechapel and gave Ms. Saunders twenty pounds for her trouble."

"She agreed to that?"

"Better than seeing the sketches in a police evidence locker until Julian and Vivienne come to trial," Grant said. "Which was her other option."

"I wouldn't have approved," my father said. "They *should* be in the evidence locker."

"The police have others," Donald said.

"Which," my father said, "is the only reason I don't report you."

"I don't suppose I'll ever see my umbrella again," Donald said.

"Probably not," Dad said. "There are items in the cellars beneath Scotland Yard that haven't been seen since the force was founded."

"An exaggeration, Dad," Pippa said.

"Elsie gave us something else," Grant said. "Show them, Donald."

Out came another folder from Donald's briefcase. Grinning, he opened it and held up the contents. A series of photographs of a Dutch old master. A stout woman, unsmiling, dressed all in black. The photographs had been taken close up, showing the details of her lace collar, the fine stitching of the handkerchief in her hand, the section of garden outside the window over her right shoulder.

"That looks like the painting I saw in Randy's apartment," I said. "I was wondering what he was working from."

"Elsie simply grabbed a folder off his table in the dealers' room and stuffed as many of his sketches as she could grab into it," Jayne said. "She assumed he was studying art techniques and was going to throw these out. She put the sketches for Donald into the same folder, not realizing the significance."

My father held out his hand. "Those I *will* take as evidence."

"Randy would be pleased," I said, "to know his sketches have gone to a good home."

"As long as we're talking about the women in Randy's life," Pippa said. "Arianna Nowacki has gone to visit her parents in Poland. I agreed it was probably wise for her to leave England."

"It wasn't Julian and Vivienne who threatened her?"

"No. Our uncle Randolph might have tried to make amends at the end of his life," Pippa said. "But he'd made too many enemies over the years. People you've cheated don't forgive and forget just because you say you're sorry."

"Well, they should," Donald said.

Mum came into the library to call us in to dinner.

* * *

We didn't linger long over after-dinner liqueurs. Ryan, who hadn't slept at all last night, almost fell asleep face first in his sticky toffee pudding. Jayne and Donald went up soon after, knowing we'd have a long day tomorrow. Mum excused herself, and Dad said he was going to take Horace out and then turn in.

Pippa, Grant, and I were left in the dining room with the bottle of Courvoisier.

"Nothing more for me, thanks." I started to stand. "I'm going to bed too."

"Have a drink, Gemma," Pippa said. "Just a small one."

I eyed her. I eyed Grant.

They were pointedly not looking at each other. Grant's hand shook ever so slightly as he poured my drink. Pippa studied the painting hanging on the wall over my head.

"Congratulations," I said. "Can I be a bridesmaid?"

"What?" Grant said.

"We're not getting married, Gemma," Pippa said.

"Oh. Sorry." I ducked my head in embarrassment. I'm not often wrong about things like that.

"But," Pippa said, "Grant does have news, don't you, Grant?"

He smiled at her. She smiled at him.

"I'm coming back to London," he said. "Permanently, I mean. To be with Pippa. I'm only renting my house on Cape Cod, so I don't have to worry about that, and I can move my book dealer business to England. If

I still have a business, considering I never did get around to making all the deals on this trip I planned on."

"We're not getting married, Gemma," Pippa said, "but we want to be together. We're going to take things slowly. I'm probably not the easiest person to be in a relationship with. My job's important to me."

"We'll work it out." Grant said. "I understand about your job."

I doubted he did. Pippa got calls in the middle of the night or in the middle of a sold-out play. She'd once been called away from the funeral of a close family friend. She worked so many hours I sometimes wondered why she bothered to keep a flat. I glanced between my sister and my friend, both of them almost glowing with the joy of being in love. Maybe they would work it out. I jumped to my feet. "I'm happy for you both." I hugged Grant. "I'll miss you so much."

"I'll miss you too," he said. "I'll miss the Cape, but I love London. And I love Phillipa Doyle."

Pippa beamed. I hugged her and she hugged me back. Her thin frame felt strange in my arms. I couldn't remember the last time my sister and I hugged.

When we separated, I failed to smother a gigantic yawn. "On that happy note, I'll again say good night."

"One thing before you go," Pippa said. "If you don't mind. Grant, can you give Gemma and me a moment, please."

"Sure," he said. "I'll see if there's any more coffee in the pot."

He left and I sat back down. "What?"

Pippa's face had settled into a serious expression, and I knew she didn't want to talk about wedding plans or the practical details of setting up housekeeping with Grant. "I've been instructed to offer you a job."

"A job? What job?"

"A government job. They want to hire you."

"To do what?"

She said nothing.

"This is unexpected."

"Your dogged determination to find Uncle Randolph's killer and to clear our father, as well as your well-thought-out deductions and attention to detail, caught the attention of powers-that-be."

I decided not to point out that if not for Donald and his black umbrella, my failure to notice the detail that Vivienne was in charge at the art gallery, not Julian, might have gotten us all killed.

"No," I said.

"If you need time to think about it . . ."

"I don't. You might think my life seems small, unimportant in the grand scheme of things, and I suppose it is. But I love owning that silly little shop. I love living on Cape Cod and in the saltbox house I share with Uncle Arthur. I love Jayne and the working relationship we have. But most of all, I love Ryan. We have our problems, to be sure, but I can't imagine leaving him. In short, Pippa, I love the life I've created for myself in West London."

"You're a lucky woman, Gemma," she said.

"I know I am," I said.

"Can I come in?" Grant called from the doorway. "I found more sticky toffee pudding."

Chapter Twenty-Two

"**I**'m back!" I unlocked the sliding door between the Sherlock Holmes Bookshop and Emporium and Mrs. Hudson's Tea Room, balancing a takeout mug of tea and a paper bag containing a blueberry muffin.

Moriarty met me at the door. He threw me a poisonous glance, hissed once, and then turned around and marched to his bed under the center table, tail held high, hips swinging.

"I've missed you, too," I said.

Jayne had headed in to work the moment we arrived in town, but I'd gone home, unpacked, taken Violet for a short walk, and had a shower, ready to get to the store in time for opening.

I hadn't seen Uncle Arthur yet. His 1977 Triumph Spitfire had been in the garage and his coat and winter boots in the mudroom, the boots standing in a puddle of melted snow, so I'd assumed he was upstairs in his own apartment. Probably enjoying the lie-in, as he hadn't had to get up to come in to work today. I was looking forward to telling him all about my trip.

I'd told Ashleigh I'd open the shop today and we'd return to the regular schedule, so I was surprised to see her burst through the front door at one minute after ten.

She was dressed in a calf-length black wool winter coat with the collar turned up and a dark gray scarf, her hair arranged in a mass of dark curls. "I couldn't stay away a moment longer," she said. "I'm so excited, I came in early. I won't even charge you for the extra time." She made no move to take off the coat. Ashleigh dressed according to her mood. I couldn't think of what her mood might be today, other than cold. And it was, if anything, too warm in the building this morning.

"Excited about what?" I asked.

"Don't pretend to be so cool, Gemma. I'm excited about Arthur's special guest, of course. Even you have to be over the moon."

"Perhaps I would be, if I knew what you're talking about."

"He didn't tell you?"

"No."

"Oh. Sorry. I'd better not say. He'll want to tell you himself."

"You can't not tell me now. What?"

"Arthur's been saving this for the right time, Gemma. He thinks you're mad at him. He'll never say so, but he's afraid you think he isn't a help in the store anymore."

"But he is a help. Didn't you say you'd been busy when he was in? They said that in the Tea Room also."

"You need to tell him, Gemma."

"I suppose I do. What's this news?"

"Okay, but you have to pretend to be surprised when he tells you." She took a deep breath. "He has some good friends who have a son who's an actor. Arthur knew the son when he was growing up, and he was sorta like an uncle to the kids."

"I get it," I said. "This actor is on British TV sometimes. If he's been a guest on *Sherlock* or in one of the

Holmes movies, it would be nice to have him visit. Aren't you going to take off that coat? You must be hot. I like what you did with your hair."

"I'm not finished. Anyway, Arthur once asked the son if he'd come to the store sometime. He hasn't been able to because he's been so busy. He's going to be making a movie in New York in June, and he's agreed to come for a visit to West London! To the Emporium! To us!" Ashleigh twirled around.

The long black coat. The scarf. The mop of curly dark hair.

"You don't mean . . ." I said.

"Benedict Cumberbatch is coming here!"

I sat down. Fortunately a chair was at hand.

I took in every detail of the shop, the shelves lined with books, the merchandise table piled high, the scent of pastries, bread dough and coffee wafting in from the tearoom next door along with the happy chatter of patrons. Moriarty peering malevolently at me from under the center table.

As I'd said to my sister, I love owning this silly little store. Never a dull moment.

"Let's get to work, shall we," I said to Ashleigh. "Those books aren't going to sell themselves."

Acknowledgments

Thanks to Alex Delany, with whom I had great fun exploring London and scouting out locations for this book. Also to Cheryl Freedman, who provided many helpful suggestions.

To Kevin Thornton, always a fun guy, for letting me play with his name. As far as I know, no one in his family is connected to the underground art word! But I wouldn't be surprised.

Read an excerpt from

A CURIOUS INCIDENT

the next

SHERLOCK HOLMES BOOKSHOP MYSTERY

by VICKI DELANY

available soon in hardcover from
Crooked Lane Books

NEW YORK

Chapter One

"I am not a consulting detective."

"Can't you at least say you'll try and help her?"

"That would be unfair to her, Jayne. I can't give the girl false hopes."

"I suppose you're right. Poor thing. I wish there was something we could do."

I glanced across the room. The little girl was perched on the stool behind the sales counter, watching us, all wide eyes, knees and elbows, long sun-kissed golden hair, and hope.

Hope that I was about to crush.

I sighed, pasted on a smile that no doubt looked as fake as it felt, and walked across the shop floor toward her, feeling perfectly terrible.

She blinked rapidly, fighting back tears.

"All I can do, Lauren," I said, "is keep my eyes open. You'll do that too, won't you, Jayne?"

"Absolutely," Jayne said.

"We'll tell all our friends to be on the lookout. Maybe you and your mum can put more posters up around town?" I'd seen plenty of those signs over the last two days. One hung in my own shop window, another in the window of Mrs. Hudson's, the tearoom next door.

"But," Lauren said, her lower lip trembling, "she's been gone for two whole days! Aunt Irene said you make it your business to know what others do not. She said you can find out things no one else can. She said you're better than the police. She said . . ."

Mentally, I cursed Irene Talbot. I might have once or twice attempted to help the West London police in the performance of their duties—okay, I solved their cases for them—but they would have arrived at it eventually. I think.

Locating a missing house cat is far out of my area of expertise.

I'm Gemma Doyle, and I'm part-owner, manager, and general dogsbody of the Sherlock Holmes Bookshop and Emporium, located at 222 Baker Street in West London, Massachusetts, and all I want is to be a shop owner. Not a consulting detective.

My assistant, Ashleigh, stood behind the girl, making frantic gestures at me. I ignored her. I would not promise to find the blasted cat, because I couldn't. Jayne, still dressed in a hairnet and apron, touched Lauren lightly on the arm in a gesture of support. When Lauren had asked if she could meet me, Jayne Wilson had come out of the kitchen of the tearoom next door to bring her to my shop.

My own cat, Moriarty, was curled up in Lauren's arms. He glared at me, no doubt also telling me to get out there and solve the case. I briefly considered offering Moriarty to Lauren as a replacement for her missing pet.

Moriarty and I weren't exactly the best of friends. He was a good shop cat and generally got on well with our patrons, many of whom adored him. But, for some unknown reason, he disliked me intensely, and he never missed an opportunity to let me know precisely what he thought of me.

If I sent Moriarty to a new home, he'd find his way back here, just to spite me.

And the poor child would have lost another cat.

"I can pay you," Lauren said. "Out of my allowance. What do you charge?"

"It's not that," I said. "I'm sorry, but I need to be completely honest with you. I can't do anything to help you."

Moriarty, Ashleigh, Jayne, and Lauren all looked at me as though I'd promised them a visit from Benedict Cumberbatch and instead sent Great-Uncle Arthur wearing a curly wig.

"That's okay." Lauren put Moriarty on the counter and gave him a sad pat. She hopped off the stool. "I understand," she said bravely. "I'll go now. Mom will be finished with her lunch soon."

"Why don't you give Gemma your phone number and address," Ashleigh said. "She can call you if she has any ideas."

I threw Ashleigh a poisonous look, which she pretended not to see.

Lauren rattled off a number and an address not far from my own house.

"I'll take you back to your mom," Jayne said. "Come on." She put her arm around Lauren's thin shoulders, and together they walked through the sliding door into the tearoom. Jayne turned her head and gave me a glare of disapproval.

"I am not a consulting detective!" I called after them.

Moriarty turned his back on me, lifted his tail high, and leapt off the counter. He stalked across the room, as disapproving as Jayne.

"Why I am feeling guilty?" I said to Ashleigh. "Why does everyone think I can find the cat? The next time I see Irene Talbot, I'm going to kill her."

"Poor little thing," Ashleigh said. "She really is upset."

I sighed. "Yeah, I know."

"I don't think Irene actually told her to ask you to help find Snowball . . ."

"Is that the cat's name? Not very original."

"The girl's eleven years old, Gemma. Originality isn't a strength at that age."

"I suppose not. Is the cat white?"

"Didn't you look at the poster in the window?"

"I might have glanced at it. As I have no interest in lost cats"—I threw a look at Moriarty, who was pretending to ignore me—"I didn't pay much attention."

The missing-cat poster was stuck to the window next to one we'd put up yesterday when a couple of women from the West London Garden Club asked if we'd help spread the word about their annual garden tour.

"I thought you noticed everything." Ashleigh always dressed to suit whatever mood she was in that morning or what was currently on her mind. Today, no doubt inspired by the garden club visit, she wore a floppy straw hat with a wide ribbon around the brim, a pair of baggy trousers tucked into yellow-and-purple rubber boots, and a T-shirt that proclaimed "Gardening is Life!" among a plethora of flowers.

"Not everything," I said. "And never info about missing cats. Or about garden clubs either, as I have no interest in gardening."

"Sounds like Irene's been spinning stories about how her good friend Gemma Doyle is smarter than the police, and when Lauren and her mom came in for lunch and Lauren found out that you work right next door, she decided to talk to you. Smart kid, I'd say."

"I liked her," I said. "I'd help her if I could, Ashleigh, but I never make promises I can't keep."

The chimes over the door tinkled. Two women came into the store, and Ashleigh and I went back to work. Moriarty did not. His job is to greet customers, but apparently he'd gone on strike today. He stayed in his bed under the big center table all afternoon, bristling with disapproval.

It was late June and the start of the summer tourist season on Cape Cod. We were busy most of the day as a steady stream of customers came into the shop. Whenever I glanced next door at 220 Baker Street, I could see a lineup at the counter for takeout, as well as people waiting patiently for tables for afternoon tea, Mrs. Hudson's specialty.

Every day at precisely 3:40, Jayne and I have our daily business partners' meeting in the tearoom. We sip tea, eat whatever remains of the day's baking, and chat. Occasionally we might even talk about the businesses. Great-Uncle Arthur and I own the Emporium, and we're half partners with Jayne in the tearoom. I run the bookshop, and Jayne's the manager and head baker at Mrs. Hudson's. The tearoom, of course, is named in honor of Sherlock Holmes's long-suffering landlady.

Our shop is dedicated, as the name indicates, to all things Sherlock: the original stories, contemporary pastiche and short-story collections, other books by Sir Arthur Conan Doyle, nonfiction relating to the author's life and times, and works of fiction set in Holmes's time frame, sometimes called the Gaslight Era. We also stock merchandise related to the Great

Detective, of which there is a substantial amount. Earlier this year, Great-Uncle Arthur received an award from an English Holmes society for helping to spread word of the Great Detective in North America. The award, an ugly glass statue, currently stands on a top shelf above the sales counter, next to the framed reproduction cover of *Beeton's Christmas Annual*, dated December 1887, in which "A Scandal in Scarlet," the first Holmes story, appeared.

Today at three thirty, the shop was comfortably busy. "I'm going to skip the partners' meeting with Jayne," I told Ashleigh.

"Alert the press," she said.

"If I did that, Irene would assume I was embarking on a case." Irene is a reporter at the *West London Star*. "I have to get home and pay some attention to Violet," I said, referring to my cocker spaniel. She's technically Great-Uncle Arthur's dog, but he travels a great deal, and most of the dog-ownership responsibility has fallen to me. I don't mind. I love Violet, and—unlike my cat—she loves me in return. Our neighbor Mrs. Ramsbatten, who pops in to give Violet a walk when Uncle Arthur's away, had gone out of town for a few days, and it wasn't fair to Violet to leave her locked up in the house all day.

"Why don't you bring her to work with you?" Ashleigh said. "She's a well-behaved dog."

Moriarty had finally emerged from his bed and was making his way across the shop floor. He leapt straight into the air, hissing and spitting.

"That's why," I said. "Back soon."

I went into the tearoom and asked Fiona, one of the waitresses, to tell Jayne that something had come up and I was going out.

"You should have said you'd help that little girl find her cat," Fiona said.

"Does everyone in West London know my business?"

"Pretty much," she replied.

I walked briskly down Baker Street toward the harbor. The town of West London is situated in the Lower Cape area of Cape Cod, nestled between the Atlantic Ocean and Nantucket Sound. It was a perfect summer's day and the tourists were out in force, popping in and out of stores, lining up for lattes at coffee shops, or enjoying cool drinks on restaurant patios. On Harbor Road they shopped for or munched on fresh fish, watched seals play in the cool waters under the pier, or explored the grounds of the historic lighthouse. The ocean was calm today, and brilliant white sails and powerful motorboats dotted the water. On the horizon, a cruise ship drifted past. I looked northeast out to sea in the general direction of dear old England and wondered how my friend Grant Thompson was getting on now that he'd taken up housekeeping with my brilliant, mercurial, single-minded sister, Pippa. My mother had reported that Pippa was happier than she'd ever known her eldest daughter to be and that Pippa wasn't working quite the long hours she always had. That pleased me very much. The cheerful tone of my parents' emails also pleased me: clearly, they'd recovered from the upsetting events of January during my last visit.

I walked down Harbor Road for a few minutes, simply enjoying the break from the shop and the beauty of the day, and then turned inland at Blue Water Place, my street. The 1756 saltbox house where I live with Great-Uncle Arthur soon came into view. Arthur is one of the world's great travelers, and at the moment he was in Thailand with friends from his Royal Navy days. Or was it Trinidad? I can never get his whereabouts straight.

Our garden was a riot of color and beautifully maintained foliage. No thanks to me; I have a pure-black thumb when it comes to gardening. Mrs. Ramsbatten and some of her garden club friends who'd recently moved into apartments but missed their gardens maintained it for us. For the heavy work, cutting the grass and such, we shared the services of a lawn maintenance company.

Butterflies flitted about, drifting from one fragrant plant to another; a bee buzzed past my ear, and a large black crow eyed me from the branch of an ancient oak as I walked up the driveway and let myself into the house through the mudroom entrance. The scent of basil rose from the herb bed Mrs. Ramsbatten and her friends had planted by the door. Violet greeted me with her usual excess of enthusiasm, and I proclaimed my joy at seeing her with a hearty thumping of her rump and sides. Mutual greetings over, she ran in excited circles while I got the leash off the hook, and we set off on our walk.

I didn't want to take too much time away from the shop, so rather than getting the car and taking Violet for a good run on a deserted stretch of the coast or along a meandering woodland trail, we stayed on our street.

Summer hours at the Emporium are long, and I like to be on hand from opening until closing, seven days a week. It's a long day alone for Violet, but fortunately Mrs. Ramsbatten is happy to pop in and give the dog some attention and a bathroom break. Mrs. Ramsbatten is in her eighties and walks with the aid of a cane, so Violet doesn't get a proper walk, but I'm happy knowing she at least gets a romp in the yard, some company, and a refreshed water bowl.

This week, my neighbor visiting her sister in Sandwich for three days, so I was trying to make a point of getting home to Violet at least once during the day.

We trotted down the sidewalk, cool in the shade of the green canopy and dappled sunlight formed by the huge trees, some of which were as old as my house. When we reached Mrs. Ramsbatten's yard, Violet jerked at the leash and tried to veer into the garden. I pulled her back. "Your friend's not there, Violet. You'll see her soon." She'd done the same thing yesterday, and I assumed Violet was wondering where Mrs. Ramsbatten was. It was nice to think that Violet was fond of the woman.

An aging Ford sedan was parked in her driveway. My neighbor didn't use her car very much these days, if at all, and it was covered by a light layer of dust.

Fifteen minutes later, we retraced our steps, heading home. As we passed in front of Mrs. Ramsbatten's neat white picket fence, intertwined with bushes bursting with red flowers, Violet whined and once again yanked at her leash. I was about to pull her back when I had a thought.

I dropped my end of the leash.

The dog scratched at the gate, and I opened it. Violet hurled herself through it and ran across the immaculate lawn and around to the back of Mrs. Ramsbatten's house. I hurried after her. By the time I reached the backyard, Violet was scratching at the door of the small black-and-white garden shed, with its cheerful red door and flower boxes overflowing with tumbling ivy and colorful annuals. When I called to her, she turned her head and looked at me. She barked once, then returned her attention to the red door.

"What have you got there?" I asked her. I put my ear to the door and listened. Inside, something rustled. Mice, probably, startled by the sound of the dog, or garden implements settling.

But perhaps not.

I keep a small flashlight attached to my set of keys. I took it out, switched it on, and turned the door handle. It wasn't locked. Slowly and carefully, I pushed open the door of the shed and shone my light in.

Two huge amber eyes stared at me from the far corner. Then the owner of the eyes, a pure-white kitten, arched its back and hissed.

I'd found Snowball.

Chapter Two

Murmuring soft words. I edged into the shed. I closed the door behind me, leaving Violet outside. I didn't want to scare the cat and chance it bolting and being lost again. Frightened eyes stared at me, and she offered no resistance as I scooped her up. The tiny body shivered, and I could feel the bones beneath the skin and fur. Today was Monday. Mrs. Ramsbatten had left on Saturday morning, and by Lauren's account, Snowball had gone missing two days ago. The little cat must have come into the shed, chasing mice perhaps, and then the door closed on her. Mrs. Ramsbatten's eyesight wasn't all that good, and she probably hadn't noticed the kitten hiding in a corner of the dark shed.

I cradled the cat to my chest and carried her to safety while Violet ran on ahead, making her way home. The first thing I did when we got to the house was pour some fresh water into a small bowl. The cat watched me warily from a corner of the kitchen. I scooped her up and put her on the counter next to the water. She gave me one dubious glance and then dove in headfirst. Next, I found a can of salmon in the pantry and dished up a small serving.

The fish disappeared in record time. The cat wouldn't have eaten for days, so I didn't want to give her too much.

When the water and salmon were gone, she sat down and began washing her whiskers. I put out one hand; she gave me a long look, then rubbed her face against my arm. She started to purr.

"You're welcome," I said. "Now it's time to get you home." I took a canvas tote bag down from a hook in the mudroom, scooped up the kitten, and dropped her into the bag. I didn't want her to escape, so I zipped the bag shut, leaving a sliver at the end open so air could get in.

"You," I said to Violet, "are the hero of the day, but I'm afraid you'll have to stay here."

The address Lauren had given me was only a couple of blocks from my house, so I walked quickly, cradling the tote bag in my arms while the little pink nose and twitching white whiskers tried to push their way out and plaintive cries broke the peace and quiet of the neighborhood.

The house I was after was a typical one for the street and the area. A late-model SUV was parked in the driveway beneath towering old oaks. The house was painted a cheerful yellow, with a dark-gray roof and matching shutters. Two stories, double garage. I estimated that it had at least four bedrooms, numerous bathrooms, and a den and TV room. The lot was large, and carefully trimmed shrubs and trees blocked the view of the neighbors. I walked along the brick pathway—not a weed pushing through the cracks—curving between shrubs of juniper and boxwood, to the wide front steps lined with terra-cotta urns overflowing with purple, yellow, and white flowers. Feeling rather pleased with myself, I walked up the steps and rang the bell.

The door opened and a woman peered out. She was in her mid-forties, nicely dressed in a typical summer-on-Cape-Cod way in white capris and a blue-

and-white-striped T-shirt—Tommy Hilfiger perhaps. She was about my height, five eight, but quite a bit heavier than she probably would have liked. Gold hoops adorned her ears, and a heavy gold chain hung around her neck. Her feet were bare, showing nails painted a bright red. Her glossy blonde hair, the color owing more to a bottle than to the sun, was pulled back into a high, sleek ponytail. Her lipstick was a fresh pale pink, and her recently applied manicure matched her pedicure.

Her clothes looked expensive, but they were too tight on her, particularly around the hips and stomach. She'd obviously put on weight since buying them, and the fact that she hadn't replaced them meant she'd been too busy to go shopping; she couldn't afford new clothes of the quality she liked; or she was in denial about having gained weight.

"Yes?" she said.

"Is Lauren at home?" My bundle squirmed, and I held it tight.

She narrowed her eyes. "Why do you want to know?"

"I'm Gemma Doyle from the Sherlock Holmes Bookshop on Baker Street. Lauren came to see me earlier today."

"If it was about that cat, I'm sorry. I wish I'd never bought the dratted thing. I told Lauren to keep it inside, but she forgot—she can be such a scatterbrain— and it got out the day before yesterday. Lauren's been in tears ever since. Nothing but high drama. As if I don't have more important things to worry about."

"Uh, okay. But I would like to talk to her. May I come in? Are you her mother?"

"I am. I'm Sheila Tierney." She spoke in a flat voice and made no attempt to crack a neighborly smile, to call Lauren, or to invite me in. *What,* I thought, *is this woman's problem?*

A tiny white paw emerged from my bag, and claws scratched at the air. Sheila Tierney blinked. "Oh," she said, "is that . . .?"

"Lauren?" I said.

The door opened, Sheila stepped back, and I came in. I closed the door behind me.

"Lauren!" Sheila called. "Lauren, get down here."

A tear-streaked face and tousled blonde hair appeared at the top of the steps.

"I brought you something." I opened the bag, and Snowball leapt out. She practically flew across the room. Lauren did fly down the stairs, screaming with joy as only an eleven-year-old girl can. She scooped the kitten up and held her so tightly I feared the little cat would be crushed.

"You found her!" Lauren squealed. "You found her. I knew you could do it!"

"Glad to be of help." I was feeling quite proud of myself. I hadn't done anything except follow my dog, but no one had to know that.

"Thank you, Ms. Doyle. I hate to be rude," Sheila said rudely, "but I'm on my way out." She opened the door.

"Wait! Wait!" Lauren called. "I said I'd pay you. I'll get your money."

"No need," I said. "This one's on me."

She gave me a radiant smile. I swear little Snowball smiled also. Shelia pointedly looked at her watch, telling me in no uncertain terms to be on my way.

"I'll never forget you," Lauren said in a low voice.

I touched my index finger to my forehead. "Gemma Doyle, Consulting Detective, at your service."